'Hugely enjoyable and gri]
believable that you forget you don't know them in
real life . . . A talented new voice in crime fiction . . .
Bloxwich kept me guessing to the end'
-Louise Voss

'As slick and hard-hitting as brass knuckles in baby
oil, *What Goes Around* is a riotous, thrilling and fresh
crime tale that brings huge entertainment, wry
humour and twists galore . . . Highly recommended'
-Rob Parker

'What Goes Around is a dark and gritty walk on the
wild side . . . Ann Bloxwich is an exciting new voice in
crime fiction and I can't wait to see what she comes
up with next'
-Howard Linskey

'What Goes Around pulls back the curtain to reveal
the darker side behind a world of glamour that few
have seen . . . This is an impressive debut with a
twisting storyline and sublime list of characters that
reach out and pull you in . . . A gripping thriller that
will keep you reading long after it's time to turn off
the light . . . Ann Bloxwich is a crime writer destined
to be a big name in the future'
-L J Morris

'Sharp characters, believable dialogue and an earthy
sense of humour combine with a strong sense of
place to create an intriguing mystery'
-Douglas Skelton

WHAT GOES AROUND

ANN BLOXWICH

Published in 2021 by Dark Edge Press.

Y Bwthyn
Caerleon road,
Newport,
Wales.

www.darkedgepress.co.uk

Text copyright © 2021 Ann Bloxwich

Cover Design: Jamie Curtis

Cover Photography: Rene Asmussen/Pexels

A CIP catalogue record for this book is available from the British Library.

ISBN (eBook): 978-1-5272-9111-9
ISBN (Paperback): 979-8-4657-9960-7

For my amazing Grandma, who taught me to read before I started school and instilled a love of books in me that continues to this day. You gave me so much strength, I hope I make you proud.

CONTENTS

20

21

22

23

24

25

26

27

28

29

30

31

32

33

34

35

36

37

38

39

40

41

42

43

44

45

46

47

48

49

50

51

52

53

54

55

56

57

58

59

60

61

62

63

64

65

66

67

68

69

70

71

72

73

74

75

76

77

78

PROLOGUE

Her mouth was open, but the scream refused to come out as she was dragged backwards on her stomach across the dimly lit path, a pair of strong hands wrapped around her bare ankles. She scrabbled frantically at the hard-packed earth, the broken glass, the barbed-wire fence, trying desperately to get a purchase on anything she could to thwart her attacker.

Her dress rucked up beneath her and she tried in vain to tug it back down, to cover what little of her modesty remained. Fingers wound their way into her hair and tightened into a fist, yanking her head back painfully as a scarf was looped around her parched throat and a heavy weight settled on her back. Her tongue lolled out as she choked and tried in vain to suck air in through her crushed airway. The scarf was pulled tighter and her eyes flickered as she began to lose consciousness, the world descending into darkness.

The last thing she heard before her body gave up the fight was a voice, coming from what seemed like miles away, calling out, 'What the fuck are you doing?'

1

Alex Peachey moved slowly through the park, eyes scanning the horizon, ears straining to alert him to any sounds. It seemed deserted, but he knew that failing to be vigilant could cost him his life. He'd called for back-up some time ago, but it had yet to arrive. He knew that the gunman was somewhere in the park, he'd chased him in here after the little boy had been shot. The weather was bitter and the ground frozen solid.

Alex used the dense foliage to his advantage as he crept forward, trying to keep his breath shallow so the enemy wouldn't spot the frosty clouds that came out of his mouth. Something caused the clump of bushes near the seesaw to tremble, so he took cover and waited. A glint of light between the leaves caught his eye. Alex felt the tension bunch in his shoulders as he prepared to take the shot.

A hand on his shoulder startled him, causing him to shout. He turned to see his wife standing behind him, a look of disapproval on her face.

'Alex, I've been calling you for ages! Now get off that damned computer, your dinner's ready.'

Alex turned back to his online game to see that the sniper had broken cover and shot his character dead.

'Bollocks,' he said, as he logged off and shut down the computer. He stood up and stretched until his fingers brushed the ceiling, feeling his joints pop and crack like breakfast cereal. He pushed his dark blond hair back off his forehead and wandered out into the kitchen.

Jayne had made Alex's favourite – shepherd's pie, with cabbage and carrots. He breathed in deeply, savouring the rich meaty smell. He stood behind his wife, wrapped his arms around her and rested his chin on top of her head.

'That looks terrific,' he said. 'You haven't got much though.'

Her plate contained a third of the food that Alex's did.

'Well, I'm trying to be good, I've still a few pounds to shift,' she replied.

He squeezed her gently. 'You look beautiful to me just the way you are, and I love the new hair colour.'

She smiled at him and touched the ends of her brunette bob. 'I fancied a change. Do you think it suits me?'

'It makes me think about skipping dinner and going straight to dessert,' he grinned.

She giggled and handed him his plate. They went through to the dining room, one of the few rooms not taken over by boxes, and sat at the table. Their son was at his friend's house for a sleepover, so they had the place to themselves for a change.

'How's Joel been today?' Alex asked between mouthfuls of food. He was trying hard not to eat it too fast, it was so good.

Jayne poured some water for them both. 'He was fine, no tantrums or anything. The staff at college said he'd been a bit loud, but nothing they couldn't deal with.'

'That's good. I did wonder if he'd be more agitated with the move looming, but he seems to be handling it well.'

'Don't speak too soon,' Jayne warned. 'You know how regimented he can be. He's going to find it difficult when his routines are disrupted.'

'More challenging than usual then . . . great. Not,' Alex said.

'Tell me about it,' Jayne grumbled as she pushed away her empty plate. 'This morning he was upset because there were no cornflakes left. I offered him toast but he says he always has cornflakes on a Friday. In the end I had to go out and buy some.'

'Don't worry, in a couple of weeks this will all be over then he'll settle down again,' Alex said, picking up the plates and carrying them through to the kitchen.

When he came back, Jayne had gone into the lounge. He flopped down onto the sofa next to her, rubbing his stomach in satisfaction. She flicked through the film channels, trying to decide what to put on.

'That was terrific,' he said with a sigh. 'How was work?'

'It was hectic. We're trying to get this book event sorted out as well as deal with Christmas shoppers, so I didn't leave until an hour after closing time. Joel being at his friend's was a blessing.'

'I'll stick a poster up in the station for you if you like.' Alex stroked Jayne's hair and kissed her before turning his attention back to the television.

'So, what are we watching tonight?'

2

Laura Morrison leaned over to catch her breath, trying at the same time to ease the pain in her big toe where her new shoes were rubbing. She never wore high heels as a rule and was regretting it bitterly. She loved them though, patent leather with a buckle strap and the same burgundy shade as her new dress and matching coat. Thank God for Christmas bonuses. The new hairdo had cost a fortune too, but she was thrilled with the result; copper highlights blended perfectly with her own natural brown tones, making it glow. She'd shunned her usual glasses for a pair of disposable contact lenses – another decision she knew she'd regret by the end of the night.

'Come on, we're really late now! There'll be no seats left if we don't get a move on!'

Vicky Wilson hurried ahead, defying gravity in a pair of white platform boots. Her huge white faux-fur coat concealed a black mini dress which clung like a second skin to Vicky's curves, the neckline so low that her breasts were barely contained. The dress would have looked cheap on anyone else, but Vicky had a way of making it look fabulous. She was stunningly pretty, almost doll-like with flame-red hair piled messily up on top of her head, leaving out a few long strands to frame her face. An oversized shoulder bag in a violent shade of orange was slung over her shoulder.

'How in hell did I let you talk me into going to a strip show? It's really not what I had in mind when I said you should organize our Christmas night out,' Laura complained as Vicky dragged her along. 'Bunch of posers waving their dicks around – not exactly cultural is it?'

Vicky giggled. 'Trust me, you'll have a great time and you've been saying you'll come for ages now. It's not just the guys, the drag artiste is great too and there's a disco afterwards. It'll be fun, trust me.' She laughed as she handed the tickets to the bored-looking man at the door and made their way into the darkened room.

The place was heaving, Laura had never seen so many women crammed into one room before. Over the top of the crowd she could just make out their friend waving madly at them, so she pushed Vicky ahead of her until they reached the front.

'About bloody time!' Helen Whittaker shouted, in a strong Birmingham accent. 'I was beginning to think you weren't coming! It's not been easy keeping these seats free you know, this lot are like fuckin' animals – yes, I mean you love!' she snarled as someone tried to slide onto one of the seats Helen had saved.

At just over six feet tall, Helen was a formidable figure. She wore faded jeans, a white vest top and black trainers. She had a hoodie tied around her slim waist and gelled her short blonde hair into spikes. Laura wondered if they were as sharp as they looked.

'Jesus, Hel, must you pick a fight everywhere we go?' Laura asked. 'Calm down, for Christ's sake, before I slap you!'

Helen roared with laughter. 'Try it, Titch, I'll get you a chair.'

'No need, I've got a portable ladder in my bag,' Laura winked. She looked around for Vicky, but she was nowhere to be seen. 'Where's Vicky gone? I wanted her to save my seat while I went to the bar.'

Helen looked over everyone's heads and shrugged. 'I can't see her. She's probably gone to the loo. You stay here, I'll get the drinks. What are you having – no, don't tell me, I'll surprise you.' She winked at Laura and headed towards the bar, casually barging people out of the way as she went. A few people threw dirty looks at Helen, then at Laura, who smiled apologetically back at them. Helen was oblivious, she really didn't care who she upset.

Laura glanced around the room. It was a lot bigger than it looked from outside, with eight huge sash windows along one wall. The opposite side was dominated by the bar, staffed by four, all working at breakneck speed. The far end of the room was where the stage was. It was impressive to say the least, designed like an old-time theatre with heavy gold curtains framing the opening. These were closed, but they were moving as if someone was behind them.

Helen strode back from the bar, expertly nudging people out of the way with her hips, drinks held high in the air. She handed Laura something bright-green and fizzy in a tall glass.

'Get that down you, it'll put hairs on your chest,' Helen said, as she gulped her beer.

'What is it? It looks like toilet cleaner!' Laura wrinkled her nose.

'It's called a Dirty Slapper. Try it, I bet you'll love it.'

'Well, if it tastes as bad as it looks then I'm having your pint!' Laura took a tiny sip and was surprised to find it tasted like sparkling lime juice. She smiled at Helen, punched her on the arm and clinked glasses with her.

'Not bad. What have you been up to lately? It seems like ages since I've seen you.'

'I've been at the Telford branch,' Helen said, downing a third of her beer in one go and burping loudly. 'Mr

Skelton's got me training the new staff over there.'

'Ugh, that sounds like fun – not,' Laura pulled a face, but Helen shook her head.

'Nah, it's really cool. For a start, it's in the shopping centre, so no cold draught every time someone opens the door. Plus, there are loads of coffee shops and stuff, so decent places to have lunch. Thirdly, he's seriously hot for an older guy. I've asked if there's a transfer available.'

'Are you serious?' Laura asked. 'You're thinking of leaving?'

'Don't be daft, I'm hardly moving to the other side of the world, just a few miles up the road. There are better opportunities for promotion, which is something I won't get if I stay where I am.' Helen laughed at Laura's long face. 'Don't worry, you won't get rid of me that easily.' She planted a wet, beery kiss on Laura's cheek, making her laugh.

'I hope not, I'm not ready to let you go just yet.' Laura glanced around the room and spotted Vicky weaving her way towards them through the crowd.

'Where did you get to? You were in such a rush to get here I thought you'd be glued to your chair.' Laura asked, turning as Vicky reached them.

Vicky tucked some loose strands of hair behind her ear. 'I popped outside to see if Ray was here but his car's not outside, so he must be running late. I thought he might have texted me to be honest, but I suppose he can't if he's driving.'

She shrugged off her coat and draped it around the back of her chair. Her dress had become twisted and she straightened it out, giving everyone in the vicinity a flash of her stocking tops.

'Crikey, I knew you liked him, but that's bordering on stalking. Be careful he doesn't report you to the police.' Laura looked concerned.

Helen snorted into her beer. 'Don't be daft! He loves

all the attention she gives him, I bet he gets a hard-on every time he sees her, knowing that someone else loves him as much as he loves himself!' Helen drained her glass and burped again. 'I'd call him a cunt, but he lacks the depth and warmth. Save my seat, I'm going for a piss.'

She stepped past her friends and strode off towards the toilets. Laura's mouth fell open in shock at Helen's choice of swear word. Although her language was colourful at the best of times, it wasn't one she'd heard her use before and the hatred in her voice was plain to hear. Vicky looked like she was going to burst into tears. Laura hugged her, telling her to take no notice.

'Don't get upset, Helen's just got a lot on her plate at the moment. I'm sure she didn't mean to snap.'

Vicky managed a weak smile. 'She doesn't know what Ray means to me; she thinks it's a silly crush. She'll soon see though, Ray's lovely once you get to know him.'

'Helen's just worried about you, that's all,' Laura replied. 'You can't blame her, given some of the things that have happened in the past. It's not as if you and he are an item, is it?'

When Vicky didn't answer, Laura tilted Vicky's chin and looked into her eyes. 'Are you?'

Vicky managed a small nod. 'Actually, we are. We haven't spent much time together, but he said after New Year we can maybe go away for a few days and get to know each other properly. You won't tell Helen, will you?'

Vicky looked worried, but Laura reassured her that her secret was safe. Helen just made it back to her seat in time as the lights dimmed and they turned to face the stage.

3

After a few seconds of silence, a fanfare of music blared out, causing Laura to jump and slop some of her drink in her lap. A single spotlight guided a tall glamourous woman onto the stage to tremendous applause. The woman had a beaming smile on her face, and it took a few moments before Laura realized that it was the drag artiste. She'd expected someone comical, but Kitty McLane was gorgeous. She was dressed in a long silver evening gown, with a pale pink feather boa and long silver gloves. She wore designer shoes, and her dark brown hair was expertly styled.

'Well, look at you!' Kitty said in a rich dark voice, 'Surely you've not all come out to see little old me, have you? No, you're here for the cock – aren't we all darling?' she continued, as a woman from the back of the room whooped in reply.

'Don't worry ladies, from what I've seen backstage, there's more than enough to go around. Tonight, seeing as it's nearly Christmas, we've got a real treat for you all. There's not just one, not even two or three. We've got four throbbing members for your delight and delectation, all straining at the zippers to meet you. But, until then, you'll have to put up with me. Allow me to introduce myself. My name is Kitty McLane, I'm a cock in a frock, a slag in drag, a chick with a dick – call me what you like. I'm here to warm you up. So while my lovely boys get ready for you, let's have some music and a sing-song. Feel free to join in.'

Kitty launched into the latest number one hit, rapidly followed by some Cher, Shirley Bassey and finishing up with Tina Turner.

Laura found herself singing along with Kitty, totally swept up in the moment. She glanced at Helen, who grinned back at her.

'Great, isn't she?' she shouted over the music. 'You can keep your strippers, I'd much rather have this.'

'She's awesome!' Laura shouted as she clapped along in time with the music.

Kitty took a bow and announced that the first two strippers were ready to take the stage. 'Come on ladies, let's show some appreciation for two lovely lads, I promise they will take excellent care of you. Please put your hands together and open your legs wide for the very talented Fire and Ice!'

Laura was dreading this part. She had no problem with the male body but thought the whole notion of stripping a bit sleazy. However, the two men who took the stage blew her away with their sharp costumes and fabulous dancing. Dressed in army fatigues, they mirrored each other's movements perfectly. The music had a lot of bass and Laura could feel it pulsing through her body.

Every woman was on her feet, clapping and shouting 'Off, off, off' to the men, who seemed only too happy to oblige. They stripped down to their tiny G-strings, showing off beautiful physiques, then ran out into the crowd to grab a couple of women to bring onstage. They sat them on chairs then gave them a lap dance. The two women looked thrilled to have a gorgeous near-naked man writhing all over them. Once they had finished, they escorted the women back to their seats, took a bow and left the stage. A young woman ran on and grabbed up their clothes, slipping and falling with a thud.

'Epic fail!' Vicky shouted, pointing at her. The woman looked embarrassed and angry as she exited the stage.

'Wow, I was not expecting that!' Laura exclaimed as she sat down and fanned herself.

'Wait until you see Ray, he's so much better than those two,' Vicky giggled. 'He taught them that routine himself, he said they were a nightmare to train as they hate each other.'

Laura wondered whether to believe Vicky or not. As far as she could see, the routine had been perfect, and the two men had appeared to get on well together. She turned to ask Helen, who had been sitting on her right, but she was at the bar again.

'Well, they looked really good together to me,' Laura replied.

Vicky got out her compact mirror and reapplied her lipstick. 'Looks can be deceiving, trust me. Ray wouldn't say it if it weren't true. You wouldn't believe some of the things he tells me.' She stood up, leaving her coat on the chair. 'Watch my seat for me, I'm just popping outside,' she said, disappearing before Laura had a chance to object.

'Here you go,' Helen said loudly, handing her a shocking pink cocktail. 'I can't remember what this one's called, but if it gets you pissed then who cares?' She laughed and belched, making herself laugh again. 'Excuse me,' she grinned.

Helen took a hefty swig of beer and sighed. 'You can keep all your fancy cocktails, nothing beats a good pint.' She slurped some more and sat back in her chair. 'What did you think of those two?' she asked, waving her glass towards the stage.

'I was very impressed,' Laura admitted. 'Their dancing was fabulous.'

'Ah, you weren't interested in the dancing, you just wanted to get a look at their dicks,' Helen chuckled.

'Hel, keep your voice down for God's sake!' Laura protested, looking around to see if anyone had overheard.

'Go on, admit it,' Helen urged. 'You wouldn't say no if it was offered. How long has it been since you had a good shag?'

'Okay, if you must know it's been a while but that doesn't mean that I fancied either of those guys.'

Helen started tickling Laura until she nearly fell off her chair.

'Okay fine, I liked them both – are you happy now?'

'Ooh, you dirty tart! Two at a time huh? Good for you girl.' Helen lifted her glass in salute and realised it was empty. 'What happened to my beer?'

'You drank it, you daft bint,' Laura laughed. She opened her bag to get her purse, but Helen wouldn't hear of it and insisted that it was her round. Laura knew better than to argue with her but made a mental note to slip some cash into Helen's pocket when she got the chance.

Vicky reappeared just as the second stripper came on. He was dressed in a fireman's costume complete with breathing apparatus and combined his act with an impressive display of fire-eating. A member of staff stood at the side of the stage, armed with an extinguisher and looking very nervous. The whole routine went smoothly, and she looked relieved that she hadn't needed to use it.

Kitty came back onstage and sang a couple of songs, then announced there would be a short interval. Vicky shot off towards the exit again.

Helen rolled her eyes. 'There she goes, off to look for knobhead again.'

Laura turned to look at Helen. 'Why do you have such a problem with her liking this guy? You don't fancy him, do you?'

Helen laughed. 'Christ no, I'd rather die! I just think it's pathetic how she fawns over him. He'd shag anything with a pulse – and probably anything without – but she can't see it.'

'Maybe he's quite nice once you get to know him,' Laura suggested.

'He's a wanker,' Helen scoffed. 'Pure and simple. He texts her, teasing her with promises of them being together soon, then he takes another bird home. She thinks he loves her, but he's laughing behind her back. I've tried talking to her about him, but she won't hear it.'

'How do you know what he's been saying?' Laura asked.

Helen nodded towards the stage. 'Kitty's a good friend of mine; we go to the same gym and have coffee together occasionally. She's known Ray for donkey's years, and you wouldn't believe some of the stuff I've heard. Kitty said that since Vicky told Ray about her inheritance from her nan, he calls her his meal ticket. He makes fun of her all the time, calling her fat, saying he wished she opened her purse as often as she opens her legs and so on. He's a nasty piece of work.'

'What a twat!' Laura retorted. 'Well, what do we do now? She's besotted with him.'

'Give it time, it'll all blow over.' Helen said, standing up and stretching her back. 'The word is that Ray has stepped on a lot of people over the years, using them to further his own career and when it comes to women, he takes what he wants then dumps them.'

'He sounds awful. How did Vicky get mixed up with him?'

'It was my fault. Kitty invited me to one of her shows and I took Vicky with me. It was a couple of months ago, when you were away with your parents. He was on the bill and he pulled Vicky up on stage for a lap dance. After the show he was having a beer in the bar and she got chatting to him. As far as I know, she's been to as many of his shows as she can since then.'

'I think I need another drink,' Laura said, holding her hand out for Helen's glass.

'Give us a tenner and I'll go; I've got more chance of getting through the crowd than you. Do you want another cocktail, or do you want something else?'

'Surprise me,' Laura joked as she thrust a handful of notes into Helen's hand. Helen headed towards the bar and Laura took the opportunity to pop to the loo. On the way back, she heard raised voices near the stage and turned to see Vicky having a heated exchange with a hefty security man guarding the stage door. When he refused to engage with her, she grabbed his arm and tried to push past him, but he stood firm and shook his head.

She snatched her phone out of her bag and took a photo of him. 'You wait till I show that to Ray, he'll have you fired. Then where will you be? Wanker!' Vicky flounced back to her seat just as Laura got there.

'What the hell was that about?' Laura demanded to know.

'He's just being a wanker,' Vicky raged. 'Ray texted me to say he's here, but that prick won't let me through. He's seen me before so it's not like I'm a stranger.'

'He's just doing his job,' Laura said, 'Don't be so hard on him.'

Vicky snorted. 'Well, he won't have his job for much longer!' She stuck her fingers up at the security man. He looked angry but stayed professional and didn't retaliate.

Laura didn't envy him one bit. She turned back to the stage as the lights went down.

4

As the film credits rolled, Alex stretched and stood up. He took Jayne's hand and helped her to her feet, encircling her with his arms. He began to dance slowly, making her giggle.

'What are you doing?' she asked, smiling as she leaned her head against his chest.

'I was going to have my wicked way with you, seeing as we get so little alone time,' Alex murmured. 'But I was trying to be subtle about it.'

'Sod being subtle,' Jayne said. 'This might be the last chance we get before we move.'

'Then why waste time going upstairs?' Alex laughed, pulling her to the floor as he kissed her.

***

'This is so nice,' Jayne said later, as they snuggled in bed together. 'I wish we could do this more often.'

'Your wish is my command, Mrs Peachey,' Alex said, propping himself up on one elbow and smiling at her. He teased a strand of hair away from her face and started kissing her neck.

Jayne gave him a playful push and he lay back down,

drawing her into his arms again. 'You know what I mean. We never seem to get quality time these days, just the two of us.'

'Maybe once the move is out of the way things will settle down and we can get some sense of normality back,' Alex said. 'Hopefully Joel will be happier too, seeing as this bungalow was designed by him.'

Alex cast his mind back to when Joel told them he wanted to build his own house, using the compensation he'd received from his birth negligence case. Alex's brother Dave had recently bought a derelict farm, complete with twenty acres of land, so had given his nephew an acre for his eighteenth birthday. It had taken a while to find an architect who specialised in accommodation for disabled people, but after a trip to a self-build exhibition they had found one who was happy to design exactly what Joel wanted. The architect was told in no uncertain terms that Uncle Dave was to build it, 'Because I trust him to do it properly.' Joel had loved visiting the site every week to see how it was progressing, and now it was almost finished.

'I'll have a talk with him, try and put his mind at rest,' Alex promised. 'But he needs to know the rules from the moment we set foot in the new place. I'll make it clear that any form of violence will not be tolerated.' Alex stroked a faded bruise on her upper arm.

'He'll have no reason to play up, he'll have his own separate living room where he can entertain his friends, and an office for his family tree stuff and whatever other projects he's got, so with any luck he'll calm down.' Jayne said.

'I hope you're right,' Alex murmured as he closed his eyes and drifted off to sleep.

5

Kitty came out onto the stage again, this time wearing a midnight-blue gown with matching feather boa. She had changed her blonde wig to a long blonde style that cascaded in waves down her back. She announced Ray Diamond, but this time there was no build-up or praise, and Laura got the feeling that Kitty didn't like Ray at all.

The lights went down again, and Vicky started bouncing around in her seat. 'Here he comes! Oh my God, I'm so excited!'

Helen stood up, knocked back the last of her beer and said, 'Right, I'll be outside. I'll come back when that prick is done.'

She walked off, leaving Vicky looking shocked. Laura patted her hand and said nothing.

The music started up and was halfway through the second verse before Ray Diamond finally appeared. He was wearing black leather trousers, a black snakeskin-print shirt open to the navel, and black boots. He also wore mirrored sunglasses, which all the strippers seemed to favour. His long blond hair was left loose and backcombed in the classic 70's style. He stood still for a few seconds, lapping up the whoops and cat calls from the audience, before launching into a gyrating dance. He quickly discarded his sunglasses and shirt, then poured baby oil down his bare chest, which he slowly rubbed in, his eyes following his hands. He grinned into the crowd and pointed at a large group, making them all scream.

Laura stifled a yawn, then realized with horror that he was looking right at her. He pulled on the waistband of his trousers and they came apart at the seams, leaving him in a tiny black thong, smaller than the ones the other guys had worn, so his cock was barely contained. He coated his chest in more oil, jumped down off the stage, strode over to Laura and sat astride her lap. He grabbed her wrists and pushed her hands onto his chest, forcing her to rub the oil in.

'Am I keeping you awake?' he drawled in a lazy voice.

He pushed her hands down towards his cock and Laura pulled her hands away in disgust. God, he really did fancy himself! He just laughed and jumped off her lap, grabbed Vicky by the wrist and pulled her back to the stage with him, moving so fast that she lost her footing. Ray pointed to her shouted, 'Epic fail!', mimicking Vicky's earlier jibe at his assistant. The audience roared with laughter, but Vicky looked upset. He kissed her on the cheek and pushed her to her knees. He produced a large flag, which he wrapped around his waist, encircling Vicky beneath it. As the music changed to something slow and suggestive, he grabbed Vicky's head and ground his hips into her face. Eventually, she emerged from underneath the flag with his thong in her teeth, a huge grin on her face. He pulled her to her feet and kissed her on the lips before facing the audience, opening the flag and flashing his naked body at them. He took a bow and ran offstage, leaving Vicky to make her own way back down. Laura rushed forward to offer her a hand and she took it gratefully.

'Isn't he amazing?' Vicky shouted over the applause. Her eyes shone like stars and Laura smiled, even though she'd thought he was terrible. The earlier performers had outshone Ray by a mile.

A few seconds later Vicky's phone beeped, and with a squeal of delight she hugged Laura and rushed off to the stage door. As Ray opened the door Vicky stuck her tongue out at the security guard and walked past him as if she owned the place.

6

The disco that followed the show had everyone on their feet, and as the night wore on Laura and Helen danced to everything from *The Macarena* to the *Cha Cha Slide*. By 11.30 p.m. Laura's head was pounding but at least her feet had stopped hurting. She tried to ring Vicky, but it went straight to voicemail.

'Balls to her then, I'm going home,' she said to herself. She looked around for Helen but couldn't see her, so went outside and rang for a taxi. As she put the phone in her bag, she spotted Helen standing in the field at the side of the club, waving at her. She had an ice bucket in her arms, gripping it as if her life depended on it and swaying dangerously.

'What are you doing in there? Come on,' Laura scolded.

Helen climbed back over the fence, caught her jeans on the wire and Laura had to grab her to stop her falling over. As they crossed the car park a fight broke out between a group of drunken women. Helen was keen to go and have a look, but Laura quickly dragged her away.

'Stay here with me. The taxi will be here in a minute and if you wander off someone will nick it.'

Helen belched loudly and was violently sick on the

path, missing the ice bucket but spattering her friend's coat with flecks of regurgitated beer. Laura stepped back quickly and fell over, causing Helen to roar with laughter before she sat down suddenly, narrowly avoiding the puddle of sick.

Laura got up and grabbed Helen's hand, pulling her up with a heave. 'Hel, the taxi's here, let's go.'

Another woman tried to open the door to the taxi, but Helen grabbed her by the lapels and leaned close to her face. 'Mine!' she hissed, breathing sour fumes into her face. The woman shrieked and pulled away, retreating to the far side of the car park.

'Hey, where's my bucket? That bitch has nicked my bucket,' Helen slurred, looking around with unfocused eyes as she climbed into the cab.

'She hasn't nicked it, I've got it. Move over so I can get in.' Laura squeezed in beside her and slammed the door shut.

The drive back to Laura's house was eventful. She lost count of how many times Helen tried to show the taxi driver her boobs, and by the time the journey was over, Laura thought the poor man looked terrified. She gave him a large tip and he sped off, leaving them both doubled up with laughter. The upstairs curtains of next door twitched, so Helen dropped her trousers and mooned at the window. Laura grabbed at her, stumbled and they both fell into the flowerbed, Helen still with her jeans around her ankles. She farted loudly as she got up, which started them off again. Eventually Laura managed to pull herself together enough to find her keys and they staggered into the hallway.

Laura kicked off her shoes and Helen headed for the kitchen. Laura found her drinking water straight from the tap, her jeans in a crumpled heap on the floor. Laura ignored her and made her way to her bedroom, where she removed half of her clothes before passing out on the bed.

7

Alex's mobile phone trilled, startling him, and waking Jayne. He grabbed it, checked the display and went into the bathroom to take the call. A few moments later Jayne heard the shower running. She sighed and turned on the lamp. The bedside clock read 12 a.m. 'So much for being on leave,' she grumbled.

Alex emerged from the bathroom, a towel around his waist, hair standing on end. 'I'm so sorry darling. Someone's found a body behind the Leamore Club in Wolverhampton. Charlie Baldwin's been rushed into surgery with gallstones, so it looks like I'm in charge.'

He dressed quickly and attempted to flatten his hair down.

'It's fine, honey. I've got Washington Poe to keep me company.' She waved a copy of the new M.W. Craven book at him.

'I'll leave you in his capable hands then,' Alex smiled as he slipped his jacket on. A car horn sounded from outside, so he kissed Jayne and hurried downstairs, leaving her with her novel.

***

Detective Sergeant Dawn Redwood sat outside Alex's house, her black Mini Cooper gleaming under the streetlight, wipers going ten to the dozen. The car was her pride and joy, a gift to herself after splitting up with her fiancé, Ben. She watched as Alex strode out of the house, pulling his coat hood up against the heavy rain. He opened the door and folded himself into the car, moving the seat back as far as it would go to accommodate his long legs. He pushed his hood off, causing his hair to stick up all over the place. Dawn laughed and flipped the passenger mirror down so he could sort it out.

'Hello boss, so much for time off huh? Trust Baldwin to get gallstones, crafty bastard. Good job I was still awake.'

Dawn hit the accelerator and the little car took off like a rocket, making Alex grab the door handle in panic. He gave her a stern look and she eased off the pedal, bringing the speed down to within the limit. He reached forward and pressed the radio button, cutting The Prodigy off mid-chorus.

Dawn inhaled deeply. 'You smell nice. Special occasion was it?' she grinned.

Alex grinned back. 'Don't be so nosey. What about you, were you doing anything special?'

Dawn shook her head, eyes on the road. 'No, just chilling with Barney, watching reruns of old television programmes and eating crap. We're not going away till you come back off leave, so it's too early to pack yet and we won't need anything special. I've booked a log cabin in the middle of the Cairngorm National Forest where we can hide away. I did look at fancy hotels, but they tend to frown on German Shepherds. If Barney had been a tiny pooch in a handbag, he'd have been okay.'

'Sounds great. What about Ben? Any word from him?'

Dawn took the next corner too sharply, causing the car to swerve. She corrected her mistake and smiled an apology at her boss.

'Sorry, it still makes me mad. No, and he won't if he values his balls. Have you got a definite moving in date yet?' she said, changing the subject. 'Give me a shout if you need a hand.'

'Will do. We were looking at the 21st, but that may have to be pushed back if we don't clear this up quickly. We can be flexible because Dave's using his van, so a lot of our stuff has already gone. Joel's will be done last. We couldn't get him into respite, so his stuff will need to be packed, moved and unpacked again in the same day. Dave took him over to the bungalow yesterday and they went through where he wants everything. Carol's bought some frames for his posters and she's made him some new curtains.'

'Sounds good, I'm looking forward to seeing it,' Dawn said as they pulled into the Leamore Club car park. It was almost deserted, apart from official vehicles and what Alex assumed were staff cars. A uniformed police officer stood to the left of the building, blowing on his hands for warmth.

Alex opened the door and got out, his knees creaking in protest. They each grabbed a Tyvek suit from the forensics van and suited up. Neither of them liked looking like giant gnomes, but CSI got upset if you didn't comply and you were simply not allowed on the scene. They both carried their paper bootees and set off across the gravel. They signed in with the officer guarding the entrance to the alleyway and he moved the crime scene tape to let them through, flashing Dawn a big smile as she passed him. She winked at him, causing him to blush to the roots of his hair.

'I think that young man likes you,' Alex murmured as they stopped to put their bootees on.

Dawn grinned, tucking her long black ponytail under her hood. Her dark brown eyes looked black in the spotlights that had been rigged up, and her olive skin gave off a glow.

'Really? I wonder why?' she joked. She gave Alex a wide grin, contorting her features until she looked like a maniacal gnome.

'You could do worse you know. He's a nice lad.'

'That's the problem, he's a lad. His mum probably still makes his packed lunch,' Dawn replied. 'I'm not ready for anyone new yet, but when I am, you'll be the last to know.'

'That's the spirit, kiddo,' he said. 'Now let's see what awaits us.'

8

The Leamore Club was situated just off Stafford Road, near junction 2 of the M54. The alleyway that ran along the side and back of the club was secluded enough to be popular with those looking to shoot up or get laid. Approximately eighty feet long, with a right-angled turn at the halfway point, the ground was littered with fag ends, used condoms, broken glass and other detritus.

Spotlights had been rigged up here and there, making it easier to see, and Alex and Dawn picked their way along, trying hard to stick to the foot plates that had been put down to preserve the scene. One side of the alley was bordered by the walls of the club, the other by concrete posts and thick rusty wire which was snapped in various places. Beyond the wire was an overgrown field, usually frequented by dog walkers and kids with nowhere else to go. A small group of teenagers stood in the field around thirty feet away, pretending not to be interested in what was going on but craning their necks all the same.

Detective Constable Gary Temple leaned against the wall of the club, watching the youths out of the corner of his eye. He wore a faded grey suit jacket, blue shirt and black trousers. His tie was askew, and his black boots were muddy. His light-brown hair had defied all attempts to make it lie flat. He stood up straight when he spotted his superior officers.

'Hello boss, you alright?' he asked. 'Shame about DI Baldwin isn't it?'

'You could say that, Gary. Has anyone spoken to them?' Alex jerked his head towards the teenagers. 'Go and have a chat, it's a long shot but you never know.'

'Okay boss,' Gary nodded, pushing down the wire and stepping over it. He waved to the youths who looked wary and ready to bolt, but Gary's easy manner seemed to work as none of them ran off and he soon had them chatting and pointing. Alex doubted that Gary would get anything of substance from them, they probably wanted their fifteen minutes of fame, but every avenue had to be explored.

Alex took a deep breath and continued down the path, his feet crunching the broken glass beneath the footplates. Around ten feet away, a tent had been erected to protect the body from the rain and looked to be a hive of activity. One of the forensics team spotted them and beckoned him forward.

'Dawn, go and talk to whoever found the body. I'm guessing that's them,' he said, pointing to where someone sat on a plastic chair. A uniformed officer crouched beside them, trying to get them to drink something from a plastic cup. Dawn nodded and went over.

Alex approached the tent and waited as a photographer snapped off a few more shots before moving in closer. It was dry inside the tent, but still cold. Little steam clouds escaped from behind the team's face masks and evaporated into the air.

The coroner spotted him and stood up.

'Evening DI Peachey, nice night for it.' Matthew Farrow said, pushing off the hood of his Tyvek suit. His cheeks were pink from the cold and his thick mop of ginger hair was flattened against his scalp. He pulled up his face mask and propped it on his forehead, his green eyes, usually so full of mischief, looked serious for a change.

'Hello Faz. What have we got?' Alex asked, crouching to look at the body. The woman was lying face down, head twisted to one side at an unnatural angle. Her naked body glowed blue in the harsh lights, a perfect contrast to her red hair, which spilled across her face.

'She's not been here long, the body's still pliable, no sign of rigour yet. There was no attempt made to conceal her, but they've been careful not to leave any obvious evidence,' Faz said. 'The damage is horrendous, as if the killer wanted to totally obliterate her face. Her nose is caved in, her cheekbones and jaw look to be broken and the back of her head has more dents than your car. There's probably a lot more damage underneath all the blood. Her fingernails are torn, as if she'd clawed at the ground, but I'll take samples and hopefully she's scratched the bugger as well. I'm sorry to say that this poor woman suffered.'

'Can you see an obvious cause of death?' Alex asked.

'There are ligature marks around her neck, and her eyes show signs of petechial haemorrhaging, so I'd go with asphyxiation at this stage. I'll know more when I get her back to the morgue.' Faz shook his head. 'Such a pity, I bet she was quite a beauty.'

'Well, someone didn't like the way she looked,' Alex replied. He walked back along the alleyway, deep in thought. Faz kept him company, there was nothing more for him to do until the body was on his table.

'How soon can you do the post-mortem?' Alex asked.

'I'll check when I get back, but probably Monday morning. I have two guests booked in at the moment, but I've finished with them and they are being collected tomorrow. It's almost Christmas, so I'm expecting a rush on middle-aged men who can't cope with the prospect of seeing their mothers-in-law on Boxing Day,' Faz mused. 'Why are you here anyway? I thought you were on leave.'

'I was, but DI Baldwin's got gallstones, so I got the short straw.'

'I've told him time and again to sort his diet out. If I'd known he suffered from gallstones, I'd have whipped them out for him. I may even have given him a sniff of anaesthetic first.' Faz smirked.

'Well, he'd better not linger on the sick for too long or I'll send the wife round. She's stressed out about this move as it is, and me being called in has buggered things right up.' Alex stood back to allow the mortuary staff to pass with the gurney. They loaded the victim onto it and wheeled her towards the car park, where a private ambulance waited.

The two of them followed the gurney across the car park, where Dawn stood with Gary. The witness had been dispatched with the uniformed officer and Dawn waited to drop Alex off. Faz shed his coveralls, revealing a smart black suit and a bow tie.

Dawn whistled at him. 'Wow, looking good Mr Farrow. Auditioning for the next James Bond movie, are you?'

'DS Redwood, lovely to see you again. If I were a single man . . .' Faz said, his eyes twinkling.

'You'd still have no chance.' Dawn laughed.

'Ouch! You certainly know how to kick a man when he's down.'

Dawn punched him playfully on the chest. 'You know I love you really. What was the occasion?'

'Steph and I went to a Casino Royale night with her mate and her husband. To be honest it was boring, loads of chinless wonders, all trying to outspend each other. Right, I'm off before my wife replaces me with Daniel Craig. See you on Monday, Alex, give Jayne my love and say hello to Joel for me. Goodnight Gary.'

He turned and walked briskly across the gravel to his

car.

'What did the witness have to say?' Alex asked, turning to Dawn.

'He said he came outside for a crafty fag, heard a noise and went to have a look. He saw the woman and rang us on his mobile. He says his boss is pissed off at him, when he told her about the body, she made him wait till closing time and the place was empty before calling us.'

Alex did a double-take. 'Really? Why was that?'

'They had a Ladies night on tonight, you know, male strippers and such, so the place was packed. By the time the first uniforms got here there were only a handful of people left in the car park, and most of them were bladdered. They did manage to get names and addresses off them though.'

'Is she still here? I want a word with her!' Alex looked furious, but Dawn shook her head.

'No, she left before we got here, she must have slipped out with the last few stragglers. Don't worry, the witness gave us her details. She'll be here first thing tomorrow so we can talk to her then. They have CCTV, so we can check the cameras as well.'

'That will have to do for now. Gary, did you have any luck with those kids?' Alex asked.

'They were more helpful than I expected,' Gary said. 'They saw people in the alleyway on and off all evening. There was a lot of activity between 5.30 p.m. up to 9 p.m., then around 10.30 p.m. they saw one person, too dark to tell if it was a man or a woman though. They went along the alleyway towards the car park. Then around 11 p.m. there were two people, a man and a woman. From what they said they were having very noisy sex.'

'Any chance that they could have been witnessing the murder?'

Gary shook his head. 'No, they said the man went back inside again afterwards, through a door at the far end of the club and the woman headed round to the front doors. I've had a quick look, that door leads to the back of the stage, so the strippers would've used it to get in and out of the club.'

'Did they see anything after that?' Alex asked.

'No. A couple of their mates had to go, so they all walked up to the chippy on Station Road. By the time they walked back our lot had turned up, so they stood in the field to see what was going on. The club had an extension on until 12 a.m. because of the Ladies night, so it didn't close until 12.30 a.m. There weren't many people left by then, the actual show finished around 11 p.m., then there was a disco on. There were a lot of taxis about, it might be worth speaking to some of the local firms to see if they noticed anything. I know it's a stretch but . . .'

'No, it's a good idea,' Alex interrupted. 'See if anyone ordered a taxi but didn't show up. Our victim might have booked one earlier in the evening.'

'Okay boss. Anything else?' Gary put his notebook in his pocket and fished out his car keys, hopefully.

'No, that's it for now,' Alex said. 'Let's go home and get some sleep while we can. It's going to be an early start, so I hope you haven't got any important plans.'

'Jo and I were going shopping for wedding rings,' Gary protested. 'It's only three months till we get married and she says I need to get more involved, so I promised I'd go tomorrow. She's going to kill me.'

'She'll understand, she's marrying a copper after all, so she'll need to get used to it. If we can make some headway in the morning, I might be able to let you slip away for a couple of hours in the afternoon.'

Gary's face lit up. 'Oh, thanks boss, Jo will be pleased!' He looked like he'd won the lottery and Alex laughed and gave him a friendly shove.

'Get off home now, I'll see you in the morning. Give Jo a kiss from me.'

Gary rushed off, a spring in his step. Alex remembered what it was like to have exciting plans and he envied Gary a little bit.

'You get off too, Dawn, I'll grab a lift with one of this lot.'

'You sure? I can hang around and keep you company,' Dawn offered. 'McDonalds on the Stafford Road is open all night, I can go and get some coffee if you like.'

'Go on then, I think we'll be needing it.'

9

The sun shone brightly through the bedroom window and Laura awoke with a groan. She tried to sit up, but the room swam violently so she lay back down. After a few minutes, she attempted to sit up again, more slowly this time. Her eyes were sore, and she realized that she'd forgotten to take out her disposable lenses before going to sleep. She managed to stand but her feet felt like someone had taken a blowtorch to the soles. She felt her stomach rushing up to meet her, so hobbled to the bathroom as quickly as she could, before throwing up. It was nearly half an hour before she felt confident enough to let go of the toilet bowl and make her way downstairs.

Helen was in the kitchen making breakfast, dressed in just her vest top and knickers, singing tunelessly along to a Bon Jovi song that was playing on the radio. She spotted Laura and laughed before placing a mug of black coffee in front of her. Laura tried to pick the mug up, but her hands were shaking too much, so she set it back down and leaned over it so she could slurp at the hot liquid.

Helen turned her attention back to the stove and it wasn't long before Laura was presented with the biggest fry-up she'd ever seen. Her stomach lurched, and she pushed the plate away, wishing she could eat it but not sure if it would stay down. Helen was attacking her own food enthusiastically, shovelling down eggs, bacon, sausages and mushrooms as if her life depended on it. She looked up when she realized Laura wasn't eating.

'What's up mate?' she asked, through a mouthful of toast, 'No appetite? Never mind, I'll finish that lot off.'

She cleared her own plate then picked up Laura's and started tucking in. 'You should eat, a good fry-up is the best cure for a hangover. At least have some toast,' she said, pushing a stacked plate towards her.

Laura shook her head. 'Maybe later. I'll stick with coffee for now.'

'Your loss, this is terrific, even if I say so myself.'

Helen finished the last forkful and washed it down with orange juice. It was incredible how much Helen could eat yet never seemed to gain an ounce. Laura only had to walk past the cake shop in town and would put on three pounds. To be fair, Helen ran at least five miles a day and swam twice a week. The closest Laura got to exercise was walking to and from the bus stop. Wolverhampton wasn't brilliant for long-term parking, so Laura used the bus for work and saved the car for the weekends.

'What time is it?' Laura squinted at the kitchen clock. 'Oh God, it's barely 9.30 a.m. How can you be so chipper at this time of day? I feel like death!'

Helen got up and refilled the kettle. 'I was drinking beer, it doesn't give me a hangover. I haven't had that much fun since that weekend in Blackpool. Remember that young bloke you snogged? You thought he was about thirty but he was only eighteen. And your cousin shagged that black guy? If her husband ever found out about that he'd go mental, he's the biggest racist there is!'

Laura started looking around the kitchen. 'What did I do with my coat? I hope I didn't leave it at the club, it was brand-new.'

Helen shrugged. 'I think you had it in the taxi. Maybe you dropped it outside, I'll go and have a look.' She darted outside and was back in a flash, holding the coat up in victory. 'Got it, it was in next door's flowerbed. It's got sick on it, sorry if that was me. I'll pay to have it cleaned. Talking of sick, I washed my jeans, I hope that was okay. They're in the dryer now.'

Laura groaned as she started to recall Helen's antics from last night. 'It was definitely you. You were sick twice, once before we got in the taxi and once when we got out. Do you remember anything at all?'

Helen sipped her coffee and thought for a minute. 'Did I flash my arse at him next door?' She giggled when Laura nodded at her.

'You puked in his flowerbed too. I think you've got some serious apologising to do there.'

Helen had the decency to blush. 'Oh no, don't make me do that, you know he fancies me! He might make me do something kinky to make up for it.'

Laura spluttered into her coffee and Helen had to thump her on the back to stop her choking.

'He's sixty if he's a day!' Laura said. 'Whatever makes you think he fancies you?'

'He asked me once if I was married. When I said no, he suggested that I needed a good strong man to smack my bum occasionally.'

Laura roared with laughter. 'The dirty old sod! I'll never look at him in the same way again.'

Laura's phoned beeped, and the two of them searched for ages before they found it under the sideboard in the hallway. Laura read the message out loud.

'Hi girls, sorry I left without telling you. Ray is so amazing though. Speak soon xxx.'

Helen raised one eyebrow. 'Well, it sounds like someone spent the night sliding up and down a greasy pole. I hope she's got some antibiotics handy.'

'Oh, come off it, he can't be that bad. I admit I think he's creepy, but Vicky seems to like him.'

Helen shuddered. 'Everyone knows he's not the cleanest in the business. I knew a woman who went with him and caught crabs. He's disgusting.'

Now it was Laura's turn to shudder. 'Ugh. Why didn't you say something to her? You know she's crazy about him.'

Helen drained her coffee mug. 'Don't you think I tried? You've known Vicky for as long as I have, so you know what she's like. She sees a guy, falls head over heels in love with him and starts planning weddings and babies. They know they'll get what they want for as long as they want it, then drop her. We pick her up, put her back together and the whole scenario starts again.'

Laura knew that Helen was right. Vicky did have a habit of jumping in with both feet. 'She does know how to pick them, she sighed. 'I'm going for a shower. Are you staying here for a bit? We can slob around the garden and you can flash your bum at him next door again.'

Helen stood up and headed for the door. 'No thanks, I'm going home to get changed then go for a swim, try and work some of that breakfast off.'

Laura looked at her. 'Well at least put your jeans on before you leave.'

10

Alex rubbed his eyes wearily. He'd made the mistake of logging back into his game when he got home and had subsequently lost track of time. He heard movement from upstairs, looked at his watch and saw that it was almost 7 a.m. He hastily logged off, lay on the sofa and closed his eyes just as Jayne came into the room.

Jayne kicked his foot when she came downstairs. 'Nice try, Buster, the computer's still shutting down, so don't try that trick with me.'

Alex opened one eye and smiled apologetically, but she didn't look amused.

'That computer will be the death of you. Now, get upstairs and have a shower while I make some tea.'

When he came back down half an hour later, Jayne had already left for work, but there was a mug of tea waiting for him. There was also a plate of toast, but their cat Jack was on the counter, happily licking the butter off it. Alex shooed off the cat and tipped the toast into the bin.

It was a hectic time of year for Jayne, with a selection of authors coming in to do book launches over the next few months. Being a book lover herself, it was as exciting for her as it was for the customers, especially since she got to spend time with the authors she admired. Alex couldn't remember who she'd said was coming, no doubt he'd find out when a new stack of books appeared on the coffee table.

He gulped down half of his tea, grabbed his keys and headed outside. The temperature had dropped again since he got home, and the road and pavement sparkled with frost. A thick fog had come down, making it impossible for him to see to the end of his road.

'At least it's not raining,' he said, as he unlocked his ageing dark blue Vauxhall Astra and started it up, leaving it to run while he scraped the ice off the windscreen. He climbed into his car and sat listening to his favourite Queen CD as he waited for the windows to clear.

They lived in a quiet cul-de-sac, where you rarely saw anyone apart from the old woman with Alzheimer's at number 56 who sometimes wandered up and down, and the kids across the road who played with their remote-controlled cars in the road. The house had belonged to his parents and he'd be sorry to move, but Joel's needs were far more important. The new bungalow was away from the main road, and they'd have Dave and Carol as neighbours, which would be good for all of them.

Driving to work took longer than Alex had hoped because of the fog, so it was after 9 a.m. when he pulled into the car park at the back of the police station. Dawn's car was already there, as was Gary's. Both were frosted up, which told Alex that they'd been there some time.

He punched the code into the keypad, went inside and took the stairs two at a time, colliding with DS Craig Muir, who was coming out of the canteen with two mugs of coffee. Craig did a little backwards jig to try to avoid him and managed to spill coffee down the front of his designer suit jacket.

'Bollocks! I've only just got this back from the dry cleaners too!' Craig complained.

'Sorry Craig, but technically you bumped into me. You came out of the door backwards and hit me as you turned. Maybe now you'll take my advice and stop wearing your best clothes to work.' Alex relieved him of one of the mugs and took a sip. 'Anything to report yet?'

Craig pulled a green silk handkerchief out of his top pocket and wiped the front of his pale grey jacket. 'Too early to say. Faz has set up the post-mortem for tomorrow lunchtime, he said that's the earliest he can do. I hope this stain comes out,' he grumbled, tucking the handkerchief back into his pocket.

Craig Muir was just over six feet tall, slim and well-toned. He had short black hair, which was always neatly gelled into place, and green eyes which seemed to smile even when he was being serious. Alex often berated him about wearing designer clothes to work, but Craig had told him he'd rather die than wear anything from a chain store.

Alex's stomach growled. 'The cat ate my breakfast, so I'll need a bacon roll before I do anything. After the briefing, you and Gary go and see the staff at the club. Lean on the manager, she has a lot to answer for. We'll meet back here after lunch and see what we've got.'

Alex walked into the room that housed the Wolverhampton Major Crimes Unit, although to call it a room was an understatement. When Major Crimes had started out, it had been in a cramped office in the basement of the old police station. As soon as a move to new premises had been announced, Alex and his colleague, DI Baldwin, had bagged the top two floors of the new building.

Originally a flour mill, it was a huge, open-plan space, with most of the floor taken up by desks in a double line down the centre. A bank of printers and other technology sat on top of a long surface along the left-hand side of the room and Alex had an office on the opposite wall. The room was partially divided halfway down, with a small kitchen beyond. This area also had sofas and a television where the officers could relax on the rare occasion that it was quiet. Light flooded in from the eight large windows that punctuated the white-painted brickwork at regular intervals at near-ceiling height.

Alex made sure his team were all present before starting the briefing. Once he'd given tasks to each of them, he spent a couple of hours dealing with paperwork, talking to his superiors and liaising with his colleagues in uniform. After lunch he popped along to New Cross Hospital to see how DI Baldwin was doing.

'Hey skiver, how are you feeling? You lazy sod, lying around in bed all day while we have a murder to solve. Anyone would think you'd planned it,' Alex said as he strolled onto the ward.

Charlie managed a half-smile and tried to sit up without wincing. 'Hey Alex, thanks for coming. Trust me, I'd swap places with you any day. This is not a pleasant experience at all. The doctor said my gallbladder was close to rupturing. Still, it's gone now.'

Charlie's dark skin made it difficult to tell if he was looking pale or not. He lay back against the pillows, looking older than his forty-eight years. 'Man, I feel like crap,' he said.

'You look like crap,' Alex laughed.

Charlie rolled his eyes at him. 'If wit was shit, you'd be constipated mate. Tell me about the case.'

The two friends discussed what Alex had so far, which by Alex's own admission, wasn't much.

'It's early days yet though, I'm hoping to move forward once Faz has done the PM. Meanwhile we do the legwork, you know how it is. Faz sends his regards and says next time you're in need of surgery, he's more than happy to step in.'

'Faz can fuck right off,' Charlie said, trying not to

cough. 'I wouldn't trust him to neuter my dog.'

'You don't have a dog.'

'Exactly. I'm hoping I can get out of here tomorrow, then back at work in six weeks, provided I take it easy. I am sorry Alex; I know you're up to your eyes at the minute with your house move.'

Alex patted him on the arm. 'No need to apologise mate, it's just one of those things. At least it was nothing life-threatening.'

'It felt like it at the time. I'm just glad that Jackie was home. If she hadn't been . . .'

'Stop being a drama queen. You're fine now, so just concentrate on getting better so I can have my time off.'

'You're all heart, Alex Peachey, do you know that?' Charlie laughed, regretting it immediately. He pressed his buzzer for the nurse. 'Now bugger off back to work and let me get some rest.'

11

Laura swallowed two high-strength painkillers and finally started to feel human again. Saturday had passed her by in a blur, with only a bottle of paracetamol and a bucket for company. She felt like she'd been hit by a bus, but she used to be able to drink three times what she'd had last night with no ill-effects at all. She was glad she'd got two weeks off work. At this rate she might need that long to recover.

The smell of next door's dinner wafted through the open back door and Laura's stomach growled. She knew she probably should eat something but didn't trust anything to stay down. In the end she made herself a slice of toast and ate it dry, praying it wouldn't come back up again.

She stood at the kitchen sink and drank another pint of water, wondering why Vicky hadn't returned her calls. She rang Helen, taking three attempts before Helen answered, sounding out of breath.

'What's up?' she puffed.

'I've still not heard from Vicky and I'm worried. Will you come with me to her flat?'

'Can it wait an hour? I'm in the middle of something. I'll meet you there when I'm done.' The line went dead, but not before Laura thought she heard another person in the background. She dismissed it as noise from the television. Helen was a fitness fanatic, so she was probably doing an exercise DVD.

***

Laura met Helen outside Vicky's in the car park that served the tall block of flats. These, unlike its neighbouring block, had recently been rendered and looked fresh. Laura used Vicky's spare keys to open the communal door and headed towards the lift. Helen hung back, saying she'd take the stairs.

Shrugging, Laura stepped into the lift and rode up to the third floor. Helen was waiting outside when the doors opened, only slightly out of breath. As they approached the door to number 17, they could hear a low wailing sound. Laura rang the doorbell then banged on the door a couple of times before using her key. A large ginger cat shot out of the door as soon as Laura opened it and legged it down the stairs.

'Oh shit, Milo's not supposed to go out, he's an indoor cat,' Laura said.

'Bollocks!' Helen retorted. 'It's a sodding cat, they go where they like. It's not natural to keep them cooped up. He'd be a lot healthier if he went out and got some exercise, he's far too fat. Let's face it, if you lived here wouldn't you get stir-crazy after a while? Leave the door open and he'll come back in a minute when he realises he can't get out of the main door downstairs.'

Laura shook her head, 'No, we'd better go back down and get him. Someone might let him out by mistake, and Vicky would never forgive us if he got out and was hit by a car.'

Helen rolled her eyes. 'Fine. You stay here, I'll go. He'd better not scratch me though or I'll run him over myself.'

Helen jogged down the stairs, calling the cat as she went.

Laura called out to Vicky as she walked into the hallway but got no reply. There was a small pile of post on the mat, and Laura scooped it up and put it on top of the low bookcase behind the front door.

The flat was small but well-laid out, with a kitchen and living room on the right side of the hallway and two bedrooms to the left. The bathroom was at the end, facing the front door. Laura looked in each room in the order she came to it, rearing back in horror when she entered the kitchen.

'Jesus Christ!' She clapped her hand to her nose to block the smell coming from the litter tray in the corner. It was overflowing and didn't look as if it had been changed for a while.

'No wonder he was grumpy,' Helen said, sticking her head around the doorframe, Milo wedged firmly under her arm, 'I wouldn't want to shit in there either.'

Laura grabbed a bin liner and quickly dealt with the tray. As soon as she put the tray back on the floor, Milo sniffed the fresh litter and looked suspiciously at Laura before walking away with his tail held high. 'Typical male,' Laura said.

Helen had never been to the flat before and shrieked with laughter when she saw the lounge. It was very old-fashioned, with peach floral wallpaper, matching floral curtains, a green suite and peach floral-patterned carpet. The sofa had cream-coloured lace cushions at either end, and a row of dolls, all wearing dresses and hats, sitting in the centre.

'Fuck me, it looks like an old granny lives here. I bet she never brings stripper boy home, he'd think he was shagging Mrs Doubtfire! I wonder what the bedroom's like?' She darted off to look and a few seconds later shouted to Laura.

'Check out this boudoir man, it's Barbie's world!

Laura followed her into the bedroom and glanced around, taking in the candy-striped pink walls, pink and white bedspread, cream long-haired rug and crystal-effect lampshades. The top of the bookcase and wardrobe were piled high with soft toys.

'So? Vicky's a girly girl at heart. What do you care?' Laura was annoyed at Helen's lack of respect for their friend. Helen saw her dark look and looked sorry.

'Well, it's like . . . well it seems weird that's all. It's like a kid's room. In fact, the whole flat is like an old-fashioned doll's house. It's not what I thought it would look like, that's all.'

'Don't be so judgemental. Vicky inherited the flat from her gran, maybe she wanted to keep it this way to remember her.'

Laura turned around and went to check the bathroom. Finding nothing unusual, she went back to the kitchen to feed the cat and found him taking advantage of the clean litter.

'Thanks Milo,' she said, giving him a dirty look. The cat just looked back at her with indifference as he scraped dirt over the puddle in the tray. Laura rifled through the cupboards, looking for cat food before finding a can in the fridge. It was next to a can of chilli con carne, and Laura wondered if Vicky had ever fed the cat from the wrong tin. It would certainly explain the contents of the litter tray. She put the food down for him, but he ignored it.

'Stuff you then,' she said.

Helen was still in the bedroom and on her phone. She hung up when Laura walked in.

'Who was that?' Laura asked as Helen put the phone back in her pocket. They went into the living room and Laura sat down in the armchair nearest the window.

'No-one,' Helen replied. 'Just a running friend I was meant to meet later. It doesn't look like she's been back, does it? There's no dirty washing, the kitchen is spotless, and her toothbrush is still in the bathroom.'

'I was going to ring her parents, but I don't want to worry them. They're so overprotective of her and are bound to overreact. I've tried her phone so many times, at first it rang but now it goes straight to voicemail.'

Helen pulled her phone out again and started flicking through her contacts before hitting dial. 'No point, her parents are on that cruise she bought them. I'll see if Neil knows anything. Sorry, I meant to say Kitty. Neil's his real name.'

'What could he know that we don't?' Laura asked. The room was very warm, and she was struggling to stay awake.

'Maybe Ray mentioned where they were going last night after the show. Damn, no answer. I'll text him and get him to call me.' She sent the text, pushed the dolls to one side and flopped onto the sofa. Within a few minutes she was snoring softly.

Maybe she was being paranoid, but Laura had a bad feeling about it. Every other time Vicky had gone off with someone she'd texted Laura to look after Milo. The fact that this time she hadn't was worrying. He was her baby, there was no way she'd leave him overnight without making arrangements for him. Maybe Vicky had asked a neighbour to feed him and they'd forgotten? She left Helen sleeping and popped out to speak to the three neighbours on Vicky's floor, but no-one had spoken to her.

Laura leaned back in the chair and closed her eyes, deciding that when Helen woke up, they would go to the police station. In the meantime, she may as well grab forty winks herself.

12

Ray Diamond lay back against the pillows and lit another cigarette. As he watched the plume of smoke rise to the ceiling, he could hear the shower running in the adjoining bathroom. He reached for the glass on the bedside table and took a swig of the clear liquid, rinsing it around his mouth before swallowing it. The neat vodka made him wince, but it also refreshed him.

He threw back the duvet and lay naked for a few minutes, enjoying the feeling of sweat drying on his skin. He got out of bed, wandered over to the dressing table and started nosing through the various objects strewn on the top, idly scratching at his balls as he did so. When he found nothing of interest, he opened the drawers one by one and poked around.

He found a large wad of cash and a cheque book in an envelope under the clothes. Ignoring the cash, he opened the cheque book and noticed that the one on the top was signed. He grinned to himself then very carefully removed two cheques from different places in the book, along with the stubs. He lay the cheques alongside the top one, then skilfully copied the signature onto the two blanks. He folded the forgeries, picked up his jeans and slid the cheques into the pocket. He heard the shower turn off, so he dropped his jeans back on the floor and lay back down on the bed.

The bathroom door opened, and a young man emerged, a towel around his large waist. His short black hair stuck up at odd angles and his skin was glowing from the heat of the shower.

'Shower's all yours,' he announced, smiling at Ray as he removed his towel and rubbed his hair vigorously with it. His flabby body shook like a jelly and Ray closed his eyes for a moment in disgust.

'Cheers babe,' he said in a breezy voice, trying to mask his revulsion. He stood up and walked towards the bathroom door. 'Is there a clean towel in there?'

The man opened a cupboard door and grabbed a large towel from a stack inside. 'Here you go hun, let me know if you need me to scrub your back.' He gave Ray a cheeky wink and turned to get some clothes out of the dressing table.

Ray closed the bathroom door behind him and sighed. Switching the shower on, he used his client's toothbrush while he waited for the shower to reach the right temperature.

He thought about Liam, the young man in the other room, and shuddered. Ray's services didn't come cheap and, although he despised fat people, they were willing to pay whatever he asked for a few hours with him. He preferred women to men but made an exception if the price was right. Despite being the highest-paid male stripper in the country, he spent his money as fast as he earned it. It was all about the image when you were as successful as he was, and image cost money.

Ray climbed into the shower and let the water run all over his body. He was in excellent shape for his age, going to the gym four days a week, having regular top-ups at the tanning salon and getting his long blond hair done by a top hairdresser. The designer clothes he favoured made him look even better and Ray knew it. He soaped himself all over, watching himself in the mirrored tiles. He masturbated at his own reflection, feeling euphoric as he climaxed.

Rinsing himself off, he stepped out of the shower and dried himself, finally wrapping the towel around his head before going back into the bedroom.

Liam sat on the chair next to the bed, dressed for work. He looked up from his magazine when the door opened. 'Feel better now, hun?' he asked with a smile.

'Yeah, much better.'

Ray threw the towel on the bed and started pulling on his clothes, smirking to himself as Liam lowered his gaze.

'I'm popping to town before work, if you fancy some lunch,' Liam said hopefully but Ray shook his head as he finished dressing and pulled his trainers on.

'Sorry babe, I've got a gig tonight, so need to hit the gym. I've got a busy period ahead, so give me a ring after New Year if you want to see me again. Oh, and can you make sure you have a shave next time? Your stubble plays havoc with my cock. Don't wanna damage the goods now, do we?' Ray winked at Liam and the young man blushed furiously.

'No problem at all, I'll do anything for you, you know that. It was even better this time, you're a wonderful lover.' Liam looked at his feet, embarrassment etched on his face.

'You were pretty good yourself. Most women can't suck my cock as well as you do, you've got an amazing tongue.' Liam went even redder and Ray laughed. He punched him lightly on the arm. 'Now pay up or I won't let you play with my toys again.'

'Oh, sorry,' Liam said, standing up and pulling his wallet out of his jacket pocket. 'There's a hundred there, is that okay? I'm pretty skint till payday.'

He thrust the money into Ray's hand. Ray wondered

about the cash in the drawer but didn't mention it or Liam would know he'd been snooping.

'Yeah that's great, thanks. Later babe,' he said as he opened the bedroom door and headed out, leaving Liam looking wistfully after him.

13

Alex put the phone down and scratched his head, ruffling his hair. Another dead end, he thought, crossing the name off the list in front of him. The team had spent most of yesterday canvassing the area surrounding the club, or speaking to the attendees from Friday night, but they'd all claimed to have been too drunk to remember much of anything.

Alex wondered how people could get into such a state, then he remembered he'd been in many a state himself when he'd been out with his brother. Dave could drink like a fish and still walk home in a straight line. Alex was a complete lightweight in comparison.

He glanced around as he headed towards the kitchen area. Dawn was perched on the edge of her desk, talking to someone on the phone. She looked up and Alex raised his mug towards her. She shook her head and went back to her conversation.

DC Maureen Ross, one of the newest team members, was sitting at the computer, typing at breakneck speed. She had a pencil balanced behind her right ear and a pair of glasses propped on the top of her head. He wandered over to see what she was working on. She was in her late thirties, but her slim frame and short black spiky hair made her look like a teenager. Being the weekend, she was dressed in skinny jeans and a band T-shirt instead of the usual smart black trouser suit.

Alex was surprised to see the twin photo frame on her desk had a picture of Mo's girlfriend Isobel in one half, and the actor Lewis Collins in the other. Mo saw him looking and blushed.

'He is the only man I have ever loved,' she said.

Alex wasn't sure if she was joking, so made no comment. 'Where are you with everything?' he asked instead.

'I've left a message for the show's organisers, I figured they'd be able to put us in touch with the acts that were on. In the meantime, I thought I'd get started on typing up these reports from people we've spoken to already.'

'Excellent work, Mo. Where's Les? I haven't seen him for a while.'

'He's gone to see if forensics have anything for us yet. I know it's early days, but we may get lucky. He's put feelers out to the local taxi companies to see if anyone reported a no-show from the club and he's talked to the press liaison office and asked them to set up a hotline.'

'To be honest, I'd be happy with identification at this stage. There was nothing on the body to tell us who she is, and as far as I know no-one's been reported missing. Once we know who she is then we'll have something to go on. I'm getting myself a drink; do you want anything?'

'Coffee would be great, thanks, boss. Milk and two sugars please.'

***

Mo loved working here. Alex and the team were so easy to get along with, unlike her previous colleagues who had been more interested in the fact that she was gay than how good she was at her job. She and Les Morris were both DCs and had joined Alex's team six months ago, but from different areas. Les had joined the force after leaving the Navy and specialised in Cyber Crime. He'd previously worked in his home town of Carlisle. Mo was Scottish by birth, hailing from Fraserburgh, but had been stationed in Coventry with the Sex Crimes Unit after graduating.

Mo was around two-thirds of the way through the witness statements when Alex came back with the coffee. As he approached her desk, she looked up at him.

'A few of the witnesses mentioned they had tickets for Friday night. I'm wondering if the tickets were numbered, and if so, where did they buy them from. Maybe whoever sold the tickets will have names that we can check, so by process of elimination we might be able to find out who the victim is, or at the very least narrow it down to a group of people, if they were a party.'

Alex looked impressed and told her so. Not used to being praised, she mumbled her thanks and carried on digging.

***

Alex carried his coffee over to his office, kicked the door shut behind him and sat down at his desk to drink it. As a rule, he only usually closed the door when he was on the phone to the top brass or when he was giving someone a bollocking. Now, he just needed five minutes to gather his thoughts.

The fact that he'd been thrown back into work when he'd mentally powered down was a pain in the backside, and no doubt Jayne would be upset too. They'd promised Joel he'd be in his new house before Christmas, but now Alex doubted that would happen. He fired off a text to his brother David, asking him to ring him when he had a few minutes. Dave was probably up a ladder, he'd mentioned he was fitting some guttering this weekend, so he wouldn't be able to talk until he was done.

Alex drained his mug, stood up and went towards the door. As he opened it, DC Les Morris was standing there, hand raised ready to knock. He was a short, stocky man, with a shaved head and brown eyes. He had a ruddy complexion from spending hours outdoors, umpiring for his son's cricket club.

'Ah boss, sorry to disturb you,' he said in his flat Cumbrian accent. 'I've just spoken to forensics, they've got nothing definite yet, there was a lot of rubbish behind the clubhouse so there's shedloads to go through. I got bugger all from the local taxi companies as well, they all say they did multiple pick-ups and drop-offs that night, many of whom could have been redheads like our victim. Sorry, boss.'

Les looked apologetic but Alex shook his head at him. 'Nothing to apologise for, at this stage it's all a bit vague. Let's concentrate on who organised the show. Mo's looking at ticket sales, can you give her a hand with that? With any luck we'll be able to match ticket numbers to credit cards and eliminate people that way.'

'When I was with the Crime Unit in Carlisle, we had a case of a promotions company being fiddled out of ticket money, something to do with the online ticket provider duplicating tickets so they were selling a hundred tickets but numbered them one to fifty twice. The promoter thought he'd sold fifty tickets for his event, but one hundred people turned up. It didn't take long to figure it out, but it caused the venue a lot of hassle.'

'Is Craig still at the club? Give him a ring and ask him to check and see if the venue had a list of ticketholders, or maybe there was one left behind. Ask him who the promoter was as well, then you can ring and set up an appointment with them. I'm not sure how long he and Gary will be, and I'm keen to get interviews sorted before everyone sods off for Christmas. I could kick Charlie Baldwin in the balls for dropping this on me but having seen the state of him I'd say he's suffering enough.'

Alex raised his mug to his lips before remembering it was empty. 'I'm off for a refill, do you want one?'

'No thanks, I've not long had one. I'll ring Craig now and get back to you.' Les headed towards his desk when his phone started to ring. He picked it up then turned to Alex.

'Boss, you're wanted downstairs. Someone just came in to report a missing person.'

14

John Jackson slammed down the phone and swore loudly. He jumped up out of his chair, strode over to the filing cabinet and punched it several times. His assistant Shona looked up from her scheduling in surprise. She could guess what was coming next, so she got up and put the kettle on, bracing herself for the outburst, which wasn't long in coming.

'Bastard! You wait till I get my hands on him, I'll fuckin' kill him!'

There was only one person who ever made John angry, and that was Ray Diamond. He looked furious, the tendons in his neck stood out like steel cords and his blue eyes blazed. The sweat glistened on his freshly-shaved head as he paced back and forth across the small office.

'What's Ray done now? It *is* him, isn't it? No-one else winds you up like he does,' Shona asked, pouring boiling water into two mugs.

'Too fuckin' right it's him! He's only gone and nicked another club from under us, telling them that they can save money by dealing directly with him instead of going through an agency. That's twice this week he's pissed me off. I swear I'll rip his head off!' He threw himself back into his chair and banged his hands on the table.

Although John was the sole owner of Bulldog Promotions, he'd started out as a stripper himself, working under the legendary entrepreneur Steve Gifford, before a back injury had forced him to hang up his G-string. John had a brilliant head for business, so Steve took him on as a partner and had proved a great mentor, and John had taken over after Steve died.

John had a good reputation on the circuit and many of the acts on his books had become good friends. In the beginning, it had been the big names like Ray who had guaranteed a full house, while ensuring that the newer guys were seen. John's strippers were fiercely loyal to the company and would never poach work from elsewhere. He was a fair man and made sure that everyone had regular work, using them equally in rotation on the weekly shows in Birmingham, Bristol, Swansea, Plymouth and now Nottingham. They had recently expanded to Liverpool and Dublin, and a tour of Greece and Switzerland had been confirmed this week.

The problems had started when a few of their regular venues started cancelling shows and booking directly with the strippers themselves, wooed by the prospect of no agency fees. There were still a lot of freelancers out there who were happy to work without an agent, but they ran the risk of a venue refusing to pay, or them not getting the agreed fee after the show.

Shona placed a mug of coffee down in front of John. He picked it up and smiled as he breathed in the aroma. It was laced with Jack Daniels and he took a large mouthful and nodded.

'Thanks Shona, that's just what the doctor ordered.'

'So, what's the other thing Ray's done to upset you?'

'He's nicked that job at the bingo hall from Adam. He rang them up pretending to be him and said he couldn't do the job because he was ill, but his friend Ray Diamond was going to fill in for him,' John said bitterly.

'What? Oh, for God's sake! Adam was relying on that job to see him through Christmas and the New Year! Why would Ray do that?'

Shona felt sorry for Adam. He was a sweet guy and a real grafter. His ex-girlfriend had recently had a baby, and she squeezed him for every penny he earned. He'd been a skilled painter and decorator when John met him, so John helped get him work decorating whenever he could, and insisted he kept that money for himself.

'He caught Adam doing an impersonation of him backstage at the last show they worked together. Even though Adam insisted that he was doing it because he admired him, Ray took it badly and won't let it go. This is the third job of Adam's that he's poached. I'm going to have to have a quiet word with Ray and make him see sense. If I'd had a pound for every time someone's taken the piss out of me when I was stripping, I'd be a rich man. Adam's young and impressionable, he hasn't got a malicious bone in his body.'

John drained his mug and carried it over to the sink to rinse it out.

'I think Ray can't handle the fact that he's past his prime,' Shona mused. 'He's so jealous of all the young talent coming up nowadays. He still thinks he's the best, but to be honest he may still have a good body, but his routine is old, and it borders on sleazy. He refuses to change it because he thinks his fans love the old one. It's time he realised that most of his original fans have moved on. The women who come to the shows now are mostly hen parties, young women who don't want to see someone the same age as their dad.'

John nodded. 'You're spot on, but he can't see it. As far as Ray's concerned, Adam made a fool of him and he won't let him forget it. If it wasn't for the fact that he's freelance I'd fire him. I'll tell you one thing though. After he's done the jobs we've contracted him for I won't be using Ray again.'

'What are you going to tell Adam? He'll be devastated.'

'The truth. It's a shitty situation, but there's no point in lying to him, because he'll find out eventually.'

Shona went through the upcoming schedules. 'According to this, Adam, Jamie and Pete were on that job. We've only had one booking today and they asked for two white guys, so I can't put Adam on that, but I can give it to the others and maybe we can pull Mark off that works do and put Adam on it. We might get something else in before Christmas, but I doubt it.'

'You can't move Mark, they asked for him specifically and it's a solo job. It's okay, I'll ring Adam and tell him. He'll be royally pissed off to say the least but there's nothing I can do about it.'

John rang Adam and spoke to him, letting the young man down as gently as he could, but Shona could hear him swearing down the phone. John put the phone down and looked unhappy. He hated it when someone hurt his lads.

'I really hope someone gives Ray a taste of his own medicine one day, and soon.' Shona said. 'He's a complete dickhead.'

'Hang on, I've got an idea, one which will put Ray Diamond right on his arse.' John reached for the phone and scrolled through his contacts. He found the number he was looking for, picked up the office phone and pressed some buttons.

Shona looked over the rim of her glasses at him. 'Really? I'm intrigued. Is it one of your lightbulb moments?'

John waited for the person at the other end to pick up. 'One thousand kilowatts, baby,' he grinned.

15

By the time Alex got down the stairs and along the corridor to the front desk his knees were throbbing, and he bent over to rub them. Dawn strolled along behind him, notebook in hand, like she didn't have a care in the world.

'Rheumatics playing up, are they?' Dawn laughed, 'You need to get fit, boss, it'll do you good, especially at your age.'

'Bugger off, cheeky cow! I'm in the prime of my life.' Alex stretched upwards and his back gave a loud crack, making him wince.

'So I see,' Dawn smirked. She spotted two women seated in the reception area through the double doors and stopped smiling. 'How do you want to proceed?'

'Let's tread carefully. If the victim is their friend, then I suggest we keep it to ourselves for now.' Alex said quietly as he pushed the door open.

The two women were seated in the reception area. One looked worried, the other seemed to be playing a game on her phone. They both looked up as Alex and Dawn came through the door.

'Good morning, I'm Detective Inspector Alex Peachey and this is Detective Sergeant Dawn Redwood. I understand you're here to report a missing person, is that right?'

The worried-looking one spoke up first. 'Yes, our friend Vicky. We haven't seen her since Friday night.'

'Let's go somewhere more private,' Alex suggested, pointing to a set of double doors opposite the ones they had just come through. 'If you'd like to come this way please.'

Alex held the door open and Dawn led the way to an interview room. This was the nicest one of the three they had, usually reserved for circumstances such as giving out bad news, interviewing children and so on. The room was bright and airy, having recently been given a makeover by a group of local college students as part of their community project. The off-white walls were decorated with swirling patterns of colour, and new blinds hung at the door and window. An abstract painting by one of the students was displayed on one wall. Three pale grey sofas made up a U-shape in the middle of the room, with a small coffee table in the centre. Along the back wall were several boxes of children's toys.

A uniformed officer arrived with some plastic cups and bottles of water on a tray, then took his leave again. Alex gestured for everyone to sit down before he did. Sometimes the way people sat in relation to each other told you a lot about them and he noticed that these two women were very different. The tall one had wandered in without a care in the world and slumped at one end of one sofa, phone still in hand, whereas the brunette sat next to her but perched like a bird on the edge, handbag clutched in front of her as if she was on trial.

Dawn sat on the middle sofa, close to the brunette and Alex took the remaining sofa opposite the two women. Dawn opened her notebook and sat with her pen poised. She was much quicker than Alex, and her shorthand was only legible to a select few.

The brunette seemed agitated, but the other one didn't seem to notice, instead, she sat back and scrolled through her phone. Alex sat patiently, looking at her and saying nothing until the woman looked up and saw he was waiting to start. She shoved the phone in the back pocket of her jeans and sat up a bit straighter.

'Now, let's start with your names, then you can tell us about your friend.'

'My name is Laura Morrison, and this is Helen Whittaker,' the brunette woman said. 'Our friend Vicky Wilson is missing.' She was struggling to make herself heard.

'Perhaps I should tell them, seeing as my gob's bigger than yours.'

Helen sat forward, resting her elbows on her knees and grinned at her friend. Laura sat back and let Helen take over. 'We were out with our mate on Friday night. We went to a Ladies Night at the Leamore Club. Vicky ended up backstage with one of the strippers. We didn't see her after that, so we figured she'd gone home with him. She a massive fan of his and she follows him all over the place, going to as many of his shows as she can. The other week he finally noticed her and gave her his phone number. She said she's been seeing him on his nights off, but I take a lot of what Vicky says with a pinch of salt. She fantasises a lot.'

'How can you say that?' Laura piped up angrily. 'Vicky never fantasised about anything in her life!'

Helen laughed at her. 'Oh yeah? What about the time she was going out with a "famous" singer?' she said, making quotation marks in the air. 'Turned out it was someone from the Karaoke club. Remember the "famous" snooker player she was seeing? He was just a fan who had once played a couple of frames with Jimmy White in a pub in London. Then there was the "famous" footballer who was my cousin Ronnie's friend. He's a cleaner at The

Molineux for Christ's sake!' Helen sat back, visibly angry.

Laura poured herself a cup of water and took a small sip. Her cheeks were very pink, as if she had been slapped.

'Take us through the events of Friday night,' Dawn coaxed.

Laura nodded, cleared her throat and closed her eyes, trying to recall the details. 'Vicky got ready at mine because I live nearer to the Leamore Club. The taxi was late so Helen was already there, saving us some seats. We got some drinks and watched the show. Vicky was pulled up onstage by the stripper, then after his routine he went backstage, he sent for her a few minutes later and off she went. The drag artiste had come back on by then, so we forgot about Vicky. When the show finished, we carried on drinking and dancing until the disco finished, then we got a taxi back to mine. Helen stayed over as we were both so drunk.'

Laura took a huge breath as if she'd felt a weight lift from her shoulders.

Dawn finished writing then looked up. 'What time was it when you left?'

Helen shrugged.

'To be fair I was steaming, so I don't remember much. I think it was around 12.30 a.m. Didn't she have a go at the security man at some point?' she asked, looking at Laura.

'Oh God, yes she did. He was standing by the stage door, making sure no-one could go in or out that wasn't supposed to. Vicky got in his face when he wouldn't let her backstage. She shoved him as well. She said she would get Ray to have him fired. She does have a temper when she starts.'

Alex spoke up. 'I see. What makes you think that Vicky is missing?'

Laura looked at Helen before answering. 'I didn't hear

76

from her on Saturday, apart from a text message that morning, but then again I didn't expect to. I had a colossal hangover, so I spent the day in bed with painkillers for company. When I still hadn't heard from her by lunchtime today, I called Helen and we went to Vicky's flat, that's when I knew for definite. We let ourselves in – I have a spare key as I look after her cat if she's away. Milo was very distressed, he'd not been fed, and his litter tray was disgusting.' Laura looked like she was about to burst into tears.

'You don't seem quite so concerned as your friend. Why is that?' Alex asked, as Helen rolled her eyes.

She sighed. 'It's not the first time Vicky's scared us like this. About eighteen months ago, Vicky was seeing this guy from the snooker club – the one I mentioned before. She hadn't been seeing him long when she disappeared. Her mum was going spare with worry. After about a week, Vicky turns up, tanned and smiling as if she didn't have a care in the world. Apparently, her boyfriend had gone to Malta to watch a snooker tournament, and she'd gone with him. She thought it was funny that everyone had been so worried, until her dad read her the riot act. She was in pieces when he'd finished tearing a strip off her and she moved in with her nan shortly afterwards. Her mum is lovely and so's her dad to be fair, but it doesn't pay to cross him. He's ex-army and I swear he thinks he's still in. Anyway, when Vicky's nan died, she left her everything, including the flat. Now she only sees her parents on Sundays. That's why I'm convinced that she'll turn up at some point, with a big grin on her face and a fanny like a clown's pocket.'

'Helen!' shrieked Laura, putting her hand over her mouth and looking mortified. Helen started giggling and soon Laura was joining in. It seemed to have broken the tension in the room.

'Interesting turn of phrase,' Alex said. 'Can you give us

a description of Vicky and what she was wearing when you saw her last?'

'She's twenty-six, the same as me. She was wearing a black dress, a white coat and white boots. She had a massive orange handbag. She's got long red hair and green eyes. Hang on, I've got a photo,' Laura said, delving into her handbag and retrieving her phone. She swiped through some pictures then handed it to Alex. 'Here you go. I took a selfie while we were waiting for the taxi on Friday.'

Alex looked at the photo then passed the phone to Dawn. It was difficult to tell if the woman in the photo was the same one that was in the morgue, but there was a definite similarity. She looked so happy that it made Alex's chest hurt. He handed the phone back.

'Tell us about the stripper she was with,' Dawn said, drawing a line under what she'd written so far.

Helen gave a snort. 'His name is Ray Diamond. I'm not sure how old he is, but I'd guess at late forties, and he's got long blond hair. He's around six feet tall, but I could be a few inches off. I'm just under six feet and he's taller than me, not that I've got that close to him.' She gave a shudder of disgust.

'If you don't like him why did you go to see him?' Dawn asked.

'I didn't go to see him, I went to see Kitty McLane, the drag artiste. She's a friend of mine. It was a coincidence that Ray was on the bill. Vicky was thrilled, she idolises Ray and she goes to see him whenever she can. To be honest I tend to zone out when she starts prattling on about him.'

'I see. You said there were other entertainers on, do you know their names?' Dawn asked.

Laura spoke up this time. 'There was Kitty, then a double act, one black guy and one white. I don't remember what they were called. There was a guy who did fire-eating, then Ray Diamond and then a disco. I think the DJ was a friend of the fire-eating guy because he came and stood with him until the end of the night. Kitty might know more.'

'I can ring Kitty if you like,' Helen said, pulling out her phone.

'We'll speak to Kitty. Do you have a number for her?' Alex asked.

'I'll give you her number, but I'll text her first and ask if it's okay.' Helen fired off a text as she spoke and got an almost immediate reply. 'She said it's fine, but she's going to be driving all day so can you leave her a message and she'll ring you when she's home. Don't be surprised if she's a bit frosty with you, she's got a lot on her plate at the moment.' Helen handed her phone over so Dawn could copy the number down.

'We'd better go, I'll need to feed Milo again soon. Will you let us know if you find her?' Laura asked as she stood up.

'I'll make sure you're kept in the loop. We'd better have contact details for Vicky's parents too, in case we need to speak to them.' Alex led them back to Reception and saw them out.

'What do you think?' Alex puffed as they climbed the stairs to the office.

'I'm pretty sure it's the same person.' Dawn answered.

'I agree. Vicky Wilson was wearing very distinctive earrings in that photo, but I'm sure there were none on the body. I want to double check those hair pins too, there were loads, so it's a safe bet that some of them might still be there. I can see someone nicking her earrings, but to take the time to remove all of those pins would make the risk of being caught very high.' Alex added. His stomach gave a hefty growl.

'Go and get something to eat before you head off to the morgue,' Dawn laughed. 'If you pass out at the post-mortem, Faz is likely to remove some of your vital organs.'

16

Alex bolted down one half of a cheese sandwich on his way to the morgue, shoving the other half in his pocket for later. He crunched on a mint and hoped he wasn't in for a long stay.

At least it wasn't far to go, just across the huge quadrangle from the station. Adjacent to the morgue on one side was the Magistrates Court, and the remaining side was home to various cafes and restaurants. There was a large green area in the centre, complete with fountain and benches. It was a nice space to relax on a sunny day.

The bright lights in the morgue made Alex wince. It always amazed him that it could be so very clean, despite what went on in here. He took his hat off to the cleaning staff, they did a fantastic job. Nothing was ever out of place. Jars and bowls were neatly lined up, ready to receive organs, fluids and other such things. Alex was certain it was cleaner than any operating theatre.

Faz stood behind the large steel table, talking to his assistant who was commonly known as Ziggy because his real name was too difficult for most people to pronounce. They looked up as Alex threw open the door and strode in, puffing heavily and offering apologies.

The young woman lay on the table in the centre of the room, so pale she almost glowed under the harsh lights. Faz and his assistant had taken fingerprints, fingernail scrapings, swabs and completed all the other preliminary tasks before washing her down. Her hair was carefully combed back, allowing the injuries to her face to be seen properly. She looked as if she had been stamped on repeatedly and Alex could see there was bruising around her neck.

'Alex, good of you to join us!' Faz's booming voice echoed around the room. 'I was beginning to think you'd got gallstones too, but then I remembered you were more likely to have stayed up all night killing imaginary people on that computer of yours!'

'Guilty as charged, Faz,' Alex admitted. 'But never fear, the wife has already passed sentence on me. I expect this evening I'll be painting walls or putting up shelves in the new place.'

Faz laughed. 'Excellent, a woman after my own heart. If ever she leaves you, I want to marry her.'

'You keep telling me that, but it'll never happen. She's already told me that leaving me would mean unleashing me on the unsuspecting female public, and she couldn't inflict that burden on another woman.'

'She's very thoughtful, becoming a martyr for the sake of womankind.'

Alex told Faz about the missing person's report and mentioned the hairpins.

'Everything we've removed from the body has been bagged and tagged but Ziggy has a printout for you. Now, are you sitting comfortably? Let's begin.'

He pulled down his clear face mask and picked up the scalpel. Alex perched on the edge of a nearby stool and folded his arms.

Faz made quick work of the Y-incision and began removing organs with a speed to be admired. Ziggy was equally swift, weighing and cataloguing everything handed to him. Alex tried hard not to zone out, regretting not going straight to bed now. Occasionally a container would be placed on a separate table, ready to be sent off for analysis. As he worked, Faz dictated his findings into an overhead microphone. His voice became soft and soothing, lulling Alex almost to sleep.

'Hello, Earth to DI Peachey,' Faz called, jolting Alex back to the present. 'I'm done. As I suspected, cause of death was asphyxiation. Both orbital sockets are broken, as are most of her ribs to front and back. Both legs, arms and pelvis show multiple fractures. This was pure rage Alex; I've not seen injuries like this since that maniac with a lump hammer was at large a few years back.'

Faz handed him a folder. 'I could see you were flagging, so I had Ziggy take notes on your behalf as we went along. The list of items that she had with her is also in there. I'll let you know when I've written up the full report.'

'Thanks, tell Ziggy he's a life saver.' Alex looked at his watch. 'Shit, it's after six already. I'd better go and debrief the team. I'm going to try and bring someone in to ID her tomorrow if that's okay.'

'Sure, I'll make sure our guest is ready. Come on sweetheart,' Faz said, as he gently pulled the sheet up over the body. 'Let's put you back to bed.'

17

The following morning, Alex and Dawn pulled up outside Laura Morrison's house in a cul-de-sac on the outskirts of Pendeford. The houses were all former council houses, most of them having been snapped up when Margaret Thatcher had given the go-ahead for them to be sold off in the Eighties. Laura's was one of the few that had become private rentals. The small front garden had no fence or gate to enclose it but was well-kept, with a small flowerbed running around the edges and a miniature tree growing in the centre of the lawn.

Alex smiled as he recognised the woman getting out of a red hatchback parked further along the road. She walked towards Alex, returning his grin.

'Hello, sir,' she said in a sing-song Devonshire accent. 'Makes a change to be in a nice part of town.'

'Hello Tess, good to see you again.' He turned to Dawn. 'This is DC Tess Hicks, acting FLO, originally from Plymouth as you can probably tell by the accent, but now living in Perton. Tess, this is DS Dawn Redwood, she's been with us for around three years now, and is one of the best.'

Tess was short and well-rounded, with dark curly hair pulled back into a ponytail.

The two women shook hands. 'Wow, praise from Alex is high praise indeed,' Tess said with a smile. 'He doesn't usually like anyone.'

'Hey, watch it, or I'll kick your backside,' Alex laughed. 'And I don't know what you're laughing at, DS Redwood, it's not too late to deny your leave, you know.'

Dawn winked at Tess. 'In that case, you can tell Barney he's not going on holiday.'

'Okay, there's no need to threaten me with Barney,' Alex said, holding his hands up.

Tess looked at her. 'Is that your fella?'

'He's my dog,' Dawn said. 'German Shepherd ex-police dog. Less trouble than a man.'

'I bet,' Tess agreed. She looked at Alex. 'I read your notes while I was waiting for you. The victim's parents are away, is that right? Are you going to ask one of the friends to do a formal ID?'

Alex glanced at the house. 'Let's get this part over with first and see how it goes,' he said.

***

Laura sat in her back garden, her mug of tea slowly going cold in her hands as tears slid down her face. She still couldn't get her head around the fact that Vicky was most likely dead, that she'd never see her again. She tried hard to recall her friend's sunny smile, rich laugh and warm hugs. She closed her eyes as she remembered arguing with DS Redwood, convinced that it was a case of mistaken identity. In the end, she'd lost her temper and sent them all packing.

The doorbell rang in the distance, but she ignored it, knowing that if she tried to stand up her legs might give way from under her. After a few minutes, the doorbell ceased.

'Hey, what's up?' Helen's face appeared over the top of

the high wooden gate. 'How come you didn't answer the door, you lazy cow? I might have known you'd be out here, talking to your flowers again.'

Helen reached over the gate and slid the bolt back, allowing the gate to swing open. She strolled in, smiling until she saw Laura's face.

'What's happened?' Helen dropped to her knees and smoothed Laura's hair off her face. 'Why are you crying?'

'They think Vicky's dead, Hel. They found a body behind the Leamore Club.' Laura broke down and Helen hugged her.

'Don't talk bollocks,' Helen said, pulling away to look at Laura properly. 'Who told you that nonsense?'

'The police came around about an hour ago and told me. They tried to ring you, but your phone was off. They want us to go in and identify her.'

Helen rubbed her hand across her face, her eyes wide. 'No, no that can't be right. Tell me exactly what they said.'

Laura repeated what Alex and Dawn had told her, and Helen dropped her head between her knees and clasped her hands around it for a moment before standing up suddenly and kicking the fence in fury. Her eyes glittered with unshed tears.

'That bastard!' she shouted. 'He did this, I know it! Wait till I get my hands on that creep!' Helen pulled her phone out of her pocket, stabbing at the screen with her finger. 'I'm going to kill him with my bare hands!'

'Whoa, calm down!' Laura grabbed at Helen's arm. 'We don't know it was him. Who are you ringing?'

'Damn, no answer. I'll text him instead.' Helen's fingers skittered over the screen, then she put the phone away again. 'I was ringing Neil to find out where that dickhead is working next. I'm gonna fuckin' have him, just you wait and see if I don't!

'Can you stop yelling? You're giving me a headache!'

'Sorry. It just makes me so mad!'

'Me too, but shouting won't help. They asked if we knew much about Ray though. I know she told you stuff about him, so I wondered if she'd told you where he lived or anything like that.'

Helen wiped her eyes angrily. 'I don't know anything about him, except that he's a twat. She tried to tell me how great he was and all that bollocks, but I told her I didn't care, so she stopped talking about him in the end.'

'Oh well, it was worth a shot. Hang on a minute. I got a text from Vicky on Saturday morning, do you remember?'

'Vaguely, I think I was still drunk. What about it?'

'If Vicky was dead then who sent it?'

'I dunno, maybe someone nicked her phone and sent it for a laugh. We won't know for sure until we check, so get your coat on.'

18

They took Laura's car, but Helen drove as Laura was still too shaken up to think straight. Dawn met them at the front desk and took them across the green to the morgue, where she introduced them to a guy named Ziggy, who was waiting for them.

'I'll go in,' Helen said to Laura as they approached the viewing area. 'You wait here.'

Laura started to protest but Helen was firm. 'They've already told us that she's a mess. You don't want to remember her like that. I've got a stronger stomach than you.' She pushed Laura towards some seats. 'Sit down, I won't be long.'

Ziggy led Helen through some double doors while Dawn waited with Laura. After a few minutes Helen came back, her face white and her breath shallow.

'Wow, I don't know how anyone can work with that smell? It must cling to your skin.' She sat down next to Laura and nodded her head. 'It's Vicky, mate.'

'Are you sure?' Dawn asked. 'She was quite severely beaten, so it would be easy to make a mistake.'

'I'm sure,' Helen replied, pulling a sobbing Laura into her arms.

They walked back across to the station, Helen taking

big gulps of air to try and eradicate the clinical smell that was stuck in her nostrils, Laura said nothing, but she was as white as a sheet. Dawn led them through to the same interview room as before. Mo was already there and had organised tea and coffee. She poured the drinks while the two women took their coats off and sat down.

'This is Detective Constable Maureen Ross, she's working on Vicky's case with us,' Dawn explained.

Mo smiled at everyone, helped herself to a cup of tea and sat on one of the armchairs. She was so tiny it almost swallowed her, and her feet didn't reach the floor.

'I'm so sorry for your loss,' Mo said. The two friends nodded at her in acknowledgement. 'I have a couple of extra questions if that's okay, but maybe you could take us through the evening again, mainly for my benefit as I've not heard it first-hand.'

'Sure, but we all know who did it. It was that tosser Ray Diamond,' Helen said, jumping up out of her seat and pacing the room. 'She went off with him and the next thing she's dead. Stands to reason really, he's a user.' She stared at Mo as if daring her to disagree.

'We don't know for definite that it was Mr Diamond, that's why we've asked you to come in,' Mo said in a clear, calm voice. 'Rest assured, we will be speaking to him very soon. In the meantime, come and sit down, and let's get started.'

'Sorry if I sound like a bitch,' Helen replied, plopping back down on the sofa. 'It's just that – well, I just wish that Vicky could've seen him for what he is, a waste of space.'

'Do you know him personally? It sounds like you've crossed paths with him before.' Dawn asked.

'I don't know him, but I know someone who does,' Helen admitted. 'I've been friends with Neil Stone for ages, we met at my work and hit it off straightaway. We've become good friends and he confides in me. He's told me some horror stories about Ray Diamond that would make your hair curl.'

'Mr Stone is the drag artiste?' Mo asked, scribbling in her notebook.

Helen nodded. 'Yes, he is, his stage name is Kitty McLane. He's terrific, you should go and see him sometime.'

'I might just do that,' Mo grinned in return. 'Now, tell us about that night. Let's see if we can't stir up a detail that may have been overlooked the first time.'

'Actually, there is something I should tell you,' Laura piped up. 'On the Saturday morning, I got a text message from Vicky's phone. But it can't have been from her if she was dead, can it?' Her eyes filled with tears.

Mo made a note of the new information. 'Do you still have the message?'

Laura scrolled through her texts then handed her phone over. 'Here you go.'

Mo read the message then passed the phone to Dawn. She handed the phone back to Laura.

'We didn't find a phone at the scene, and her handbag was missing too,' Dawn said.

'I said to Laura that it could have been nicked. Some people would have your fillings if you yawned widely enough. Of course, Ray could have it,' Helen suggested.

'We're running a trace on her phone, but it seems to be switched off. We will be notified if it's turned back on, then we'll be able to get a location on it,' Dawn said.

'Should we tell her mum and dad?' Laura asked. 'Then there's Milo, Vicky's cat. Who's going to look after him?' She started to cry again and Helen pulled her into a rough embrace.

'We will contact Vicky's parents, but I'm sure they would appreciate it if you took care of Milo for the time being,' Dawn said. 'Now, let's start at the beginning.'

***

By the time they had given their statements, Laura was emotionally drained, and Helen seemed even angrier than before. She kept insisting that Ray Diamond had killed Vicky, and it took a lot of effort to persuade her not to confront him. Dawn and Mo had asked them both to keep Vicky's death to themselves for the time being, until her parents had been notified.

'Can't you wait until they get home?' Helen had asked. 'It seems wrong to spoil their holiday when they haven't long gone away.'

'Imagine how they will feel if we don't tell them, especially if her mum is used to hearing from Vicky every day. There's also the worry that the press may get hold of the information and we don't want them finding out that way,' Dawn explained. 'I'll contact the travel company and get a message to them onboard.'

'Helen Whittaker really doesn't like Ray Diamond, does she?' Mo remarked after they'd seen the two women out. 'I wonder what he's done to upset her.'

'Who knows?' Dawn replied, as they headed back upstairs. 'But from the sound of it, he upsets everyone he meets.'

19

The morning briefing was in full swing and Alex had the floor. Detective Chief Inspector Andrew Oliver, Alex's boss, had been in and said his piece, and had been happy for Alex to take it from there.

Alex flipped through the notes he'd brought back from the morgue the day before. 'This list confirms that there were hairpins in the victim's hair that match Vicky Wilson's, although some may have been ripped out in the struggle. There were no earrings on the body, were there any logged at the scene?'

'Nope. Maybe they ended up in the field. More than likely the killer took them, trophies perhaps?' Dawn shrugged.

'Possibly. He confirms that cause of death was due to strangulation, possibly with a pair of tights or a scarf. There was extensive bruising to her abdomen area, lower back and between her shoulders.' Alex read through the rough notes he'd made. 'Multiple breaks, pretty much every bone in her body. Abrasions to her hands and knees and the bald patches on her head suggest that she was dragged backwards by her hair. Her face had been battered repeatedly with a heavy object, to the point that her face was practically obliterated. That tells me this was personal. There was semen in her throat but not anywhere else. Did Vicky's friends say how long she'd been seeing the stripper for?' Alex asked.

Dawn shook her head. 'No, they didn't, just that he'd given Vicky his number a couple of weeks ago.'

'Les, have you had any luck with tracing Vicky's phone?'

Les cleared his throat. 'Not yet, boss, it's either been dismantled or the battery's dead.

He looked frustrated, but Alex put his mind at rest. 'Never mind, it was worth a shot. Craig, what have you got for us?'

'I've managed to track down the club's manager, she's agreed to meet me at the club this morning and said she'll make sure all the staff from Friday night will be there. She said that the security staff were provided by Bulldog Promotions, the same agency that the strippers were from.' Craig scanned his notes. 'I've also set up a meeting with the agency's owner, Mr John Jackson, for this afternoon at 2 p.m. at their office in Wolverhampton. Do you want me to go and see him after I've spoken to the club manager?'

'No, it's fine, I'll go and see him. You and Gary take the club. Dawn, did you speak to Neil Stone, the drag artiste?' Alex asked.

'Yes, I did, he didn't seem too eager to talk to me, but he did give me Ray Diamond's address. It's one of those big houses on the Wombourne Road. I'm going to see him this morning. Can I take Mo, or do you need her for something else? I'm thinking two women might get more out of him. Apparently, his ego needs a lot of stroking.'

Dawn laughed as Mo pulled a horrified face.

'Good idea, we can put Mo's incredible talents to use – I meant mental talents Mo, don't look so shocked.' Everyone laughed at the thought of Mo trying to chat Ray up.

'Don't worry boss, he may not be my cup of tea, but I don't mind taking one for the team,' she said with a wink, causing a ripple of laughter to go around the room.

'I'll speak to Mr Stone after I've been to see Mr Jackson. We need contact details for the other acts that were there too, including the DJ,' Alex said, skimming through his list. 'Right, have I missed anything?'

'Boss, is it worth doing a radio appeal for witnesses?' Les piped up. 'There were a lot of women there that night, and we haven't tracked down all the attendees yet. It might help us to fast-track through the list.'

'Yes, speak to the press officer and ask them to set that up, get them to set up a hotline for information as well. I know I don't have to tell you to withhold some details to weed out the crank callers.'

Alex glanced at his notes once more to check he'd covered everything. 'Right, fuel up with bacon rolls, tea, coffee or whatever and let's get some results. My wife has promised that my balls will be hanging on the Christmas tree if I'm not home on time tonight, so unless you want a boss who sings soprano, I suggest you get a move on.'

20

DS Craig Muir and DC Gary Temple were attempting to interview the staff of the Leamore Club but were making very slow progress. No-one seemed willing to speak up and eventually Craig lost his temper. He threatened to haul everyone down to the station and interview them under caution. Suddenly, everyone was more than happy to help. After a couple of hours, they were down to the last two members of staff.

'Gary, you take the barman and I'll take the manager.'

'Righto,' Gary chirped and beckoned to the man lurking near the bar. 'Excuse me, sir, could you come here please?'

The man didn't look very happy but followed Gary to the side of the room. He sat down, lolling to one side as if it were too much effort to sit up unaided.

'Right then, let's start with your name, shall we?' Gary always sounded cheerful, even when he wasn't. He sat opposite the young man, pen poised, and waited for him to speak.

'Simon Tate,' the young man replied with a sigh. He was dressed all in black and wore more eyeliner than Alice Cooper. His greasy black hair was cut short on one side and long on the other, and his fringe kept falling over his face.

Gary wrote the details in his notebook. 'Now then, Mr Tate, tell me about Friday night.'

'I was working the bar. It was packed so I didn't see anything.' Simon sat back and folded his arms, making a huffing noise.

Gary was irritated by his attitude but was determined not to show it. 'Is that a special skill?'

'Is what a special skill?

'Working the bar with your eyes shut. I mean, they must have been shut if you didn't see anything.'

'Don't be ridiculous, of course they weren't shut! Do you think I'm an idiot?' Simon asked, sighing loudly again. He did that a lot, Gary noticed. It was almost theatrical, and it was getting on Gary's nerves.

Gary rested his arms on the table and leaned forward, making his suit jacket strain at the seams. He may not have been as slim as Craig, but not an ounce of his bulk was fat. His colleague could outrun most people, but Gary was the muscle. He was proud of his strength and could bench press one hundred and sixty kilos without breaking a sweat.

Simon looked at the bulging arms and swallowed hard.

'Listen son, stop being a smartarse and answer the questions. Start by telling me what time you were here from and when you left, and everything you did in between. And stop bloody sighing.' Gary raised his voice, his usual cheeriness momentarily deserting him. Simon moved his chair back a bit.

'You can't speak to me like that!' Simon croaked, his voice abandoning him for a second.

'You're right, I'm sorry if I caused you any offence, sir,' Gary said, relaxing once more and sitting back slightly. 'Now then, where were we?'

Simon cleared his throat a couple of times. 'I was

meant to come in around 5.30 p.m., but Sally called me in early. The guy who does the stock run had phoned in sick, so I had to do it. I ended up doing two runs to the warehouse – in my own car too. I bet I don't get any extra money to cover my petrol,' he whined.

'What time did people start arriving?' Gary asked. 'I mean the acts, not the staff.'

'One bloke was here when I got back from the first run, so I let him in and went off to get the next lot. That was around 6 p.m., I reckon. I don't know what time the others got here; they were all here when I got back.' He looked like it was a real effort to speak for so long without sighing.

Gary wrote the word *Prick* in the margin of his notebook before motioning for Simon to continue.

'Oh yeah, before I did the warehouse run, I made sure the back room was ready for the performers. They usually give us a list of what they need before they arrive. It saves them having to ask us later when we're busy serving customers.'

'What sort of stuff did they want? I'm curious, that's all.' Gary added as Simon gave him a funny look.

Simon thought for a moment. 'The drag queen's assistant had phoned and asked for a table and two chairs, both without arms. She also wanted a table-top mirror and asked us to make sure there was plenty of decent lighting. The blokes didn't ask for anything, they rarely do. I put a couple of bin bags and some toilet rolls in there, but they still left loads of mess. I think your guys took the bags away, they're not there now.'

Gary flicked through his list of questions. 'What about during the show? Did you see anything out of the ordinary?'

'Not a lot, it was manic. One thing I will say though – that woman who died was being a bitch to the staff. She pushed in at the bar a couple of times, which pissed a lot of the other customers off, and she was rude when Angela asked her to wait her turn. She was going on about needing to get a drink for one of the strippers, so she needed to be served first. In the end, I came and served her just to get rid of her before she caused a fight. And she had a go at the security man. He was really angry.' Simon sat back in his chair again.

'Do you know what she said to him?' Gary asked, without looking up from his notebook.

'I didn't hear her, he told me about it later when we went for a smoke outside. He said she was in his face, screaming about how the stripper had told her to come through to the dressing room, but the security guy refused to let her go in. She said she'd make sure he was fired. The thing is, none of the strippers had told him about her, so he was right not to let her through.' Simon looked at Gary, as if waiting for him to agree with him.

'Don't worry, we'll be speaking to him in due course. Do you know his name?' Gary asked.

'I think it was Alan, or it could've been Aaron. He doesn't work for us, I think the drag act hired him. Sorry if that's not very helpful.'

'No problem, we'll track him down. Now, did you see anything unusual when you went for a smoke?'

'No, I don't think so. To be fair I was a bit preoccupied.' Simon looked embarrassed. 'This bird came out while I was having my break. She was a bit drunk, started coming on to me, you know? She was very fit, so we had a bit of a moment.'

'Really? Was that all? How long were you outside, and whereabouts did this "moment" take place?' Gary paused from writing and looked hard at Simon.

'I'll show you if you like,' Simon said, standing up but Gary waved him back down into his seat.

'In a bit, Mr Tate, let's get this done first. So, you and this lass – what was her name?'

'I don't know, I didn't ask. I was just happy to get a bit of action. Afterwards, she went back inside while I got my breath back. She was a bit of a looker, not the sort that usually bothers with guys like me.' Simon had a faraway look on his face as he recalled the memory.

'What about at the end of the evening, once the show was over?' Gary asked. 'Did you see the victim after your run-in with her at the bar?'

'No, I didn't see her after that. She disappeared backstage with the stripper around half ten. It started to empty out around midnight, and she didn't come back to the bar. Her mates did though, they were steaming. Especially the blonde one, she was completely off her face. I gave her an ice bucket in case she was sick. I bet she had a hell of a hangover the next day,' he grinned.

***

DS Craig Muir was in the function room and was faring a little better with the bar manager.

Sally Cameron was a short, large-breasted woman in a clingy dress designed for someone both younger and slimmer, with shoulder-length black hair that flicked up at the ends. She teetered on her six-inch stilettos, and her vivid green eyes roamed over Craig as if he were a prime steak. The expression "Cougar" came to Craig's mind. He tried to keep a respectable distance between them, but Sally seemed to find any excuse to move closer to him.

'Yes, I booked the show, it's very popular at this time of year,' she said, her voice like nails down a blackboard. 'Mind you, I'm a red-blooded woman, so the opportunity to have some gorgeous men getting their clothes off was right up my street! They were really fit too. Do you know if they were married? I don't do married men. That drag queen was a right diva, so full of himself. Or should that be herself? Anyway, I'm thinking of booking another show for New Year. What do you think? Will it seem disrespectful, on account of that woman getting herself murdered like that?'

She paused to take a breath and Craig jumped in quickly. 'To be honest, I'd rather stick to the questions if you don't mind. Was there any trouble that you are aware of? Any fighting, or arguments at all?'

'Oh, there's always a scrap or two at these events. Women getting drunk and losing control, thinking they'll get off with one of the guys, then losing it when the guy makes eyes at their mate. It happens more than you know. The security man was very good, so professional. He had to escort a couple of women off the premises, they were doing drugs in the toilets. I don't have any of that nonsense here. If they want to kill themselves, they should do it somewhere else. Oops, that sounds bad, given the circumstances, but you know where I'm coming from don't you?' Sally had the grace to blush.

'Anything else?' Craig asked.

'To be honest it was so busy I had to help out behind the bar to keep the queues down. It's been our best night of the year sales-wise. I think the dead woman had a row with one of the security men, but I don't know which one. They all look alike to me, those coloured blokes.'

Craig bristled at her ignorance, but kept his mouth shut. 'How many people were backstage?'

'There was the drag queen and her friend, that cute blond guy with the tattoos, a big black man – he was gorgeous – and a dark-haired guy who looked a bit miserable. Ray turned up later with his assistant.' Sally scrunched her face up in thought, causing her thick make-up to crack. She looked a lot older than the thirty-eight years old she'd claimed to be.

'You said earlier that you didn't know the strippers' names,' Craig said.

'I said I didn't know the other strippers, but everyone

knows Ray Diamond. He's been stripping for years, and he's still the best out there. You'd make a good stripper; you've got a lovely figure.' Sally stroked Craig's lapels and he felt his balls shrink back up into his body.

'My charms are for my wife's eyes only,' he said, stepping back out of her reach. His back bumped the bar.

'Pity, I could teach you a thing or two. Anyway, are we done? I've got loads to do, can't stand around being chatted up by you all day.' Sally laughed.

'Just one more thing,' Craig said, pulling his wallet out and pointing to the shelf behind the bar. 'Give us a couple of those cheese rolls, will you? I'm starving.'

21

Alex stood on the dance floor at the comedy club in Bradstock, listening to a band on the stage. He was waiting for Neil Stone to turn up and had been drawn towards the stage when he heard some of the numbers the band were practising. They were very good, and Alex found himself humming along under his breath. The lead singer bounced around the stage like a teenager, and Alex wished he had half his energy. It was refreshing to see a band with an older line-up, not the boy bands that seem to be popular these days.

As they finished the Ramones number, the lead singer spotted him and climbed down from the stage and bounded over towards Alex. He was older than he'd first appeared, around forty years old, and was dressed in black jeans, a blue Superman T-shirt and red trainers. His jet-black hair was styled to look like he'd just got out of bed, and his green eyes sparkled with adrenalin.

'Hi mate, how did we sound? Not too many bum notes I hope,' he said, pushing his glasses back into place. 'I'm Dean Smith, and we,' he gestured towards the stage, 'are Nowhere Fast.'

Alex introduced himself and explained he was waiting for Neil Stone. 'You can carry on if you like, I'm happy just listening to you, although I'm more of a Queen fan myself. You're all really good. Have you been together long?'

Dean gave a small bow. 'Thank you very much. We've been together around six years. There's been a few line-up changes, but we've got a good mix now. We're playing a charity gig here on Saturday if you fancy coming along.' He searched in the pockets of his jeans. 'I did have some tickets here somewhere, I'm happy to give you a couple on the house.'

Alex shook his head and pulled his wallet out. 'No need for freebies, I'm happy to pay for them. I'll take six please, some of my colleagues might want to come too.'

Dean was delighted. 'No problem, hang on, I'll grab some tickets from Matt.'

He rushed back to the stage and was back in a flash with six tickets. 'They're a fiver each, so that's thirty quid in total.'

'What are the chances of you doing a Queen number? I'll give you an extra tenner for your charity if you can manage it.'

Dean scratched his head. 'We can try, but it'll be tough. They aren't really our style.'

Alex grinned. 'There's a lot more to them than you think. I recommend you listen to the album titled: A Night at the Opera, I think you'll be surprised how diverse they were.'

'Cool, I'll see what the lads think.'

'I'll make it twenty quid if you can do a Beatles track for my wife, too.' Alex laughed at the expression on Dean's face.

'Challenge accepted, but don't blame us if she never speaks to you again,' he said.

Alex took the tickets and handed over the money. Even if the others couldn't make it, he was happy to support local talent. He looked at the tickets Dean had given him.

'Bulldog Promotions – would that be John Jackson's agency? He's next on my list of people to talk to.'

Dean nodded. 'Yeah it is. We did a free gig for one of his charity shows, and he took us under his wing. Most agents wouldn't look at an older band like us, but he's been great.'

'Brilliant. Well, I'd better get back to it. I'll see you on Saturday.' They shook hands again, and Dean went back to the stage and started talking to his bandmates.

Alex turned away from the stage and almost collided with a woman standing behind him, startling her and causing her to drop her handbag. He bent down and picked it up, handing it back with an apology.

'No need to apologise. I'm so sorry I'm late, one of the old dears at the bingo hall had a funny turn, and we had to send her off to hospital,' the woman said, in a dark smoky voice. Alex did a double-take and the woman smirked at him.

'Detective Inspector Peachey I presume? Kitty McLane at your service, or Neil Stone if you prefer. Shall we go through to my dressing room?'

The small room that served as a dressing room was bleak to say the least. There was no window, and the only lighting came from a solitary bulb hanging from the ceiling. A distinct lack of ventilation meant the smell was quite nauseating, like old socks, stale beer and cheap perfume all rolled together. The small folding table along one wall was heaped with sequinned dresses, feather boas, wigs and what looked like bags of bird seed. Alex perched on the edge of a wooden box that stood along one wall and took out his notebook and pen.

Neil slipped his wig, jewellery and dress off and threw a black silk kimono on over his underwear. He sat down at the dressing table on the opposite side of the room and pulled the mirror closer, before rummaging in a box by his feet and taking out various tubs, packets and tubes, and placing them on the tabletop. He opened a large tub of cold cream and smeared a thick layer of it over his face before realising he was still wearing his false eyelashes. Neil swore softly to himself before peeling them off and dropping them on the floor, where they lay like two dead spiders.

Alex shuddered and tried not to look at them.

'You don't mind if I take my slap off while we talk, do you? I get terrible spots if I leave it on too long and I'm getting a little too old for acne,' Neil wiped off the first lot of cream and applied a different product.

'Not at all, it's fascinating to watch if I'm honest,' Alex replied, watching as Kitty slowly disappeared and Neil took her place.

'Whenever I pull a double like I have today, I try and let my skin breathe between jobs. Now then, what would you like to know?' Neil asked, bringing the conversation back to the matter in hand.

'Mr Stone, I need to ask you about the show you did last Friday night. Can you give me a run-down of the evening, please?'

'Please call me Neil. I won't bite you – unless you ask me very nicely!' Neil winked broadly at Alex and looked him up and down. 'Trust me, I'd give you anything you ask for.'

Alex looked at him with a blank expression and Neil looked sheepish. 'Sorry, force of habit to chat up handsome men,' he admitted.

Alex repeated the question and Neil put his finger to his lips and closed his eyes, deep in thought. There were still traces of silver glitter on his eyelids.

'I got there around 7.00 p.m., Des was already there, and Chad arrived a few minutes later. I started putting my face on, Ruby laid my clothes out and helped me into my frock. Once I was ready, I went out to give my music to the DJ and chatted with some of the women. A couple of them bought me drinks, bless them. I came back in to check the running order and grab my microphone, that was around 8.30 p.m. Si had just arrived; I think he'd had some trouble with his car. Des and Chad were getting ready when I went out to get the show started.'

Neil took a baby wipe from a packet on the table and smoothed it over his face and neck, removing the cream and leftover make-up. He turned from the mirror and smiled at Alex. He looked so different that Alex would never have guessed that Neil and Kitty were one and the same. Neil was around forty years old, bald and brown-eyed. He reminded Alex of one of the guys in those fast car movies that Jayne loved.

'What about Ray Diamond?' Alex asked.

Neil pulled a face as if he'd smelled something offensive. 'I don't know what time he arrived, but he was there when I came off at 9 p.m. Des and Chad went on, I got changed and had a quick snack. I went back on, did a quick introduction for Si, then once he was finished, I did twenty minutes to close the first half. Ray went on after the interval, which was around 10 p.m. or thereabouts.'

Alex wrote quickly, hoping he'd be able to decipher his scrawl later. 'Did you talk to Ray at all?' he asked.

Neil raised one perfectly plucked eyebrow. 'Darling, it's a well-known fact that Ray and I don't get on. I keep as far away as I can and pay him as little attention as possible. It's not always easy though, but I try.'

'Was there anyone else in the dressing room at all?' Alex asked.

'Only Ruby and Michelle, but that's normal. Ruby Clarke is my dresser, she comes to all my gigs, she lays out my costumes, helps me with my zips, that kind of thing. She filled in when I split up with my partner, and she's been with me ever since. She knocked Ray out once, he made some remark about her being related to the chimps from the tea advert. You probably don't remember those adverts, do you? I expect you're too young.'

'I remember them, I'm older than you think,' Alex admitted, causing Neil to raise his eyebrow again.

'Why are all the good men straight? Such a waste,' Neil lamented before continuing.

'Michelle Simmons is Ray's dresser, but more so. She does whatever Ray tells her to do. She's a little darling, she'd do anything for anyone, and she's the only person who can calm Ray down when he loses his temper.'

'Is Michelle romantically involved with Ray Diamond?'

Neil started packing his toiletries away again, balling up the used tissues and cotton wool and dropping it into the wastepaper basket under the table. 'No, definitely not, although I expect he's tried. He's so stupid, he thinks he can get into anyone's knickers just by batting his eyelashes at them. Michelle knows what he's like, she's quite often had to wait in the car while he gives some little scrubber a quick one in the car park. I don't know how she puts up with it to be honest, he treats her like shit.'

Alex glanced at his notebook again. 'What about Vicky Wilson? I understand she came backstage to see him.'

Neil nodded. 'Yes, Vicky was one of what I call his little pets. Most of the time, Ray likes to love them and leave them, but now and then he gets his hooks into a woman who hangs on his every word and treats him like a God. He keeps them around for a while, getting them to spend their money on him and in return they do everything he asks. Vicky was sweet, but she had a nasty tongue on her. I was standing by the dressing room door when I heard her having a go at the security man. She said some vile things to him, I'm surprised he didn't throw her out.'

'Do you know his name?' Alex asked, but Neil shook his head.

'No, not someone I'd seen before. He might be part of

John's crew. I'm freelance nowadays, so I work for whoever hires me,' Neil said.

'Fair enough,' Alex said. 'Did you see Vicky leave?'

'No, I was onstage doing my last spot. The only people left here when I came back out, besides Ruby, was Si. He was getting a lift with the DJ, so he was out the front by the disco booth. Everyone else had gone home. The lads went out through the front doors, they like to talk to the women after the show, not necessarily to chat them up, they're just nice guys. Ray crawled out the back way as usual, he's too important to mix with the audience, unless he wants something of course. Vicky went with him as far as I know. I didn't see her again.'

Alex closed his notebook. 'I think that's it for now, but I may have to come back to you at some point. Can I just ask what Ray did for you to hate him so much? It's written all over your face, to be honest.'

Neil took a deep breath, stood up and walked over to Alex. He opened his kimono and let it fall to his waist, turning his back on Alex as he did so. He lifted up his vest and Alex sucked his breath hard. Neil's back was a mass of welts and scars, almost like a noughts and crosses board.

'What the hell happened?' Alex looked at the puckered skin on Neil's back. He couldn't see where one scar ended and another began.

Neil let his vest drop down and put his kimono back on, tying it tightly at the front. 'Like I said before, Ray has a temper. We used to work together a lot, toured abroad and everything. I got him his big break, introduced him to the right people, you know how it goes. Anyway, about three years ago, we did a show together, a charity one. He was high as a kite on something or other, he likes a quick snort now and again. I don't know how he managed to do his spot to tell you the truth. He came up to me afterwards and asked if I'd lend him some money. He said

113

he owed it to some shady characters, and they wanted it back. I said no, I have Mum to think about. She's in a residential home and every penny goes towards her care. He seemed fine about me refusing, and we went our separate ways. I arrived home around midnight after dropping Ruby off and Ray was parked outside my house in his flash car. If I owed anyone money, that would be the first thing I'd get rid of.'

Neil paused for a moment, trying to keep his voice from shaking. Alex told him to take his time.

'He asked me again to help him out, I refused again but he kept asking, begging even. In the end, he said he would let me fuck him – his words, not mine. I was so taken aback that I laughed. That was my big mistake. He lost his rag, he grabbed me by the throat and started shaking me like a rag doll. Back then he was doing steroids and was strong. I couldn't make him let go. He threw me on the ground and started kicking me, I wrapped my arms around my head and curled up as small as I could. He was snarling like a wild animal, I thought he was going to kill me. He tore my shirt off my back, beat me with his belt then lit a cigarette and burned me. Then he opened his trousers, pulled out his cock and he pissed on me. Can you believe that? I was so humiliated I just lay there, not moving or speaking. Once he was done, he told me to keep my mouth shut or he'd pay my mum a visit and give her a taste of a real man.'

Alex was appalled. 'You should have reported him.'

'How could I, given that he'd pretty much threatened to rape my elderly mother?' Neil shivered at the thought and a tear slid down his cheek.

'How come no-one saw him? Surely your neighbours would have heard the commotion or seen something through their windows?'

Neil smiled bitterly. 'I live in a rough part of town where you keep your nose to yourself unless you want trouble, and I'm no snitch.'

'Why do you still work with him? You must be terrified. I know I would be,' Alex admitted.

Neil lit a cigarette and watched as the smoke curled upwards. After a moment he spoke again. 'I'll admit that for a week I couldn't even go outside, but the drag community is fabulous. We look after each other, a lot of us have had abusive relationships or come from broken homes. I was meant to be doing a gig in London for a dear friend, but I cancelled it. He kept ringing me and when I didn't answer he turned up on my doorstep. Next thing I know I'm in London in his spare room, being cared for by some of the most wonderful queens in the business. It was the best therapy I could have had. It was a month before I could work again, and I got such a warm reception that I knew I'd be okay.'

'What happened when you saw Ray next?'

Neil took another drag on his cigarette. 'I'll admit I was terrified, but the beauty of being a drag queen is that your make up acts like an invisible shield you can hide behind, it protects you from anything and everything. Neil Stone might be scared of Ray Diamond, but Kitty McLane certainly isn't. I'm damned if I'm going to let him stop me being who I am.'

'Would you like to report it now, to me?' Alex asked. 'I'll throw the book at him.'

Neil shook his head. 'No need, it's in the past now. Ray Diamond will get his comeuppance one of these days, of that you can be certain. I only hope I'm there to watch.'

22

Dawn flipped her visor down to protect her eyes from the harsh winter sun and turned the radio up. She was in good spirits and hummed along to the music, as she relished the thought of interviewing Ray Diamond. She'd met blokes like him before, they loved to brag about their conquests. He was more likely to let his guard down if he was showing off.

Dawn glanced at Mo sitting next to her, singing along to the radio. Even though she was wearing her usual work attire of black trousers, white shirt and black jacket, Mo still looked like a teenager.

Dawn knew it was Mo's first big interview since she had joined Alex's team, and guessed she was eager to prove herself. They got on very well, and Dawn marvelled at Mo's perceptiveness. It was like having Dustin Hoffman on the team, and Dawn sometimes referred to her as Rainman, much to Mo's amusement. Having Mo on the team meant that paperwork didn't have time to build up; she typed at lightning speed and could produce reports almost before they'd been asked for. She always noticed the finer details, the ones that might possibly escape a casual observer. Mo only had to glance at a crime scene and she'd be able to recall exactly where every single item was from memory.

'This must be the place,' Dawn said as she indicated left and pulled over at the side of the road. She'd double-checked the address before they set off, not quite believing that someone like Ray would live in such a prestigious neighbourhood.

Wyndham Lane was a long leafy road on the outskirts of Wolverhampton, with open fields beyond, just off a stretch of road known as the Dog Leg due to its many twists and turns. It was popular with confident commuters wanting to get to Stourbridge, but without the long queues through the city. All the homes in the lane were formidable to say the least, many of them having the long sweeping driveways and symmetrical trees lining the way.

They were both impressed as they drove through the tall wrought-iron gates that stood proudly open at the mouth of the property, but their admiration quickly faded as they realised that the high stone wall that shielded the house from the rest of the road had been hiding what could only be described as a total disaster.

Whatever Ray did with his time when he wasn't strutting his stuff, it certainly wasn't looking after his property. The long, honey-coloured gravel driveway that swept up towards the house in a gentle curve was pockmarked where weeds had pushed their way up through the stones. The miniature fir trees that lined the driveway all appeared to be dead or well on their way to dying. What few flowerbeds there were had been left to their own devices, all life choked out of the flowers by the weeds that had taken them over.

The only orderly thing were three cars, a van and a motorbike parked neatly in a row against the hedge bordering the left-hand side of the garden. The fishpond in front of the house had a shop mannequin half-submerged upside down in it, the legs making a crude V sign. Green mould coated the mannequin. A bright-red Porsche Carrera was parked close to the edge of the pond, the driver's door wide open and loud music blaring from it, which could be heard from inside Dawn's car.

She parked and walked over to the Porsche, sticking her head inside for a moment. It stank of weed and booze and she stepped back hurriedly.

Mo climbed out of the car too and looked at the front of the house. It was Georgian in style with large sash windows on either side of the wide front door. There was a small balcony above the door which looked as if it had been recently added but was in keeping with the rest of the house. Mo stood very still as she scanned the house and cars from left to right and back again. Dawn smiled to herself, she knew that Mo was capturing every minute detail.

'Come on, let's get this over with,' Dawn said, crunching her way across the gravel to the front door and indicating for Mo to follow. Dawn had never met Ray Diamond but, according to Heather in the canteen, he was the best thing since sliced bread.

Heather had almost fainted when Dawn had said where they were going, and had brought in a promotional photo which she thrust at her, begging her to get his autograph. Dawn had looked at the photo and rolled her eyes in disbelief. To say it was cheesy was an understatement. In the shot, Ray knelt sideways on, with his head tilted back and his eyes closed. He was wearing only a pair of white jeans, with the top button left undone and the zip down. A tuft of pubic hair peeked out of the opening. He held a bottle of water high above his chest, the contents trickling down over his six-pack. His trademark honey-coloured hair billowed out behind him, fluffed to within an inch of its life. To make it worse, he appeared to be sporting a pair of white angel wings. Dawn thought he looked like an extra from a cheap porn film.

Mo rang the bell and a deep chime sounded inside. It was a good five minutes before the door creaked open and a mousy-haired, harassed-looking woman peered around it. Both officers held up their ID cards for inspection.

'Hello, I'm Detective Sergeant Dawn Redwood from Wolverhampton MCU, and this is Detective Constable Maureen Ross. We need to speak to Mr Ray Diamond please.'

The woman didn't look surprised, as if having the police call round was an everyday occurrence. She opened the door wider and motioned for them to come in, hitching the basket of laundry she was carrying further up on her hip. She looked around twenty-five years old and wore a yellow T-shirt which matched her rubber gloves. Her baggy black jeans were held up with a brown leather belt.

'I'm Michelle Simmons. You'd better come in. Excuse the mess, I'm a bit behind today. You'd best come through the kitchen to avoid getting paint on your clothes.'

Michelle tucked a lock of hair that had escaped her ponytail back behind her ear and walked off towards the back of the house, her black trainers squeaking on the wooden floor, leaving Dawn and Mo to follow behind.

Michelle walked along the corridor to the left of the staircase, which swept around and upwards in a gentle curve. The hall was in the throes of being decorated. The walls had been recently plastered and there were several pots of paint stacked up beneath the window. A pair of stepladders stood near the door and a slim, dark-haired man was balanced on them, brush in hand and a look of concentration on his face as he painted the architrave above the door. He glanced at them as they passed but said nothing.

The kitchen was bright and airy, the large window allowing shafts of sunlight to stream into the room. It was fitted out with every modern convenience you could think of, and it was spotlessly clean. Both the washing machine and tumble dryer were on the go, and whatever Michelle had cooking in the oven smelled heavenly.

Mo commented on it and Michelle smiled as she told her that she had been trying out some new bread recipes. 'Not that any of them will appreciate it,' she added, as she tipped the full laundry basket onto the kitchen floor by the washing machine.

'Bunch of heathens. I usually freeze it and have it myself when Ray's not here, the cheese loaf is lovely with tomato soup. Ray's got some friends over at the minute, but I think they're going home soon.'

Michelle opened a door at the side of the kitchen and showed them into a huge room that was separated into two by folding doors which stood open.

The décor in the room was stunning. Michelle explained that Jason, the decorator, had only finished it the week before. The walls were white, with inset panels in a pale green that looked like polished plaster. The three floor-length sash windows were dressed in dark green damask, held with cream tie backs. The high ceiling had plasterwork fruit and leaves around the edges, and a magnificent chandelier in the centre. The floor was stripped oak, polished to a high sheen.

Two large cream leather sofas were set at slight angles with each other to face the sixty-eight inch television dominating the wall above the open fireplace. A long oak coffee table stood in front of the larger sofa, and a dining table and six chairs graced the area near the window.

A suit of armour stood against the wall between the windows. It had a large dildo sticking out where the codpiece should be, and a pair of knickers on its head. At the other end of the room, through the open double doors, was a full-sized pool table, around which stood three men, two white and one black.

Dawn wondered if they were the other strippers from the night of Vicky's murder. The black man potted a ball, laughed then moonwalked around the table. The other two groaned in disbelief and got their wallets out.

'Ray, visitors for you,' Michelle called as she crossed the room and disappeared back through the kitchen door.

The two officers took a moment to survey the messy room properly. Dishevelled clothes were scattered here and there, hanging off the backs of chairs and in small piles on the floor. Beer bottles, empty cans and takeaway cartons littered the open fireplace, spilling their remains on the white marble hearth. The two large ashtrays on the coffee table were overflowing with discarded cigarette butts, and the whole room smelled like a wrestler's armpit.

Michelle reappeared, armed with an empty laundry basket. She circled the room, gathering up clothes as she went, folding the clean ones and placing them on the arm of the sofa and depositing the dirty ones in the basket. She lugged the basket away and returned with a black bin liner. She scooped up the rubbish with lightning speed – she obviously had to deal with this on a regular basis and had it down to a fine art. In less than five minutes the room looked habitable again. She lit a large candle on the mantelpiece, the scent of which soon masked the smell of sweaty feet.

Dawn was impressed. She wondered if Michelle did house calls and how much she charged.

'Ray, I said you have visitors,' Michelle said, much louder this time.

Half-sitting, half-lying across one of the sofas and oblivious to all around him was Ray Diamond. He was swigging from a beer bottle and absent-mindedly twirling his hair while he watched a video of his own show. The volume was so loud that Ray hadn't noticed Dawn and Mo enter the room, so when Michelle spoke for the second time, he jumped so violently that he spilled beer all down his black frilled shirt.

'Fuck! You stupid bitch, now look what you've done!' he shouted, standing up and wiping his shirt, he turned angrily towards Michelle.

Spotting Dawn and Mo, he instantly replaced the scowl with a huge Oscar-winning smile, and Michelle took the opportunity to disappear again.

'Hello ladies!' he exclaimed, stumbling sideways and crashing into the coffee table. 'I'm sorry if I scared you just then. Michelle should have told me I had guests. Guys, we have company!' he shouted across the room, waving his beer bottle to get the attention of his friends. They looked over, waved back and returned to their game.

'That's Des, Si and Chad,' he explained.

Before Dawn could identify herself, Ray looked back at the television. 'I'm just watching a video of my routine, seeing if I can improve it, but you can't improve on something that's already perfect, can you? If you ladies want to take a seat, I'll give you a private show,' he said, gyrating slowly but struggling to stay upright. 'Hey, is that one of my promo pictures? Allow me to sign it for you.'

He scattered the rubbish on the table, knocking most of it to the floor and locating a pen. He waved his hand at Dawn for her to give him the picture. 'Who shall I make it out to?'

Dawn told him, and he scrawled his name, adding a plethora of kisses underneath.

'There you go, that will be worth a fortune one day. Now, don't go touching yourself when you look at it, you'll go blind.'

He winked broadly, making Dawn feel sick. She took the photo back, holding it by the corner as if it were contaminated and placed it on the back of the sofa.

Dawn couldn't decide whether it was part of the act or he really was as drunk as he looked. His hair was matted and greasy, his eyes were glazed, and his clothes looked like he'd slept in them for a week. She really didn't want to know what the stains on his white jeans were.

She took out her ID card and held it up to Ray but before she could speak, she felt hot breath on her neck. One of Ray's mates had come up behind her and was standing very close. He put his hands on her hips and pressed against her, swaying in time to the music from the television and humming into her ear. When she turned around to face him, he grinned at her, showing very white teeth.

Dawn gave him an award-winning smile of her own and flashed her warrant card at him. He let go as if he'd been scalded, stepped back and promptly fell over the rubbish bag that Michelle had left on the floor.

He got up to laughter and jeers from his friends. Despite being slightly shorter than the others, he was bulkier, with larger biceps and a palette of colourful tattoos snaking down each arm. His black jeans hugged his body as if scared to let go, and his black vest top looked painted on. His blond fringe fell lazily over his forehead and his green eyes twinkled in mischief. He winked at Dawn and jogged back towards the pool table.

'Well done Si, you twat,' the taller of the white guys said, clapping him on the back. Si turned, gave Dawn a sweeping bow and blew her a kiss. Dawn bit back a smile and told Mo to go and talk them.

'Yeah, come on Detective, see if you can beat the reigning champion,' Si laughed, pointing at the tall black man.

Dawn waited until Mo had gone into the other room before turning her attention back to Ray.

23

Ray stood watching Dawn, his smile wavering slightly. He clearly had no idea why she was there, either that or he was a bloody good actor, Dawn thought. She identified herself, showing him her warrant card. They stared at each other for a few seconds before Ray suddenly seemed to wake up and, shoving the pile of clean laundry onto the floor, invited Dawn to sit down.

Dawn perched on the edge of the sofa and Ray surveyed her through half-closed eyes as he retook his seat.

'I'm making enquiries about a suspicious death on Friday 20th December at the Leamore Club on Stafford Road. I've been led to believe you were working there that night.'

Ray looked blankly at her. 'I dunno, was I? It's possible, but I've had a drink since then,' he said. He glanced around the room. 'Michelle will know for definite. Shelley!' he bellowed for his assistant and she stuck her head around the kitchen door.

'You called, O Master?' she replied, her sarcasm lost on Ray. 'How can I best serve thee?' She spotted the clean laundry on the floor and hurried over to pick it up.

Ray's face lit up. 'Ah Princess, there you are. Where

was I working last Friday? Be a good girl and bring me the diary, will you? Then, can you pop to Asda and get some more beer, we're nearly out. Don't worry about cooking tonight, we'll get a curry in, again. If you're quick I'll let you suck my cock again, I know how you love it.'

He erupted into fits of laughter as Michelle stuck her tongue out at him and went back into the kitchen. She came back a few seconds later, dropped a red diary onto the sofa with a thud, scooped up the bin bag that Si had fallen over and left again. She looked angry and embarrassed. The front door slammed and a few seconds later a car roared off.

Dawn made a note to speak to Michelle in private as soon as possible.

Ray saw Dawn's expression and laughed. 'Don't mind her, she loves it really. Shelley's like a mum to me – with added benefits, if you get my drift. Lads, tell the nice police officers how much Michelle loves me.'

The guys shouted that Michelle loved him loads, and he saluted in return. Dawn gave an inward shudder and returned to the task in hand.

'Right, Mr Diamond, the reason for our visit is, as I said before, to discuss the incident that took place at the Leamore Club,' she said. She looked up and saw that Ray wasn't listening. He was watching the television screen and idly stroking his crotch.

Dawn reached for the remote control and flicked the television off. The room was plunged into silence, apart from the murmurings coming from the other end of the room. Ray looked as if she'd slapped him. 'I do need your full attention, if you don't mind.'

Ray looked contrite and sat up a bit straighter, picking up a new beer bottle as he did so. 'Okay babe, I'm all yours. Do with me what you will.'

He twisted the top off the bottle and took a long drink, his eyes running over Dawn's body.

Dawn resisted the urge to punch him in his smug face. She pointed to the diary lying between them and he shrugged. 'Go ahead, no secrets in there. I keep my naughty stuff in my bedroom,' he said with a wink.

Dawn picked up the diary and scanned the pages until she found the date in question. 'It says here that you were working with four others, is that right?' She pointed to the entry. 'Can you talk me through what happened that night, starting from the time you arrived?'

Ray took the book from her and read through the details. 'I remember now. It was a straightforward show. I got there around 8.30 p.m., had a few beers out the back with the lads.'

'The ones who are talking to my colleague?' Dawn asked.

Ray nodded. 'Yeah, you can ask them, they'll tell you. I got ready while they were doing their spots. Chad and Des have a terrific double act, well worth watching. Si's not bad, he's lost his edge recently though. If I were him, I'd quit now while I was ahead. No-one wants to see you when you're past your best. I always go on last, seeing as I'm the star. I did my stuff, nipped backstage to put some shorts on, then went back out to do photos with the women.'

Dawn wrote it down. 'What time did you leave, and was anyone with you?'

'I left around half eleven, I think. Michelle drove me home, I was really drunk by then. The drag act will vouch for me – although I think he'd already gone by then, probably had rent boys to pick up. Have you asked Michelle? Where is she anyway?'

Ray looked surprised when Dawn reminded him that she'd gone to the shop.

'Look, what's this all about? Has some little tart shouted rape or something? If she has then she's lying, because no-one says no to me, they all want a piece of this.'

He cupped his crotch arrogantly and glared at her.

Dawn slowed her breathing down to calm herself. She really wanted to beat the shit out of him. 'If you'd been listening, you'd know that we're here about a suspicious death that occurred that night. I believe you knew the victim, a Miss Vicky Wilson?'

'Vicky? Cute little redhead? Oh yeah, she's been at all my shows for the past six months or so, and for the last couple she's been backstage with me. She's sweet, mouth like a vacuum cleaner. Is she in trouble? If she is it has nothing to do with me,' Ray stated, as if he hadn't heard what Dawn had told him.

'It's clear to me that you're not listening to me. I've just informed you that she's dead, Mr Diamond. You may have been the last person to see her alive,' Dawn replied, getting more and more irritated by the minute.

'Don't be daft, of course she's not dead!' Ray laughed at the idea. 'I saw her on Monday, she came around when Michelle was . . . well, wherever she was, and I spent all morning screwing her brains out, first on the pool table, and then right there on that rug.'

He pointed to a spot in front of the fireplace. 'She left before Michelle got back, then I went for a shower.'

Dawn looked hard at him. 'Are you sure that was Vicky? Because her friend has positively identified her body at the morgue.'

Ray tried to run his hand through his hair, but it was too tangled, so he pushed it back off his face instead. 'Maybe you're right, it could have been a different bird.' He laughed nervously. 'I have a few on the go, it's hard to keep track sometimes. I'll tell you what, check the inside of her thigh. I gave her a cracking love-bite, you should still be able to see it. There's probably a couple on her tits as well.'

His eyes strayed back towards the television and he

groped blindly for the remote control.

Dawn stood up, her patience at its limit. 'We'll no doubt have further questions for you, so I'll need a contact number if you don't mind. I'll let you get back to your video.'

She picked up the remote and tossed it back to Ray, who fumbled and dropped it on the floor. As he scrambled to pick it up, she walked towards the other end of the room, turning to close the double doors behind her so that the sudden increase in volume from the television was lessened. She stood for a second and took a few deep breaths, before joining Mo at the pool table.

They had abandoned the game now and were sitting on stools next to the bar in the corner. Si looked furious, he'd obviously overheard what Ray had said about him and he gripped his pool cue tightly.

Des had a hand on his shoulder, trying to calm him down. 'Listen man, you know your routine knocks spots off his, don't let him wind you up.'

Si smiled at him gratefully, his colour starting to return to normal. 'Cheers dude, nice to know someone appreciates me.'

'I love you man, you're a credit to the profession.' Chad put his hand on his heart, then pointed to Si.

Si blushed to the roots of his hair. 'Shut up you poof, I know you fancy me but there's no way that massive dick of yours is going anywhere near my ass!'

The men fell about laughing, their amusement rubbing off on Dawn and Mo.

Chad stood up and offered his stool to Dawn, and he leaned against the pool table. The three men listened carefully as she repeated what she'd told Ray. At least they were taking her seriously, judging by the look on their faces.

'Poor woman,' Chad murmured, when she'd finished speaking. 'She seemed like a nice kid. I hope you get whoever did it.'

'Me too,' Dawn agreed. 'Now, let's get some details if that's okay. Des, can we start with you?'

Des was tall and broad, with short dark hair, and had that weathered look about him that came from working outside. His brown eyes had a sharpness about them, and Dawn figured he didn't miss a thing. He wore a red polo shirt and faded blue jeans. His brown boots bore traces of concrete dust. 'Actually, do you mind if I nip to the loo first?' he asked, giving them an apologetic smile. 'I think that curry last night has rotted my insides.'

He stubbed his cigarette out in the ashtray and left the room in a hurry.

Dawn turned to face Chad. He was so tall that she had to crane her neck to see his face.

'Hang on, let me sit my black ass down so we can talk face to face.'

He smiled, his dark eyes twinkling, before dragging another stool over to sit next to her. He was slimmer than his friends; almost whippet-like. His tangerine-coloured tracksuit was from a high-end retailer and he wore hi-tops to match his clothes. His black hair was corn-rolled into tiny rows across his scalp.

Mo turned to a clean page in her notebook and waited.

'I didn't have my kids that weekend, so I knew I could get a bit of a lie-in on Saturday morning,' Chad explained. 'I think it was around midnight when I left. I talked to Kitty for a while, she was on about setting up some self-defence lessons at the local LGBT club. I'm a Karate master, so I said I'd be happy to get involved, but it would be after New Year, I'm having my kids over Christmas this year, so my ex can get a holiday with her fella.' Chad looked sheepish. 'Sorry I can't be of more help.'

'That's fine, we may need to come back to you at some point, so make sure we have your details. That goes for all of you,' Dawn said. 'Right, your turn,' she said to Si, indicating for him to sit with her away from the others as Chad had, so they couldn't influence each other.

'My bloody car broke down, so I was late,' Si explained. 'By the time my brother had come to get me I was cutting it too fine to make the first spot, so I rang Chad to tell him. He suggested switching the running order, so I didn't lose any money. They had just come off when I arrived. I threw my gear on and went out. I was debuting my fire-eating act, nearly burned the place down. Hey, do you want to see it? I've got my stuff in the car.'

He went to stand up, but Dawn held her hand up to stop him. 'Maybe another time. Did you see Vicky at all?'

'Very briefly, when she came backstage. I went out to talk to the DJ so didn't spend very long in the dressing room. I was out front when Ray called her through. She pissed off the security bloke though, I heard him slagging her off to his mate. He said she was a right bitch.'

'Interesting, thank you. What time did you leave?'

'I stayed till the DJ finished. He offered me a lift home, so I said I'd help him pack up. The place was almost empty when we went. I've got his number here,' he said, pulling his wallet out and removing a card. He handed it to Mo.

'Thanks. Did anyone see Ray arrive, and was he with anyone?' Dawn asked.

'I did,' Chad said, 'It must've been around 9.30 p.m. or maybe later. Si was onstage when he came in. Michelle was with him; he was shouting at her for making them late. She told us later that he'd made her follow him in her car, then he stopped for cigarettes. He'd spent twenty minutes getting Michelle to take photos of him with the shop assistant. He was chatting to some of the women out the front for a while, and Michelle had to call him a couple of times before he came in to get ready. As a result, Kitty didn't start her final spot until after 10.30

p.m. She normally likes to be done and out the door by 11 p.m. at the latest. She was furious with him, but he just laughed in her face.'

Des came back in, looking ashen. 'I really must stop eating all this crap,' he said. 'It's playing havoc with my insides.'

He reached behind the bar for a bottle of water, opened it and drank half of it in one go. Within minutes his colour had returned to somewhere near normal. 'Sorry about that. What did you want to know?'

'Did you see Ray turn up?' Dawn asked him.

'I didn't, I was at the bar with Kitty,' Des admitted. 'Some of the women bought us a drink, so we were chatting to them while we watched Si do his fire-eating. He was brilliant, apart from when he nearly took that poor bird's eyebrows off.' He laughed.

'It was an accident,' Si said, 'I told her to stay really still but she grabbed my cock, and I wobbled a bit. She was fine, I was the one who nearly roasted my own chestnuts!'

The guys fell about laughing, and Dawn and Mo tried to hide their smiles. Si winked at them both.

Des picked up his jacket from a nearby stool and put it on. 'I'm sorry, but do you mind if I head off? I really don't feel too good. I'm going to walk round this way, so we don't have to disturb Ray.'

'We still need your account of events, but you can pop into the station if it's easier. We'll need to speak to Michelle too. Have any of you got a number for her?'

Si picked up his phone and showed the number to Mo, who wrote it in her notebook.

Des threw open the patio doors that led out into the back garden and fresh air came rushing in, clearing the fog of cigarette smoke that lingered in the room.

Si and Chad said they may as well leave too, so the five of them followed the overgrown gravel path around to the front of the house. The back garden was immense, stretching as far as the eye could see and blending into the treeline at the bottom where it met the woods.

'Beautiful place,' Mo said as they all approached their cars. 'Pity it's a mess.'

'Glyn would go mental if he saw it,' Des said. He explained that the house was owned by Glyn Mason, local casino owner and self-made man. It had been a wreck when Glyn first bought it, but it was being brought back to its former glory with the help of Ray's daughter. Hope had recently graduated from University. She divided her time between living with her mother in America and with Ray in England. She loved old houses, so Glyn had bought Mason Manor specifically for Hope to restore.

'Glyn is Hope's godfather,' Des explained. 'He dotes on her. Rumour has it that when he pops his clogs he's leaving everything to her. Ray told Hope that he had nowhere to live after his last girlfriend kicked him out, so she asked Glyn if he could stay at the house. Glyn's been in Jamaica for the last few years, but he's due back soon. Hope is studying to be an architect, so Glyn has pretty much given her his chequebook. He trusts her to do the job properly.'

'They named their baby Hope Diamond? Was that Ray's idea?' Mo asked.

Chad laughed. 'I hadn't even thought about it, but probably not, he's not that intelligent. To be fair it suits her as she is both beautiful and precious, not at all like her old man.'

As they approached their respective vehicles, Dawn had one final question for them: 'How did Michelle come to be working for him?'

Chad spoke up. 'Ah, now that's a story none of us knows. She turned up at a show with Ray around five years ago and has been working for him ever since. I think he put out an ad for a housekeeper when he moved in here. Michelle got the job, though why she stays is a mystery. You've seen how he treats her, yet she takes it all on the chin. All I can say is he must pay her very well.'

'So, no romantic involvement then?' Mo asked, looking up at him.

'God forbid,' Chad replied. 'He reckons there is, but I asked her once and she was adamant that there never was and never will be anything other than a working relationship between them. She was upset that people thought it too, but given the crap she puts up with, you can see why they think it.'

He pulled out a bunch of keys and pressed a button on the key fob. A black sports car nearby reacted with a beep and a flash of the hazard lights.

Mo whistled. 'Nice car. Dodge Challenger, 2008 model, if I'm not mistaken?'

Chad looked impressed. 'Girl, you know your motors. 6.1 V-8 engine, 425 horsepower and after next months' pay packet it's all mine.'

'I've got a 1979 Ford Capri 3.0L S. It was a wreck when I got it, but my big brother spent over a year restoring it for me and I finally picked it up last week,' Mo said. 'He's upgraded the safety features, putting in a roll cage and five-point harness, but everything else is the same as the original.'

'Didn't Bodie, or was it Doyle, from that old television series *The Professionals* have one of those?' Chad asked.

'Bodie did.' Dawn said with a smile. 'Mo is a tiny bit obsessed with him.'

'Fair play,' Chad nodded. 'It was a great programme, they don't make them like that anymore. Most women I know liked his sidekick.'

'Not me. Bodie is my idol,' Mo said, a dreamy expression on her face.

Dawn rolled her eyes. 'Don't get her started, you'll be here all day. She's a right petrolhead.'

'Really?' Chad grinned. 'We should get together and talk cars sometime.'

'You're on,' Mo said. 'But I should warn you, you're not my type.'

'Because I'm black?'

'Because you're male.'

Si roared with laughter at Chad's expression. 'Bad luck mate,' he said, wiping a tear away.

Dawn and Mo asked all three men to come in and give formal interviews. They watched each of them drive away before climbing back into Dawn's Mini.

'What about Ray Diamond?' Mo asked.

'He's in no fit state to take us seriously at the moment so I'll speak to Michelle Simmons and arrange it through her, seeing as she handles his appointments.' Dawn turned out of the gate and back onto the main road, opting to go through town this time.

'It's a curious set-up,' Mo said as Dawn drove along the dual carriageway. 'She didn't seem unhappy, but I couldn't work for someone like him. He's horrible.'

'He is,' Dawn agreed. 'But maybe we're just lucky to have a decent boss.'

24

Alex Peachey finally got home at around 9 p.m. to find his wife sitting at the dining table, her head in her hands. The radio was on, but it didn't disguise the shouting and swearing coming from Joel's room. Alex knelt beside her and put his arms around her.

'I'm so sorry I'm late sweetheart, I got home as quickly as I could. It's been a shitty day, but it sounds like a holiday compared to yours. What started him off this time?'

Jayne sighed and leaned her head on his shoulder.

'He's upset because Kirsty can't take him to the disco tomorrow as it's her grandfather's funeral. His argument is that the funeral's in the afternoon, so she should be fine to take him out later. I thought I'd try to explain that she would still be upset, and his reply was that everyone dies so Kirsty should just get over it. I told him that he needs to be more sympathetic and he kicked off. I dread to think what damage he's doing in there. All I can say is thank God we weren't planning to sell this house just yet, there won't be anything left of it at this rate.'

'At least we don't have neighbours at the new house,' Alex replied, as a new stream of expletives came from Joel's room. 'Strange how he swears really fluently, yet he struggles to make himself understood with everyday words.'

Jayne smiled sadly. 'I wish it was the other way around. At least then I wouldn't know when he was calling me names.'

Alex stood up again, ignoring the creak in his knees. 'Go and put your feet up in the other room. I'll put the kettle on and we'll have a cuppa, then I'll go and talk to him.'

He kissed the top of her head and went through to the kitchen. While he waited for the kettle to boil, he thought about his son and wondered how much longer they would be able to cope with his rages. Alex knew it was time to get some professional advice. Jayne was struggling to manage him, despite her protests to the contrary. She did well to play it down, but he'd noticed the fresh bruises on her forearms and the way her T-shirt had been pulled out of shape where Joel had grabbed it.

He arranged the tea things on a tray, along with a plate of biscuits and carried it through to the lounge. Jayne was already asleep on the sofa, worn out from her altercation with Joel. Alex put the tray down and left the room, closing the door behind him.

He knocked loudly on the door to his son's room, causing the shouting to stop immediately. He opened the door and stepped into the room, his heart sinking when he saw the devastation. Joel had systematically pulled every packed box apart, spilling the contents across the room in a maelstrom of rage. The curtain pole had been ripped from the wall and lay across the bed, curtains still attached. Drawers had been emptied and clothes were strewn everywhere. It looked like a hurricane had torn through the room.

Joel sat in the middle of the floor, his blue Adidas T-shirt torn open at the neck and his black jogging trousers wet. His knuckles were bleeding and he had small cuts on the tops of his bare feet from where he'd crawled around on the broken CD cases. His glasses were bent out of shape and his face was smeared with snot and drool. His short, sweat-dampened brown hair stuck up at different angles. He sat very still, panting heavily, looking up at his father with a murderous glare.

'I'm sorry,' Joel said, although he looked anything but.

Alex said nothing. He looked squarely at Joel, keeping his expression neutral.

'Why are you sitting on the floor? You should be in your wheelchair.'

'I don't like using it in this house because I can't get around quickly enough. That's why we're moving, remember?' Joel snapped.

Alex ignored his son's tone. 'Fair point. It just doesn't seem very dignified, that's all. It was fine when you were little, but it can't be very good for your knees.'

'I don't care, I prefer it because it's easier for me,' Joel replied. 'My legs don't work anyway, so I don't care if my knees get damaged.'

'Your mother tells me that you're upset with Kirsty. Do you want to talk about it?'

Alex had to chew on the inside of his cheek to stop himself from losing his temper.

'Kirsty is being a bitch, she doesn't want to take me to the disco tomorrow night just because it's her granddad's funeral.'

'Kirsty is upset about her granddad dying so it's only right that she has the night off. I'm sure she'd still like to take you, but her family might think she's being disrespectful. Her grandma will be upset, so she might need someone to look after her. I know you don't understand the need to grieve, but one day you might lose someone you love and then you'll understand how it feels.'

Joel huffed. 'I doubt it. When you're dead, you're dead.'

'Maybe in your eyes, and you are entitled to your own opinion, but the rest of us feel differently. Kirsty needs to be with her family, and you need to look at it from her point of view, even if you think it's silly. If you get angry at Kirsty, she might decide that she doesn't want to be your helper anymore and then you'll have no-one to take you out.'

Joel looked thoughtful. 'What can I do to help her feel better? I don't want her to still feel sad next week. It's the Christmas party and I really want to go.'

'Well, you could get her a sympathy card. Maybe your mum will pick one up for you tomorrow.'

Joel started crawling towards the door. 'I need to say sorry to Mum,' he said.

'Leave it for now. She was very upset when I came in, so I sent her for a lie-down. Why does she have bruises on her arm?' Alex asked, careful to keep his voice calm even though he wasn't feeling it.

'It was an accident,' Joel said. 'I grabbed her arm because she tried to walk away when I was talking to her. I didn't mean to hurt her.'

'Well, you did. You're an adult now, Joel, it's time you realised that. Make sure it doesn't happen again.'

'It won't and that's a promise!' Joel's voice rose as he started to become agitated again. Alex held his gaze steadily and he quietened down. 'I'm sorry,' he said.

'Good. Now I'm going to order pizza for dinner while you start tidying this lot up. I'll bring you some bin bags for the broken stuff.'

'I need some new boxes. These all got ripped. By accident,' Joel said the last two words through gritted teeth, as if challenging Alex to argue with him.

'No problem, there are loads in the garage. I'll bring some through later. You should wash your hands before dinner and get that blood off.'

Alex left the room and closed the door quietly behind

him, ignoring the barrage of rude names that echoed down the hallway behind him.

25

The football club was almost empty, apart from a couple of members of staff. All the acts had gone home, and Michelle was alone in the changing room. She packed up Ray's things, making sure she'd picked up all the discarded clothes from the stage. Last week he'd gone mad when she'd left his gloves behind in Sheffield, and he'd refused her offer to buy him a new pair.

'No, you'll go all the fucking way back and get mine. That will teach you to be more careful, you stupid bitch,' he had said, before getting in his car, roaring off to Birmingham and getting blind drunk.

Later he'd rung and asked her to come and pick him up as if the earlier outburst had never happened. He'd blown his top again when she'd said she was just leaving Sheffield so wouldn't be able to, and suggested he get a taxi. He'd screamed drunken abuse down the phone at her, calling her names she'd never heard of and slammed the phone down.

Michelle grinned to herself as she hung up and walked back into the lounge. She'd had no intention of driving all the way back for the sake of a pair of gloves, so she'd phoned Des to see if he had a spare pair. Des had arrived an hour later with the promised gloves, then he'd phoned

Chad and Si and told them to pick up a curry and come over. They'd spent the evening watching old movies and laughing together. She loved hanging out with them, they treated her like one of the lads and she knew she could depend on them if needs be, like the big brothers she'd never had.

She double-checked the room again, dragged the heavy bag across the car park and threw it into the boot of her car. She had two days to get everything sorted out ready for the Christmas show on Friday. Ray had left ahead of her, getting a lift with another stripper, saying he had something to take care of.

As she drove back to Ray's house, Michelle hummed along to the late-night show on the radio, enjoying the opportunity to listen to what she liked for a change. She made a mental note to go shopping in the morning. Ray's daughter, Hope, was coming for Christmas and Ray would be keen to impress her as usual. Hope was the only person who could turn Ray into a decent human being, and Michelle was looking forward to having some female company.

She arrived at the house and parked by the side door. Ray's car was still parked half in the hedge where he'd left it that afternoon, but she thought twice about moving it. Last time she'd got behind the wheel of his precious car he'd gone mad at her. She called out to him as she dragged the bag into the kitchen but there was no answer, so she assumed he was either still out or already in bed.

Michelle made a cup of tea, then set about sorting out the gear for the following night. The bag was a mess, so she upended it on the kitchen floor. As well as dirty clothes, there was baby lotion and oil bottles, some empty and some half-full, a cock pump, wads of used tissues, creased porn magazines, three odd socks, five white gloves and a load of hair bobbles all knotted together. Ray's diary, wallet and a set of keys that Michelle didn't recognise were also among the mess. She sighed to herself, put on a pair of rubber gloves and picked out all the rubbish, then sprayed the holdall's PVC interior with anti-bacterial cleaner. She noticed a lump underneath the liner at the bottom of the bag, so she pulled it out to see what it was. Caught in the threads underneath was a small silver bracelet.

Michelle got some scissors and carefully cut it loose, trying not to damage it. It was caked in mud, so she ran it under the tap to clean it, then patted it with kitchen roll to dry it. She turned it over in her hand, admiring the tiny charms hanging from it. The chain was snapped halfway along it and it looked like a couple of the charms were missing.

'What's that you've got there?'

Michelle jumped out of her skin at the sound of Ray's voice behind her. She turned to see him leaning against the door frame, wearing nothing but a pair of black boxer shorts. He was watching her like a snake watches a mouse and she tried hard not to shudder.

'Jesus Christ, you scared the life out of me. I didn't know you were home.' Michelle placed her hand on her chest as if to slow her heart rate down.

'I asked what you had in your hand, Shelley,' Ray repeated.

Michelle held the bracelet up. 'I found this in your bag, it was caught in the threads underneath the liner.'

Ray padded over to take a closer look. Michelle dropped it into his outstretched hand and turned back towards the pile of laundry on the floor. She watched Ray out of the corner of her eye as he turned the bracelet over in his palm, poking at it with his finger.

'It's probably a souvenir from a fan,' he said. 'It looks cheap though, may as well throw it away.' He headed back towards the stairs, dropping the bracelet in the kitchen bin as he passed.

'Goodnight,' he called out.

Michelle heard him bound up the stairs and slam his door. She loaded the washing machine and switched it on, her mind racing. She knew Ray better than he knew himself, she'd noticed the split-second look of panic on his face when he'd first spotted the jewellery, and how quickly he'd regained his composure. Something had rattled him.

As she headed to bed, she stopped by the bin, retrieved the bracelet and slipped it into the pocket of her jeans.

26

Alex arrived early at the station again the following morning, keen to get things underway. He wanted to have interviews done and at least some progress made by the end of the day. He intended to pop in and see Charlie Baldwin on his way home, he was out of hospital now and recuperating under the watchful eye of his wife, Jackie.

As Alex walked into the room, he noticed that everyone else was in early too, a sign that his team were as committed as he was. The printer rattled off sheets of paper, Mo was typing furiously and Les was on the phone arguing with someone. Craig was reading through paperwork and Gary was at the far end of the room, making drinks.

Alex loved the dedication his team put in, despite the time of year. Each and every one of them did him proud on a daily basis.

Gary called out to him that he had some important messages on his desk, so he went into his office to tackle them first. He set the ones from Laura Morrison to one side and glanced at the rest. One name jumped out at him. He leaned out of his office and shouted across the room.

'Dawn, come in here a minute, would you?'

Dawn went into Alex's office to see what he wanted. He was scanning through her notes from the day before.

'When you went to Mr Diamond's house the other day, you said that there was a housekeeper.'

'Yes, her name's Michelle Simmons. I haven't spoken to her yet, but she's on my list of people to chase today. Why, what's up?'

'She's left a message asking if she can come in and talk to us. She specifically asked for you and Mo, so if you're not busy can you arrange that for this morning? I don't want to make her wait in case it's important.'

He handed the number to her.

'Sure, I'll ring her now. I mentioned to Ray's friends that I'd need to speak to her. I'll call Des Clarke too, he wasn't feeling well so we didn't get his statement.'

Dawn stood up and headed back to her desk to call Michelle Simmons. Alex looked down the list of people yet to be spoken to, then passed the list to Les so he could set up the interviews. He had just finished talking to his boss when his mobile rang. He frowned when he saw his sister-in-law's number displayed.

'Hi Carol, is everything okay? Say that again? Christ, I only left an hour ago. Right, I'm on my way.'

Alex grabbed his jacket and car keys. 'Family emergency, I'll be back in a bit,' he called out as he rushed through the office, bumping into Craig and making him spill his coffee for the second time in a week.

'Sorry Craig,' he called back over his shoulder, leaving Craig cursing and wiping coffee off his new shirt.

Alex parked his car half on the path and half on the road and hurried towards the front door. He threw it open and rushed into the living room. Carol sat next to Jayne on the sofa, holding a tissue to Jayne's nose. They both looked up as Alex came in.

'Where is he?' he demanded, his face almost black

with fury.

'Dave's taken him out for a couple of hours. Don't worry, he'll soon straighten him out,' Carol said. 'In the meantime, tell this stubborn bugger to let me call the doctor.'

Alex knelt in front of his wife and gently tilted her face towards him. Her nose had stopped bleeding but looked as if it may be broken. Her eyes were starting to bruise and were red from crying. She looked fragile and Alex knew that if Joel had been there at that moment, he would have beaten him senseless, regardless of his disability.

'I'm fine darling, honestly I am. I just wasn't expecting it. It was my fault for trying to take his posters down. He said he still needed them, and I told him he didn't, that I was packing them away. As I leaned over to pull one off the wall, he head-butted me. He swears it was an accident, that he was trying to move out of my way.'

'I don't care what he said, he's not getting away with it!' Alex shouted, unable to stop himself.

Jayne struggled to her feet, her legs visibly wobbly. Carol held out a hand to help but Jayne waved it away. She squared up to Alex as best she could, fixing him with a cold stare.

'If you'd been here then maybe he wouldn't have done it!' Jayne shouted back. 'For fuck's sake Alex, you're meant to be on leave! I don't care if Charlie Baldwin's dying, you promised you'd be here and you're not!'

Jayne sat down again with a bump and burst into tears. Carol glanced at Alex as she handed Jayne another tissue. He nodded at her and she picked up her handbag and left the room. She squeezed Alex's arm as she passed him, letting him know that she was there for him too.

Alex sat down next to his wife, waiting for her to stop crying. She leaned against him, so he wrapped his arm around her shoulders and kissed the top of her head.

'I'm so sorry darling, I really want to be here to help, but my hands are tied with Charlie off sick. I'll tell the boss that I'm only doing half days from now on.' Alex coughed to try and clear the lump that had formed in his throat.

'Don't be daft. We've been married long enough for me to know how important your job is, but sometimes I just feel so alone.' Jayne sighed.

'I think I should call social services. They may be able to get a temporary placement for him somewhere.'

'But I'm his mother, and I'm not going to put him in care.'

'No-one's saying you should, but maybe we need to think about what Joel needs. He wants his own life with as little input from us as possible. That's why we built the bungalow, so he could have more independence. But he also needs people around him who are trained to deal with his type of behaviour. Let's face it, we're not. We simply can't cope for much longer.'

Alex felt Jayne stiffen next to him and waited for her to argue, but she didn't have to. Her face gave away how angry she was.

'Go back to work Alex, we'll talk about it tonight. Dave has promised to keep Joel out until you get home, and I could do with a proper lie-down.' Jayne stood up, walked past him and headed up the stairs.

Alex thought about following her but decided against it. Instead, he went outside, got in his car and drove back to the station.

27

Les called out to Alex as he walked in. 'Boss, I've set up interviews with the acts from the Leamore Club as requested, and I'm about to call John Jackson, the agent from the promotions company. Any preference on who talks to who?'

'You and Mo take one stripper and give one to Craig and Dawn. I'll go and see the agent. Dawn and Mo are talking to Michelle Simmons later today, then I'll take whoever's left. Have you included Ray Diamond in the interviews?'

'No, I hadn't. I thought Dawn had already interviewed him, he's not on my list,' Les replied, looking at his computer screen.

'She has, but that was on his turf. I want to talk to him on mine. He was three sheets to the wind when she and Mo went over there, so I want to make him aware that this isn't a silly game. Stick him down for 9 a.m. tomorrow, let's see how cocky he is first thing in the morning. Put me and Craig down for that one.'

Alex looked around for Gary, spotting him by the printer. 'Have you typed up those interviews from the Leamore Club yet, Gary?' he called out as he crossed the floor towards his office.

Gary stuck his pen between his teeth, grabbed the sheaf of paper that the printer had spewed out, and hurried after Alex, veering towards his own desk to deposit the papers in his hand and pick up the recently typed interviews. He handed them to Alex and waited anxiously while his boss flicked through them.

'Great work, I know you hate typing, but you've surpassed yourself. Well done.'

Gary looked embarrassed and fiddled with his pen, finally putting it in his jacket pocket. He had a stain on his shirt which Alex hoped was ketchup and not blood.

'Actually, boss, I got Mo to do them. Before you get mad at me, it's only because she types a lot faster than me, and she doesn't make spelling mistakes. I've promised her a box of doughnuts from that posh new shop in the town centre.'

Gary managed to look both innocent and guilty at the same time, and although Alex was cross, he couldn't help admiring his honesty.

'Next time do them yourself, no matter how long it takes. Mo has enough of her own work to do without helping you. Go and get me a sausage roll and a coffee from the canteen and be quick about it, then you can take over the phone call list from Mo.'

Alex tried to keep his voice stern, but it was difficult when Gary stood looking at his feet in shame, his light-brown hair sticking up at odd angles and his tie askew. He looked like a schoolboy caught stealing pencils.

'Righto boss, sorry boss,' Gary said, rushing off before Alex could reprimand him further. Alex shook his head in disbelief, then started sorting through the pile of messages that had accrued on his desk.

'Out goes Starsky and in walks Hutch,' Alex said as Craig strolled in, looking like a catalogue model.

Where Gary's style was laid-back, Craig's was designer catwalk. Today's ensemble was a charcoal-coloured pinstriped suit, white shirt, a perfectly knotted sapphire-blue tie, matching handkerchief and highly polished black shoes. His dark hair was gelled carefully into place. He walked towards Alex's office and Alex beckoned him in.

'Afternoon boss, sorry I wasn't here earlier. I did leave a message though.'

Alex waved him to sit down and he did, putting his right ankle up on his left knee. His trousers rode up slightly and Alex looked at his ankles.

Craig saw him looking and laughed. 'Spiderman socks, an early Christmas present from Debs. She knows how much I love Marvel films, and she bet me thirty quid I wouldn't wear them to work.'

Alex smiled. 'Very nice. Now, you were about to tell me why you weren't here on time.'

'An anonymous call came in, saying that we should check out one of the local charity shops. It seems that someone had donated a bundle of clothes that matched Vicky Wilson's missing things. I've picked up everything that was donated and it's with forensics now. I don't hold out much hope, but you never know.'

'Good work. Do they know who handed it in?'

'No, it was left outside the shop. There are cameras in the street outside, so I thought we should take a look and see who was around.'

'Get Gary to go through the footage, he's deskbound for the foreseeable future so he may as well make himself useful. That will teach him to get Mo to do his typing for him.'

Craig looked amused. 'He's a crafty sod. Mind you, she's fast, over one hundred and fifty words a minute and never a single error. I'd be stuffed without autocorrect.'

'Well, it's backfired on him now. Is it me, or do we seem to be going around in circles on this one? It's been days and not even a sniff of a suspect. We really need to solve this, Joel's giving Jayne grief at home and it's causing big problems.'

'Well, if you need a hand with the move, Gary and I are happy to help out. Just say the word.'

'Thanks, I appreciate that. Ah, Gary, there you are. I thought you'd got lost,' Alex said, as he arrived with his food.

Gary put the mug and a paper bag on the desk. 'Sorry boss, there were no sausage rolls left, so I had to nip to Greggs.'

'No problem. Craig's got a lead of sorts, he will fill you in.'

Gary nodded and followed Craig out of the office. Alex opened the bag and bit into his sausage roll, showering his desk with flakes of pastry. Les stuck his head round the doorframe.

'Sorry, boss, you said to let you know when I'd spoken to John Jackson. He said he's in the office all day, so just go along when you like. He said he leaves at 5.30 p.m., but to give you his mobile number if you need it.'

'Great, I'll get along and see him once I've eaten this. I need to sort some stuff out at home as well, so I'll nip back there once I've spoken to him. Ring me if you need to.'

'Will do. I'll get on to the phone company again and see if they've got Vicky's mobile records yet.'

Alex popped the last piece of sausage roll into his mouth, balled up the paper bag and dropped it in the bin.

'Get onto forensics again. Craig's just given them a load of new stuff to look at, but they should be done with the first lot by now. Now, let's start shaking the tree a bit harder and see what falls out.'

28

Alex swore to himself as he tried to find a parking space close to the office of Bulldog Promotions, which was above a row of shops on the approach to Birmingham's New Street station. Eventually, he gave up and parked on the fourth level in one of the city's many multi-storey car parks and hoped the parking fee wouldn't be too horrendous.

When he saw how many people were trying to cram themselves into an already overcrowded lift, he decided it would be quicker using the stairs. His knees screamed at him by the time he reached the ground floor, and it made him more determined to start a fitness regime in the New Year.

Finding the office was easy, and he was relieved that it was on the first floor, so there was only one flight of stairs to deal with. Alex was about to knock on the door, but a young woman opened it before his knuckles could strike the wood.

She was tall and thin, dressed from head to toe in shocking pink Lycra, her long blonde hair scraped back in a ponytail and secured with a scrunchie that matched her outfit.

'Hiya, are you here to see John?' she asked, smacking

her chewing gum against her teeth.

Alex pulled out his ID card to introduce himself, but she pulled the door wide and pointed to a desk near the window.

'That's him. He'll make you a cuppa, I'm off to do my Christmas shopping.'

She shot off down the stairs before Alex could think of a reply.

'Come in mate,' the man at the desk called, standing up and walking towards the kettle. Alex walked across the room, glancing at the brightly coloured posters that adorned the walls. Most of them showed half-naked men, some in groups and some alone, posing to show off their impressive physiques. Alex suppressed the urge to pull his stomach in. Other posters showed drag artistes, comedians and various tribute acts, including the one he'd met at the club a few days ago.

'Have a seat. Tea or coffee?' the man asked, the steaming kettle in his hand hovering over two mugs. He also seemed to be in peak physical condition, with bulging muscles, but looked older than the men in the posters. He was wearing grey jogging bottoms and a white sleeveless T-shirt, and had a long-sleeved top tied around his waist.

'Coffee please,' Alex said, lowering himself onto one of the two straight-backed chairs that stood in front of the desk. 'You'd be John Jackson, owner of Bulldog Promotions I assume?'

'I am indeed,' the man said in a cheery voice. 'You must be the Old Bill. I recognise the weary expression. My old man was a copper, he worked in Cornwall back in the fifties.'

John placed a mug in front of Alex and took a seat behind the desk. 'Now, what can I do for you?' he asked. He leaned back in his chair, nursing his mug in his big hands. He seemed very easy-going and Alex liked him immediately.

'I need some information about the ladies' night that took place last Friday at the Leamore club. You may have heard that a young woman was killed either during or after the show. Can you give me a run-down of the show, how it operates, who was there, etcetera?'

John's smile faltered. 'Your officer mentioned it when he called. Shocking business. That poor woman, her parents must be beside themselves. If I can help in any way, then I will, so just tell me what you need?'

He put his mug down and switched his computer screen on, scrolling down through a calendar until he found the correct date, then clicking on it. A new page opened, and John turned the screen so that Alex could read it.

'This is the contract and corresponding information for that show. I still prefer to use a diary and notebook, but Shona – that's the woman who let you in – said we should be doing everything on here now. I guess she's right, but I'm a bit of a dinosaur when it comes to technology. My kids know more than I ever will, but I'm getting the hang of it, albeit slowly.'

John talked Alex through the list of names on the screen. 'This tells me who was booked to appear, how many spots they were doing and how much they were getting paid. Some venues want each act to do two spots, in which case the guy will go onstage and do his first routine, but only strip down to his G-string. For his second spot, he'll have a different costume and music, but will take everything off. If the venue wants one spot, he'll do the full strip, unless they've asked for just a teaser. That's the name of the act, the DJ and so on,' he continued, pointing out the various people.

Alex nodded as John went through the contract. 'What about security? Do you provide that?'

'Not always. Some of the bigger clubs have their own

so we don't need to provide it. This was a smaller club, but they said they would sort out their own.'

'That's strange,' Alex said. 'The club owner said that you provided the security that night. She said that the guy had an official badge.'

John looked confused. 'The only other explanation is that one of the acts hired him. Kitty usually goes through me as I can get her a good deal. Maybe she decided to try a different firm. I'll double-check with Shona, but if we had provided them it would be on here.'

'Can I get a copy of that contract?' Alex asked. 'It will help us identify anyone we've not yet spoken to.'

'Sure, coming right up.' John clicked the mouse and the printer on the adjoining desk began whirring. He leaned across, grabbed the sheet from the printer tray and passed it to Alex, who was draining his mug.

He nodded when John stood up and offered him a refill. He waited until John had sat back down before continuing.

'What can you tell me about Ray Diamond? I understand he has a reputation of upsetting folk.'

Alex took a biscuit from the plate on the desk and dunked it in his coffee.

John laughed, but the smile never reached his eyes. 'Ah yes, the man himself. Well, where should I start? If you want to hear everything you'd be here all day. To put it mildly, he's an arsehole, he treats people like shit, but he still pulls the crowds in. He's been around for twenty-five years or so. He started out under Steve Gifford. Steve was a bodybuilder-turned-stripper back in the Seventies, one of the first in the business. Ray met him at the gym, and Steve saw the potential in him. He trained him up and got him his first few gigs by taking him along to shows with him and getting him to do teaser spots. By the time Steve died, Ray had become big enough to fill a venue by himself.'

'How did Steve die?' Alex asked.

'It was a hit and run, right outside his house. He was on his way home after a show, he decided to walk that night because it was a local gig. I don't know what sort of vehicle hit him, but he was really messed up. They said he would've died instantly, which is a blessing. It was a real shame. Steve was a genuine bloke, always pleasant to work with. He was the one who started Bulldog Promotions, or Perfection as it was back then, and I was one of his acts until I did my back in. We got on like a house on fire from the minute we met. He used to put me and Ray on shows together, until Ray decided he should be top of the bill all the time, instead of us taking joint billing. I didn't care, I was happy doing my stuff and earning a decent crust, but Ray got more and more competitive, so I stopped working with him in the end. I was also happy working the gay clubs, something Ray refused to do, and I made a lot of money that way. I met Neil Stone at one of the clubs, he was struggling to get into the drag scene, so I brought him to meet Steve. That's when Kitty was born, so to speak.'

John raised his mug to his lips and finished his drink, a faraway look on his face.

'So, you took on the agency after Steve's death,' Alex said. 'That must have been difficult.'

'Not really, I'd always been interested in learning the business side from quite early on, so after my injury I used to help Steve out in other ways, like driving other acts to gigs if they didn't have a car, doing promotional stuff like mail drops, and so on. It got me more involved in the running of it, allowing him more time with his family. He took me on as a partner and I always thought his wife would take over if anything happened to him, but when his Will was read out, I found out he'd left the whole thing to me, on the premise that I would continue to train new strippers and drag acts. Apparently, his wife didn't want anything to do with it.'

'That must have been tough, carrying on without him,' Alex murmured.

John shrugged his shoulders. 'Like I said, I knew it inside out. The tough bit was not having Steve around to run new ideas by. Some of the guys didn't like me being at the helm, so they left, and I had to fire a couple who'd been robbing Steve blind for months by putting in false expenses and charging more for jobs than they should have. I changed the name to signify a new start and I'd like to think he'd approve of me branching out and taking on musicians and tribute bands. Let's face it, strippers have a short shelf life, and strip shows may one day become as outdated as Tupperware parties.'

'Don't say that in front of my wife, she swears by her resealable sandwich boxes,' Alex grinned. 'I got the impression when I spoke to Mr Stone that he and Mr Diamond aren't the best of friends. Can you shed any light on why that might be? Mr Stone told me of an altercation between them, but I wondered if there was more to it.'

'Ah, yes. It's a rivalry that's lasted for years. One of the rumours is that Ray made advances towards Neil and was turned down. Ray would probably tell you it's the other way around. Personally, I reckon it's because when Neil created Kitty McLane, she was an instant hit. The audiences loved her from the start, and Ray was jealous when people came to his shows and complained that Kitty wasn't on the bill. We gave Kitty a few shows of her own for two reasons. One, to try and dampen the animosity between the two of them. And two, to give Kitty a chance to broaden her audience, therefore guaranteeing that more people would come to strip shows where Kitty was appearing. She's incredibly popular and Ray soon noticed that shows with Kitty on had the biggest audiences, so he agreed to work with her again.'

John laughed to himself. 'Between you and me, he asked to work with her again, but he'd never admit that to anyone because it would make him look needy.'

'It must be lonely at the top,' Alex mused.

'Especially if you tread on people in order to get there,' John added.

Alex placed his empty mug on the desk and stood up. His knees cracked loudly, and John raised an eyebrow in sympathy.

'You sound as bad as me, that's why I don't spend as much time at the gym as I used to. My joints are just about shot nowadays but I still have a few fans, so I take part in our Christmas Charity Show. This year we raised over £3,000 for Birmingham Children's Hospital.'

John indicated the charity tin on the desk opposite and Alex nodded approvingly.

'Right, well, I may come back to you at some point, depending on what we find. But if you find out who provided the security that night, I'd be grateful if you'd give me a ring.'

'No problem.' John extended his hand and Alex shook it warmly. 'Let me know if you need anything else.'

'Will do, and thanks for the list.'

29

Jayne closed her eyes and sighed heavily as the noise from the bathroom got louder and louder. At first, they'd thought it was Joel's way of dealing with his frustration at being disabled, but since he'd never known any different she didn't believe it. She had her own theory, that he could swear all he wanted to his reflection and it wouldn't tell him off. It was a shame that the only time that Joel's speech became crystal clear was when he was cursing.

Jayne peered into the chest freezer, trying to locate a tray of pigs-in-blankets, when the door flew open and banged against the wall, scaring her half to death and causing her to hit her head on the freezer lid.

'Ow! Bloody hell, Joel, you scared the crap out of me!' She rubbed her head, feeling a lump already beginning to form.

'Sorry. When you go shopping, can you get me some more plastic wallets please? I need two hundred, and I need some more shower gel too.'

Joel knelt on the floor, watching her intently. Jayne noticed that his glasses frames were bent again, meaning that at some point in the last couple of days, he had tried to destroy them. That meant another trip to the opticians for yet another repair. Joel couldn't help being heavy-handed but sometimes it was a pain in the backside, especially when she knew that it wasn't always an accident when things got broken.

'I got you some wallets last week, you can't have used them all already. You'll have to wait until we've moved now, I've got too much to do as it is, and with your Dad having to work I'm having to do most of it myself.'

Jayne finally spotted the pigs in blankets and pulled them out with a flourish.

'I need the wallets now, I've got loads of documents to print off for my family tree,' Joel said in his drunken-sounding drawl.

'Joel, that's a lot of paper to print off. Don't you think it would be safer to keep it in the Cloud? That way there's no chance of it getting lost.'

Joel's face darkened. 'I'm sorry if you don't think it's important, but it is to me. I can't carry on until I've printed the records off.'

Jayne could see there was a storm brewing behind his eyes. 'All I'm thinking is that if you wait until after the move, you'll have a lot more room to spread things out and sort it all out. If you print it off now, it will have to be packed then moved, and it might get mixed up. Uncle Dave's built you loads of shelves in your new office, so you'll be able to organise things much more efficiently. You can ask him about it later. Now, I know you don't like Christmas pudding, so what would you like instead?'

Joel thought for a moment then grinned at her. 'That's true. I'll wait till we're in the new house. Can I have apple crumble?'

Jayne smiled at him. 'Sure. Now, go and get dressed, you'll be late for your club.'

***

Dinner was the furthest thing from Alex's mind at that moment. The interviews were set up for the following day. Gary was busy following up on phone calls, most of which seemed to be hoaxes. Alex could never get his head around the mentality of people who rang in and confessed to a crime they hadn't committed.

Dawn and Mo were working their way through the list of potential witnesses from the ladies' night, although most of them had been so drunk that they either didn't remember anything or were choosing not to.

Alex read and re-read the reports until he couldn't see straight any more. He was sure he was missing something, but he couldn't put his finger on what it was.

Craig breezed in, still rubbing his hands together to get the circulation going despite having levelled up two floors.

'Bugger me, it's nippy out there. I still reckon we're in for a white Christmas.'

He shrugged off his black wool overcoat and draped it over the back of the chair in the corner. Pulling out his notebook, he flicked to the right page. 'I went back to see the bar manager at the Leamore Club,' he said, still rifling through his notes. 'Ah, here it is. She said before that Vicky had a bit of an issue with the security man that night. Now her memory has improved, she's saying that the security guy was slagging Vicky off to the staff later on, saying that she was a little bitch and that given the chance he'd give her a fucking slap. He was furious that she embarrassed him in front of everyone. I've tracked him back to see who he works for and he's one of the Bulldog Promotions security team.'

'That's interesting. I've been to see John Jackson today, and he said that he doesn't know who did the security,' Alex replied.

'Do you think he's lying?' Craig asked, but Alex shook his head.

He shrugged. 'I'll give him a call.'

Alex picked up the phone and got the answerphone. He left a message for John to ring him back, then looked at his watch.

'Right, I'm going home. Dave and Carol are coming over for dinner, so we can finalise the details for the move. We're hoping that we can move in at the end of this week, once Jayne's happy that everything is where it should be.' Alex rubbed his face, surprised at how tired he felt. 'I'll be glad when we're in, I can't remember the last time I slept properly.'

'It'll be worth it, and hopefully Joel will settle down and behave himself better. Let us know when you want the roleplaying group to meet next. James from the night shift was wanting to join, so I said I'd bring him along. He tends to play a lot of Fallout New Vegas, Knights of the Old Republic and he's a bit of a Minecraft nut as well.'

'Sounds great, the more the merrier. I'm hoping we can get one final game in before Christmas, but I'll let you know. By the way, I've got tickets for a tribute band for Saturday night if you're up for it. You and Deb, me and Jayne and Gary and Jo. It's at the Comedy Club in Bradstock.'

'Sounds great, we'll be there. See you in the morning, enjoy your dinner.'

30

John Jackson smiled to himself as he brewed a fresh pot of coffee. His visitor, Vince Patterson, was due at any time, and John was sure he'd be more than happy to help him with the problem he'd got regarding Ray.

Vince had been a good friend of Steve's and had worked closely with him during the setting up of the company. Now he had his own company in Brighton, with an impressive team of his own. Vince only drank filter coffee, and John was eager to impress his old friend, so he'd invested in a fancy machine, which did everything except wash the mugs up afterwards.

The door flew open and Vince strode in with a huge smile on his handsome face. He was a fan of old-school rock music and tended to favour band T-shirts teamed with faded jeans, leather jackets and clumpy boots. His hair was long and dark, and John swore he was wearing eyeliner just like his hero, Alice Cooper.

'Vinnie boy, how are you doing?' John greeted his friend with a back-breaking hug, which was returned just as enthusiastically. 'Looking good, my man. Skinny as ever though.'

Vince grinned at him, his perfect teeth glowing ultra-white. 'John boy, how's it going?' he replied, not even trying to mask his London accent. He looked around the office and nodded. 'Very swish. How's business?'

Vince sat down while John busied himself with drinks for them both. He pulled out the bottle of Jack Daniels and waited for Vince to nod before pouring a glug into each coffee.

'Why not? It is Christmas, after all.' He took a drink and nodded his approval. 'How's my beautiful girl? Has she realised the error of her ways yet?'

'If you mean my wife, she's very well and still beautiful.' John picked up a framed photo and handed it to Vince, who whistled in appreciation. 'She was only your girl in your dreams, mate. She knows she married the right man, she wouldn't have put up with you for five minutes.'

Vince laughed at him again, handing the photo back. 'True, but then what woman could? Anyway, you said you had a business proposition for me.'

John put his coffee mug down. 'It's more of a favour actually. Ray Diamond is up to his old tricks again and I want to put a stop to it, or at least knock him off his pedestal for a bit.'

'I might have known it would be him. I didn't know he was still going, I assumed he'd either have been killed by some jealous husband or drank himself to death by now.'

'No such luck. He's been poaching work off my lads again and he seems to have it in for one lad in particular.'

Vince sat with a grave expression on his face as John filled him in on Ray's behaviour towards Adam.

'The lad looks up to him, or he did before all this started. Ray hates the fact that there are younger, more talented acts out there. He's like Bette Davis in that film where she torments her crippled sister.'

'I can see why you're upset, I would be, if this were one of my boys. I take it Ray knows the fix Adam is in?'

'He does, that's what makes it fun to him.'

Vince got up and helped himself to more coffee. 'Tell me what you need.'

'I was wondering if you'd consider taking Adam on for a while, in exchange for one of your lads. Preferably one that Ray can't intimidate.'

'Sure, I'll take your boy for a while, it'll be a pleasure. Which one of mine do you want?'

John didn't speak, he just grinned from ear to ear. Vince threw his head back and laughed.

'You want my star? You're a crafty bastard, I see exactly what you're up to.' He pulled out his phone and sent a quick text. 'It's your lucky day, he's downstairs in the car.'

31

Jayne cast her eyes over the vast array of dishes set out on the kitchen worktop. Given that the next few days would be chaotic, she'd gone all-out and done Christmas dinner, complete with all the trimmings. She didn't think she'd forgotten anything but, given the way her head felt now, she wouldn't be surprised. She checked her watch – it was almost 6 p.m. Alex should have been home by now. Cursing him under her breath, she carried the dishes through to the dining room and placed them on the table. Carol and Dave were just pulling up outside as she brought in the wine.

'Hi, come in. Alex isn't back yet,' she called out as Carol opened the front door.

'Wow, this looks fabulous!' Carol said as she took in the food and decorations on the table. 'Crackers too. You do spoil us.'

She kissed Jayne on the cheek before pulling out a chair and sitting down.

'Excellent, more for us then,' Dave's voice echoed loudly around the room, which was now devoid of everything except for the table and chairs.

Dave and Alex were like chalk and cheese, although both were tall and stocky, Dave had more muscle due to the amount of manual labour his job demanded. He and his sons had been along earlier to pick up the sideboard, bookshelves and other bits of furniture and take it to the new place. It had seemed easier to do the move one room at a time and Jayne had found it easy with Carol to help her to decide where everything should go. Pictures, ornaments and books would be unpacked in time, but at least the big furniture would be where it should be.

'If he doesn't get a move on he'll be getting nothing,' Jayne replied. 'I've made an apple crumble as well as Christmas pudding, so he'd better be here.'

'Now I'm really hoping he's not,' Dave laughed. He put his hand on his generous stomach. 'I'm a growing lad, I need all the sustenance I can get.'

Carol raised an eyebrow at Jayne. 'If he keeps growing like this he'll need a trailer for his belly.'

'You know you love me just as I am. Where's my main man?' Dave asked.

'He's in his room. Go and get him, will you? We may as well eat before it gets cold. I'll put Alex a plate of leftovers together if he's not back by the time we finish eating.'

Dave wandered off to find Joel and soon returned, carrying his nephew across his broad shoulders. He set him down on his specially adapted chair and took the chair next to him.

'You don't mind if I sit here, do you mate?' Dave asked him, a twinkle in his eye. 'That way I can nick your sprouts when you're not looking.'

He winked at Joel, who looked shocked until he realised his uncle was joking.

'Touch my food, feel my fork.' Joel said, thumping Dave on the shoulder.

Dave let out a shriek and fell off his chair. He lay on the floor, pretending to cry until Carol threw a cracker at him.

'Get up, you daft twat. You'll get no pudding if you

don't behave.'

'Sorry Mum, I'll be good, I promise,' Dave said in a child-like voice, as he clambered into his seat, causing Joel to burst into a fit of giggles.

'Men,' Carol said, rolling her eyes at him.

Dave blew her a kiss and picked up the wine, pouring a glass for each of them apart from Joel, who wanted orange juice. They each helped themselves to food and had just started eating when Alex came in, breathing heavily from rushing so much. He kissed the top of Jayne's head, ruffled Joel's hair and sat down.

'I'm so sorry folks, I had to stop for fuel and the queues were ridiculous.'

He loaded his plate with food and began to eat while Dave brought his brother up to speed in regards to the new bungalow. 'All the hardwood flooring was being put in today when I left, and the carpet fitter came to take measurements of the bedrooms. He says they can put the carpets down on Saturday morning. I'm waiting on the plasterer doing a skim on the ceiling in Joel's room now, but that should go ahead tomorrow and be dry by the day after. So, you can officially move in anytime from Sunday morning. What do you reckon, Joel? Shall I organise the move for Christmas Eve? I can drop the big fat bloke a note to tell him where to deliver your presents.'

Joel laughed, drooling gravy down his shirt. 'Don't be stupid! Santa's not real.'

Dave's face took on a look of horror. 'What do you mean, he's not real? Who brings my presents then? I think I might cry now! And if he's fake, who drinks the glass of Scotch I leave out for him every Christmas Eve?'

'That would be me, fat boy,' Carol said, coming back in with a stack of bowls. 'It's the only way I'm going to get a glass of your best whisky.'

Dave's eyes grew wide. 'Infidel!' he roared, grabbing Carol round the waist and pulling her onto his lap. 'I demand retribution!' he said, tickling her.

'Get off me, you big ape! Honestly Joel, do you see what I have to put up with?'

'You two are mad,' Joel giggled.

'You have to be mate, to live with him,' Carol said as she climbed off Dave's lap.

Alex sipped his wine as Jayne dished out the desserts. For a few moments he allowed himself to forget the case for the first time that week and enjoy some normal family time.

32

Des Carter arrived early for his interview the next day. He sat patiently in the reception area, reading from a battered paperback. His black and yellow leather jacket lay on the chair next to him, and a black crash helmet sat on top of it. His beloved bike was parked up in the secure car park across the road.

When his name was called, he grabbed his stuff and followed the young PC through to the interview room, where Les Morris and Mo Ross were waiting for him. They shook hands and Des took a seat, placing his things on the vacant chair beside him.

'Thanks for coming in, Mr Carter.'

Les opened a brown cardboard file that lay on the desk in front of him.

'I know you've already spoken to my colleagues, but we'd like to go over things in a bit more detail if that's okay. Don't worry, it's mainly so we have all the facts, and something may come back to you that you'd forgotten last time.'

'Call me Des. No problem, I'm happy to help. I wasn't feeling very well when they came to Ray's house, I had a dodgy stomach.'

'Right then. Let's start with who was backstage that

night.'

'There was me, Chad Nicholls, Si Palmer, Ray Diamond, Michelle Simmons, Neil Stone – also known as Kitty McLane, and Ruby Clarke, who's Kitty's dresser. Vicky Wilson was there as well but not for long.'

'We'll get to her in a minute. What about security people or bar staff?'

'Not all the time. One of the bar staff came to collect some glasses halfway through the night, but they weren't there very long. If they came back later, it must have been after I'd gone home. The security guy who was watching the stage door popped in at one point to ask if we needed anything. I don't know who he was, I'd not seen him before. John Jackson might know him. He's the owner of Bulldog Promotions and it was one of his shows.'

'Does Mr Jackson manage Mr Diamond?' Les asked.

'Ray is freelance same as me, but he used to be managed by Steve Gifford, the original owner of Bulldog Promotions. It used to be called something else back then. John changed the name after Steve died but he kept most of the original acts. John gave the company a proper shake-up, he fired a few guys and some jumped ship. Ray left when Steve was still in charge. He does do the odd show for John, but John tends to use his own guys wherever he can. It puts Ray's nose out of joint, but there's not much he can do about it. Not that it stops him trying,' Des said.

'In what way?' Mo asked.

Des looked uncomfortable. 'Well, I don't want to slag him off, but he can be a bit childish sometimes. He's been known to poach jobs from other strippers. He'll ring a venue up and tell them that the guy they've booked is ill, or double-booked, and when they start to panic, he'll say he can cover it, but his price is higher. They don't want to cancel so they agree to pay him.'

'I see,' Les said, chewing the inside of his cheek to stop

himself saying what he was thinking. 'What happens when the original stripper turns up for the job?'

'Ray's clever, he'll get one of his girlfriends to ring them and tell them the job's off. Nine times out of ten the poor stripper never questions it – people get ill and venues pull out occasionally, it's just one of those things. I only found out about it a couple of months ago when Si, Chad and I went out for a curry. Ray got even more hammered than usual, and he started bragging about it. When he admitted he'd poached a big job out from under Si's nose. Si flew at him, and we had to get between them to stop Si killing him. Si said if he ever found out that Ray had ever nicked any more of his jobs, he'd make him wish he'd never been born. Ray just sat there, laughing to himself until he passed out.'

'Okay, let's move on. What do you know about Vicky Wilson?'

'I've not worked with Ray for about a month, so hadn't seen her before. She seemed nice, not his usual type. He normally goes for skinny women with small boobs and short hair, but Vicky was shapely with big boobs and long hair. She reminded me of Jessica Rabbit. She was like a kid in a sweet shop. She was all over Ray like a rash. She went out through the fire exit a few minutes after Ray called her through, and he followed her out ten minutes later. When he came back in about half an hour after, he was alone. He said he'd fucked her brains out, gave us all the gory details. An hour later he was chatting up some women at the bar, but I left just after that. I helped Michelle with Ray's gear, he always leaves her to carry it and she was struggling. She did shout for him to come and give her a hand, but he pretended not to hear her.'

'Did Michelle leave at the same time as you?'

'Yes, we put the gear into the boot and she drove away. Ray's car was still there, he quite often turns up separately. Don't ask me where he'd been, but he was in a really good mood. Michelle seemed pissed off with him all night, although she refused to say why. It must have been something major, he treats her like shit most of the time, and she just takes it. This is the first time I've seen her angry with him.'

'Why does she stay if he's horrible to her?' Les asked.

'That's the question we'd all like to know the answer to. She started working for him around five years ago. He brought her along to a show one night and introduced her to everyone. He just said that she was his new assistant. Not long after that she moved in with him. We thought he was sleeping with her, but she soon put us straight on that score. Since she's been around he's looked a lot smarter on stage. She persuaded him to get new costumes and start looking after himself properly. I've seen him throw the nastiest abuse at her, but she just takes it on the chin.'

'Has anyone ever had words with him about it? Or maybe spoken to Michelle?'

'There's no point talking to Ray, he just laughs at you. As for Michelle, we've all talked to her, but she says it doesn't bother her. Me and the lads spend time with her when Ray's not around, take her for a meal or pop by and check in on her. We look upon Michelle as a little sister, but we know she can handle his sarcasm. If he ever hit her though, we'd break his neck.' Des looked at his watch. 'Is there anything else? I'm working in Manchester tonight and I need to sort my gear out.'

'I think that's all for now, you've helped to fill in some of the gaps,' Les said, closing the folder.

Des got up, pulled his jacket on and shook hands with both officers again. He tucked his book into his inside pocket and picked up his crash helmet.

Mo nodded at the helmet. 'What bike have you got?' she asked.

'A Honda Fireblade, it's awesome,' Des replied. 'Do you

ride?'

'Not for a few years, but I've been thinking about getting another bike for a while,' Mo said.

'You should see her car,' Les added.

Mo grinned as she pulled out her phone and thumbed through her photos. She held the phone up for Des to see the sidelong image and he gave a low whistle.

'I'd love a classic car, but I prefer bikes now. I'm after a Harley Davidson next, my parents live in Kent and it plays havoc with my back being hunched over on the Fireblade for so long. It's great for speed, but Harleys are better when it comes to comfort. If you're ever in the market for a bike, give me a call. I can recommend a few good garages.'

'Will do, but I'll have to ask for a pay rise first.'

Mo smiled as she walked with Des back to reception.

'Well, he was pretty helpful,' Mo said when she rejoined Les in the interview room. He was going through his own notes as he couldn't read Mo's.

'Yes, he was. I wonder why Ray Diamond went for Vicky if she's not his usual type.'

'I'm wondering what hold he has over Michelle that makes her stay. I wouldn't put up with that crap.'

'Maybe she owes him money and is working it off, or he could be blackmailing her.' Mo checked the time. 'I'm heading to the canteen, are you coming?'

'No, I want to chase up forensics again. They seem to be on a go-slow because it's Christmas.'

'Okay, see you in a bit.'

Mo turned the opposite way at the top of the stairs and Les headed back to the office. Alex was having a stern conversation with someone on the phone, so Les waited until he'd finished before going in to tell him how the interview with Des Carter went.

'The other two strippers are coming in after lunch,' Les said, looking at his sheet of names.

'I haven't had Ray Diamond's statement yet, who interviewed him this morning?'

'I booked him in for 9 a.m. as requested, but he never showed up.'

'I see. What time is Michelle Simmons coming in?'

'I booked her in for 10.30 a.m.' Les looked at his watch. 'She should be here any minute.'

'What are you doing now? If you're not busy, get your coat on. I'm going to Ray's house, and I'd like to catch him when he hasn't got Michelle Simmons to hide behind.' Alex pulled his jacket on and looked for his keys.

Gary knocked the door frame. 'Boss, Faz says can you pop over? He says he's got the preliminary post-mortem findings back and there's something you need to see.'

'Great, just what I didn't need. Tell him I'm out, but I'll catch up with him later.' Alex turned back to Les. 'Ask Dawn to find out from Michelle Simmons if Ray Diamond has a bolt-hole we don't know about, or anyone he would stay with when he's not at home. I'll meet you in the car park in ten minutes.'

33

Dawn and Mo arrived in reception at the same time as Michelle Simmons. She looked troubled but had a genuine smile for the two officers. They went through to the interview room and sat down around a scarred grey table.

'Michelle, thanks for coming in. We were going to ask you for a statement about the night Vicky Wilson was killed, but you've saved us the trouble of calling,' Dawn said. 'Is that why you're here?'

'Not exactly. I mean, that's not the reason I'm here.' Michelle seemed nervous and didn't seem to know where to look.

'It's okay, anything you tell us is confidential, so don't worry,' Mo said, trying to put her at ease.

'It's Ray,' Michelle said after a long silence. 'I'm worried that he's done something bad, but it might be nothing and I don't want to accuse him in case I'm wrong.'

'Why don't you tell us what's on your mind, and we'll sit here and listen? Ray won't know you've spoken to us.' Dawn wished she would just say what was weighing so heavily on her mind.

'He will know, because he threw it away. He'll know I

took it back out of the bin,' Michelle said, with a wobble in her voice.

'Michelle, we can't help you if you don't tell us,' Dawn persisted.

Michelle closed her eyes briefly and swallowed hard. She reached into the pocket of her jeans, pulled out a silver bracelet and placed it on the centre of the table.

'I found this under the lining in Ray's work bag,' she said.

Dawn gently moved the object around on the table with the tip of her pen, noticing the broken links where some of the charms should be. 'Who else has handled this?'

'Just Ray as far as I know. It was clogged up with mud when I found it, so I ran it under the tap. Ray came down just as I was patting it dry. He took it off me, said it must have been from one of his fans and dismissed it as cheap rubbish before dropping it into the kitchen bin.'

'What made you take it back out and bring it to us?' Mo asked.

'It was his reaction when he first saw it. It's hard to describe, but it was almost like an "Oh Shit" moment. He thinks I didn't notice, but I can read him like a book. I thought maybe he'd stolen it.'

'You didn't find any loose charms, did you? It looks like there's a couple missing.'

'No, I emptied the whole bag out to give it a thorough clean. That was caught in the threads under the liner.'

'I see. Thanks for bringing it in, we'll get it to forensics to see if they can pull anything off it, but it's unlikely, seeing as it's been washed. Don't look so worried,' Dawn added, seeing Michelle's expression. 'Like I said earlier, if Ray hasn't done anything wrong, he has nothing to worry about.'

'That's his problem, he doesn't worry about anything at all, it's one of the many things he leaves to me,'

Michelle replied. 'I'm supposed to be his housekeeper and assistant, not his bloody mother.'

'Let's talk about the night Vicky Wilson was killed,' Mo began.

Michelle gave them a rundown of the evening. It tallied with what everyone had said, but with one slight difference.

'Ray said you drove him home, but other people said you didn't. Can you clarify what happened?'

'I don't know how he got home,' Michelle said. 'I took the bag and left him there. He was talking to some women at the bar. He waved me away when I told him I was leaving so I assumed he'd pulled. The car was outside the next morning when I got up, so I figured he'd driven himself home.'

'We understood that he was dating Vicky. Did he cheat on her?' Dawn asked.

'Ray has never been exclusive to anyone, that's why his marriage failed,' Michelle said. 'He married Angie because she was pregnant, but it didn't stop him playing away. Once she had the baby, she divorced him and moved to America. I don't think he's had a serious relationship since then, but I've not known him that long.'

'When did you start working for him?' Dawn asked. 'How do you get a job like yours?'

'I was working in a pub in Birmingham, and Ray used to come in on a regular basis. One night he was in by himself and we got chatting. He said he'd just moved into a big house just outside Wolverhampton, I joked that if he needed a live-in housekeeper I'd be interested, and he said that would solve all his problems. I didn't think he was serious until he turned up again a few nights later and asked when I could start. Within a week I was living there.'

'When did you start going to shows with him?'

'It was quite early on,' Michelle said. 'His car had

broken down one evening, so he asked me if I'd give him a lift to work. Once we were there, he introduced me to the other people he was working with. After a while he was asking me to go with him every time.'

'Can I ask if there's ever been any romantic involvement between the two of you?' Mo chipped in.

Michelle looked horrified. 'There's no way I'd go out with him, he's old enough to be my father! He's never made a move on me, I'm sure he just sees me as the hired help. He used to bring women home overnight, but then one of his watches went missing. He assumed that she had stolen it, so he made sure that he stayed with them after that.'

'Why do you stay? It's been indicated to us that Ray doesn't treat you very well,' Dawn asked.

Michelle's eyes glazed over. 'That old chestnut again? Look, Ray can be brusque and filthy to say the least, but it's nothing I can't handle. When he's on his own he's different, but it's kind of like an ownership thing with him. He likes people to see that he's the boss, so he lords it over me. Trust me, I get my own back.'

'In what way?' Mo asked.

'Nothing you'd find interesting, just the odd lost message from women he gave his number to, or a job that gets cancelled,' Michelle smiled at them both. 'Now, was there anything else? I have to go to the supermarket.'

34

Alex pounded on Ray's front door but there was still no answer. Ray's car was parked in its usual manner, halfway across the balding lawn, but of the man himself there was no sign. He peered in through the windows but couldn't see anyone. Les came trudging back round from the rear of the house, his breath making little clouds in the cold air.

'Nothing, boss. Either he's not here or he's being bloody quiet.' Les cupped his hands to his mouth and blew into them to warm them up.

'Right, let's get back to the station. We've got enough work as it is without chasing around after Ray Diamond!'

Alex stomped back to the car, trying to get some feeling back in his toes. It was bitterly cold, and the grey clouds overhead threatened a downpour. The journey back to the station took a long time. The streets through the city were heaving with last-minute Christmas shoppers, and Alex swore more than once as other drivers tried to cut him up.

'For crying out loud, get out of the way! Bloody hell, anyone would think it was the end of the world! Look at that woman,' he complained, as an old lady struggled to push a shopping trolley laden with food across the crossing. 'Does anyone seriously need that much bread? She must have at least six loaves in that trolley.'

'You'd be amazed, boss. There's only four people in our house, but it soon gets eaten. Ruth is on first-name terms with our Sainsbury's delivery driver.'

Les took a packet of mints out and offered them to Alex before popping one in his mouth and crunching it noisily.

'My point is that the shops are only shut for one day, two at the most,' Alex said, as he swung the car into the car park. 'Yet people stock up as if their lives depended on it.'

'Nowt as queer as folk,' Les agreed. 'I wonder how he affords that big house – Ray, I mean. It's prime land around there. It's got to be worth at least a million, and there's loads of land at the back.'

'Dawn said it's not his, it belongs to Glyn Mason. He's godfather to Ray's daughter. Ray's living there while he's abroad.'

'I wonder what he'd make of the state of it. It's not been looked after has it?' Les punched the code into the keypad and they hurried inside where it was warm.

'I know. I wouldn't want to be in his shoes when Glyn sees it, he'll have him kneecapped.'

'Knowing his luck, he'd talk his way out of it. Our Mr Diamond seems to have a touch of the blarney about him.'

'Trust me, he won't,' Alex said, as they walked up the stairs to the office. 'I went to school with Glyn Mason, he was one of those kids that was always in trouble, even when it wasn't his fault. The teachers seemed to take a dislike to him, probably because he came from a rough family but in truth they were no rougher than the rest of us, they just weren't afraid to challenge authority. Old man Mason could break someone's neck with one hand while stroking a kitten with the other. He was old-school and believed in fighting for what you wanted. He brought his lads up to be the same. Glyn's done well for himself, he started his business from scratch and got into the casino game well ahead of the competition. If Ray is living in his house, he will expect Ray to treat it with respect. If he doesn't, Glyn will hit him first and ask questions afterwards.'

'He sounds like a decent bloke . . .'

'He is, until you upset him.'

'Is it worth contacting him to see if he's heard from Ray?'

Alex shook his head. 'Definitely not. The last thing we want at the moment is finding Ray Diamond hanging from the nearest tree. Michelle Simmons is our best bet, I'll get Dawn to ring her, unless she's still downstairs.'

They walked into the office and spotted Dawn and Mo in the kitchen area. 'Ah, she's obviously been and gone. Dawn, can you come into the office please?'

***

Dawn looked up at the sound of Alex's voice. She put her hand on Mo's arm. 'I'd better go and give him the latest news.'

'Good luck.'

'Cheers, I think I'm going to need it.'

35

Ray sprawled back on the bonnet of the car, eyes closed as the young woman leaned over him. There was nothing quite like getting a blow job in the open air, especially on a cold day like this. He glanced down, amused to see the little clouds of her breath that escaped as she pleasured him. She was certainly skilled, with a hot body and an even hotter mouth.

Ray liked women to suck him off after he'd fucked them, it got him clean and got him off at the same time. He screwed his face up as he came, gripping her hair to force himself further into her throat. Once he was fully spent, he zipped up his jeans and brushed his hair out of his face.

'Not many women can make me come twice in an hour, but babe, you are something special,' he said, wrapping his arms around her so he didn't have to kiss her. He took no pleasure in tasting his own juices.

He let her go abruptly, reached into the car for the vodka bottle and took a long drink, then climbed back into the car and waited for her to start the engine.

'What shall we do now babe?' he said. 'You've paid for two hours, it's only fair that you get your money's worth. Are you hungry? Shall we go and get some lunch? You'll have to treat me, I must have left my wallet at home.'

She didn't speak, just smiled at him before turning the car around and heading out of Wombourne Wood and back towards the main road.

After a pleasant lunch in a little pub near Bridgnorth, Ray got his companion to drop him home. He waved as she drove away and walked towards the front door. He glanced up as he did so and noticed the French windows of his bedroom were open. He frowned; certain he had closed them. Michelle must have been snooping again, he thought angrily as he let himself into the house and raced up the stairs.

He tried his bedroom door – locked, just as it had been when he went out. Shrugging, he unlocked it and went in. Nothing seemed to be out of place, although it would be difficult to tell. This was the one place Michelle wasn't allowed, so it didn't get cleaned unless Ray did it – and that was unlikely.

The master bedroom was garish, painted red and black, with furniture to match. A magnificent four-poster bed took pride of place in the centre of the room, painted red and draped in black satin. Ray flicked through the contents of his vast wardrobe, which took up an entire wall, but found nothing he wanted to wear. Eventually, he picked up a rumpled shirt from the tangle of clothes on the floor and sniffed it. It wasn't too bad, nothing a squirt of body spray wouldn't sort out. Finding a pair of black jeans in a drawer, he threw them on the bed next to the shirt.

Ray stripped and showered, smiling to himself as he recalled the morning's activities. He wrapped one towel around his waist and another around his head, then padded back to his bedroom, sat on the bed and picked up the bundle of cash to count it. £200, not bad for a morning's work. He checked his phone to see when his next appointment was, then got dressed.

A loud crash from outside the window startled him, and Ray rushed over to the window in time to see someone running away from his car. The passenger-side window was smashed, and glass littered the gravel. With a roar of annoyance, he bolted down the stairs and ran outside, but there was no-one around. He strode back into the house and tried to phone Michelle, but it went straight to answerphone. He left a string of expletives on her voicemail, hung up and walked to the kitchen. There was a bottle of white wine in the fridge, so Ray opened it, took a large swig and left the bottle on the counter. He took his phone out again, pressed a few buttons and waited for the other person to answer. 'Hi babe, I've had some car trouble. Could you come and pick me up instead? That's great, I'll give you an extra half hour free as compensation. Cheers.'

When his lift arrived, Ray strolled out of the house with a big smile on his face and climbed into the car. He didn't notice the front door wasn't quite shut, nor did he notice the figure peering around the corner of the house at him.

36

'Morning boss, how was dinner the other night? It's been so busy I forgot to ask,' Dawn said, as she got out of her car the next morning. The temperature had dropped overnight, and everything was coated in a thin layer of frost, so the two of them walked slowly across the car park, hanging on to each other for fear of falling.

'It was really good. I even managed to relax for a while. Dave says we can move in from tomorrow, but I think we'll wait until the day after Boxing Day. Joel will be wanting decorations up in the new place if we move in before that, and I can't be arsed with all that as well as everything else.'

'Is he okay about spending Christmas with Dave and Carol?'

'He'll be fine. Dave's house is massive, all the bedrooms have their own bathrooms, so he'll be very comfortable. Dave and I are planning to move Joel's furniture in on Boxing Day. We'll take him along that morning, so he can tell us where he wants things. Carol's been great, she's hung his new curtains and has promised to help him unpack his stuff and put them away. She knows that Joel is likely to behave for her, and Jayne can get some peace to do the rest of the house.'

'I can't wait to see it,' Dawn said. 'It will be good for all of you to have more space.'

'It will, and I hope it helps with his moods. We're not bothered about us, we just want Joel to be happy. We've decided to keep the old house on and rent it out, the market's not brilliant at the minute. There may also come a time when we can't look after him for whatever reason, so we'll hire live-in carers and move back into the house.'

'There's so much to think about,' Dawn said. 'I wouldn't know where to start.'

'Believe me, we've had to wing it sometimes. There are loads of books about raising children, but not many that deal with raising disabled ones.'

They walked into the office together, Dawn headed for her desk and Alex his office. He was hoping to get as much of the paperwork done today, so they weren't swamped when they came back in after Christmas. Every member of the team had been happy to come in the day after Boxing Day to help Alex out. They wanted this one solved as much as he did.

He sat at his desk and worked steadily through the various tasks, occasionally stopping for tea or coffee. At one point he looked up to see a ham sandwich sitting on his desk. He'd been so engrossed in what he'd been doing that he hadn't noticed anyone come in. By 2 p.m. he was starting to seize up, so he got up and stretched, wincing as his joints popped and cracked. He wandered out into the main body of the office and clapped his hands loudly to get everyone's attention.

'Okay folks let's have a quick round-up. I'd normally wait until the evening briefing but I'm taking my wife out tonight, so want to get home at a reasonable hour. Gary, go and put the kettle on would you, we need a brew and it's your turn.'

Gary grumbled under his breath but went off towards the kitchen. Alex brought his team up to speed with where he was, then asked them all what progress they'd made.

'We're still waiting on some forensic results, we've not yet managed to pin down Ray Diamond for an interview, and we still need to find this elusive security man. Is that it, or is there anything else?'

'Did you go and see Faz?' Craig said.

'No, I haven't had time. Can you go and see him Craig? He may have the toxicology results back as well by now.'

'Oh no, do I have to go, boss? Last time I went to the morgue, Faz put an ear in my pocket. It was my new Armani as well.'

Alex laughed. 'It was only a plastic ear. Faz would find himself struck off if he started putting real body parts in people's pockets.'

'Well, it looked real to me. I nearly shit my pants when I got home and took my jacket off. I've had it dry-cleaned twice and it still feels tainted.' Craig shuddered at the memory of it.

'I keep telling you not to wear expensive clothes to work, so it's your own fault. Faz knows how to wind you up and he'll continue to do it because he's a sadistic bastard and enjoys your pain. Now, get going.'

Gary came back, carrying a tray laden with mugs of various designs. Everyone took their own, leaving a white one with *Boss* written on it for Alex.

'Can I drink my coffee first?' Craig asked.

'Fine, but ring Faz and tell him you'll be there in a bit.'

'Great, that will give him time to find something really gruesome, like a bladder,' Craig complained as he picked up the phone.

'If he does, just pray that it's an empty one,' Alex joked. 'Dawn, can you get a photo of that bracelet and see if one of Vicky Wilson's friends can identify it?'

'No problem. Laura Morrison's house is nearest to me, so I'll call round on my way home.'

Craig put the phone down. 'Boss, Faz says you're to go and see him tomorrow instead, he's busy with a new guest at the moment.'

'Right, I'll add that to my never-ending list,' Alex said.

'No joy on any of those witnesses,' Mo said. 'They didn't see anything out of the ordinary, and door-to-door hasn't turned up anything.'

'Les, have you got anything new?'

'Apart from a bloody headache, no I haven't. I'm starting to think that security man was a figment of everyone's imagination. No-one can describe him, not in politically correct terms anyway, and no-one saw him leave. He has to be dodgy.'

'Could he be a friend of Ray Diamond's? We've asked everyone else apart from him, mainly because we haven't been able to find him yet, and no-one seems to know where he is,' Gary offered.

Alex mulled it over for a moment. 'That's a possibility. Today we make locating Ray Diamond a priority. Find out when and where he's working, and where he likes to go when he's not. Honestly, it's like trying to track down Lord Lucan!'

As 6 p.m. approached, Alex called a briefing.

'Has anyone had even a sniff of Ray Diamond?'

He looked at the blank faces and rubbed the back of his neck. 'This is getting us nowhere,' he complained.

'Boss, you look knackered. Why don't you go home? You can get your head down for an hour before that gig tonight. I'll stay and oversee things,' Dawn offered.

'I'm happy to stay as well,' Les said. 'Ruth's at yoga and the kids are out with their mates, so I've got nothing better to do.'

'Make that three,' Mo volunteered.

'Thank you, that would be good. I doubt you'll hear anything, but let me know the minute you do.

Craig and Gary, I'll see you two in a couple of hours.'

He handed them their tickets for the club. 'Save us a seat, we'll be there as soon as Joel is sorted.'

37

The club was packed, and Alex and Jayne had to squeeze their way through to the front of the room, where Craig and Gary had saved a table to the side of the stage.

'Christ, it's mad in here, anyone would think it's Christmas,' Alex complained, as he narrowly avoided getting beer slopped on him by a drunken reveller. He pushed the drunk away and glared at him, but he didn't notice. He was too busy singing along with the young man on the stage, who was doing a very respectable rendition of *Wonderwall*.

Jayne laughed. 'Well, it is a charity event, what did you expect?' She crammed herself into the corner so she could talk to Jo and Deb. 'Hey you two, you're both looking fabulous tonight,' she said, exchanging hugs with them.

'You're looking pretty hot yourself, sweetness,' Deb said in a deep smoky voice, her eyes sparkling. She was a stunning woman, with shoulder-length dark brown hair accentuated by golden highlights. She was the same height as Craig but tended to tower over him due to her penchant for stilettos. Tonight, she wore over-the-knee black patent leather boots with steel-tipped heels, black leather trousers and a grey silk tank top. She reminded

Alex of Emma Peel from *The Avengers.*

'Wow, you look gorgeous, but you always do,' Jo said, as she kissed Deb's cheek. Jo had curled her long brown hair and it bounced around her shoulders. Her blue eyes shone with happiness.

'Thank you honey, so do you,' Deb purred. 'I love your dress. Purple really suits you.' She turned to Jayne. 'Is that the same black jumpsuit you bought when we had our shopping day out at the retail outlet?'

'Thank you, it is indeed. I bought it for Jo and Gary's engagement party if you remember, but I couldn't get into it. I was determined to shift that stone this year.'

'Well, you look fabulous darling, especially with those killer heels,' Deb said.

Jo agreed. 'You look amazing Jayne, well done.'

'I just followed that plan that you gave me, I can't believe how easy it was. I thought about putting Alex on it, but I don't know what he's eating at work, so it wouldn't do any good.'

'I've told Gary he needs to cut down on the junk. If his wedding suit doesn't fit on the day, he'll only have himself to blame,' Jo said.

Gary pushed a pint towards Alex. 'I got you one in, boss, but I was starting to wonder if I was going to have to drink it for you.'

Alex took a long pull on his pint. 'You'd have found yourself on filing duty for a week if you had,' he said, giving Gary a stern look.

Gary's face fell, and Alex started laughing. 'I'm joking mate, but you can get the next round in for being cheeky.'

Gary looked relieved. 'Remind me never to play poker with you.'

'Don't tease him, boss, you know he's easier to wind up than a cheap watch,' Craig said, poking Gary in the ribs as he squeezed past and headed to the bar.

'You can talk! You're just as easy sometimes,

especially if Faz is around,' Alex noted.

'I swear he targets me with his daft pranks. I should take him to a tribunal for harassment.' Craig looked grim. 'And you wonder why I don't like going to the morgue.'

Deb leaned forward and stroked Craig on the cheek. 'As long as he doesn't harass you sexually, darling – that's my job,' she purred, making him grin like a Cheshire cat.

'Aw, Deb, I love the way you defend Craig but still manage to make it sound rude.' Jo said, giggling.

'Well, you know what they say, if you ever need an innuendo, I'm always happy to give you one,' Deb winked.

Craig leaned over towards Alex, a conspiratorial look on his face. 'Right, while Gary's out of earshot, I need to tell you about the stag do. It's the first weekend in March. I've booked a couple of stretch limos to take us to Birmingham, we're going to the Comedy Bar then onto a gentleman's club. I've arranged for him to get a private lap dance as well, then we've got an overnight stay before the limo brings us home again the next day. Sound okay?'

'Sounds great, let me know how much you want from me and I'll sort it out.'

'There's fourteen going so far, but I've asked for final numbers by the end of January. I've paid deposits on everything but don't worry about that as we can sort it out nearer the time.'

Gary came back and set three pints of beer down on the table. He pulled a bottle of Prosecco out of his pocket and placed it on the table in front of Deb. She blew him a kiss, then went back into a huddle with Jo and Jayne.

'There we go. What are they up to?' he asked.

'Hen weekend stuff. Trust me mate, you don't want to know,' Craig said, pulling a shocked face. 'Whips and chains and other implements of torture – oh hang on, that's for your honeymoon.' He laughed, winking broadly at Gary.

'Take no notice of him,' Alex said, throwing Craig a stern look. 'Craig was just telling me about your stag do. It sounds great.'

'I know, he's done me proud,' Gary beamed. 'I'm amazed though, I didn't know so many of the lads liked fishing. I'm thinking of starting up an angling club, so we can make a regular thing of it.'

Craig tried desperately not to laugh, and Alex was relieved when the lights dimmed at that point and the band came on.

As Nowhere Fast churned out one song after another, Alex was pleased to see his friends were enjoying it as much as he was. The snippet he'd heard at their rehearsal didn't do them justice, they really were talented. Craig and Gary nodded along to the music, clearly enjoying themselves as much as he was.

Alex bought the next round, and just made it back to his seat as the band came back on for the second half. Dean Smith addressed the audience with a flushed face and a beaming smile.

'Wow, what can I say? What a fantastic turnout! Thank you all for supporting Birmingham Children's Hospital, it's an excellent cause and Nowhere Fast are proud to do their bit. I'd like to thank our agent, John Jackson of Bulldog Promotions for arranging the event, and to the club for their warm hospitality. There are collection buckets all around the room, so please feel free to drop your change into them, even a few coppers will make a difference.'

Dean paused for a moment before looking at Alex with a twinkle in his eye. 'Speaking of coppers, we have some of west Midlands' finest with us this evening, so these next few songs are for them. It's not the sort of stuff we usually do, but never let it be said that we don't listen to our audience. I hope you like our versions.'

Dean saluted at Alex before launching into *Get Back* by

The Beatles, followed by *Back in the USSR.*'

Jayne blew Dean a kiss and he returned the gesture with a grin. Next, they turned their attention to Queen, much to Alex's delight, and sang *Death on Two Legs* before finishing with *Stone Cold Crazy*. They received a standing ovation when they finished and did a couple of Sex Pistols numbers as an encore.

When Dean came over to shake Alex's hand at the end of the night, he was promptly mobbed by Jayne, Deb and Jo, and smothered with kisses and hugs. He thanked them all and gave them business cards, then rushed off to help his bandmates pack up the equipment.

'I had a brilliant night,' Jayne said. 'We should do this more often, maybe just us girls next time. You guys have your roleplaying thing every week, it's only fair that we have a regular meet-up.'

'Hear, hear,' agreed Deb. 'Starting next week. Part one of the hen celebrations is next Thursday night, the 28th.'

'Sounds great, we'll be moved in by then. Where are we going?'

38

Jayne dropped the dirty cloth into the bucket, sat back on her heels and blew a strand of hair out of her eyes. It might have been lunchtime, but she was ready for bed. Dave had been over and collected the washing machine, tumble dryer and fridge freezer that morning, and was busy installing them in the bungalow. Jayne had cleaned the kitchen windows, wall tiles, counter tops and woodwork, and all the cupboards inside and out. Now the floor was done she could relax for a while.

They hadn't put the house on the market yet, but Jayne figured it was easier to clean each room as it was cleared, so she didn't have to worry about it after Christmas. She glanced round the kitchen, empty now except for the few boxes containing her best china, which stood in the corner. Alex had been tasked with taking them over when he got home. They hadn't moved out yet, but it already felt like they'd never lived here at all.

A car pulled up outside, signalling that Joel was home from his morning club. Jayne opened the front door and he drove his electric wheelchair into the house, climbed out and crawled along the narrow hallway towards his room. He stopped dead when he got to the kitchen.

'Where's the fridge?' he asked, looking around. 'I

wanted a drink and a sandwich.'

'It's gone to the bungalow. Don't worry, I made some sandwiches before it went and put them on your desk in your room. There's a carton of juice as well. Uncle Dave will be here in an hour to take you to his place. Did you have a good time?'

'It was good. Andy brought Trivial Pursuit in, so we played that. It was a Doctor Who version, but I didn't win because I don't watch that.'

'Never mind, maybe you can take one of your games in next time. Now, go and eat your lunch, then pack what you want to take to Dave and Carol's.'

'What about you and Dad?'

'We're coming with you. We're spending Christmas Eve, Christmas Day and Boxing Day at Dave and Carol's too, remember. Dave took our bag over earlier when he picked up the kitchen stuff.'

'Okay.' Joel made his way through to his room, then shouted in annoyance. Jayne hurried through to see what the matter was, just as Jack ran out, a piece of ham hanging from his jaws. Jayne closed her eyes in disbelief. She'd forgotten about the cat.

'I'm so sorry, son, I must have forgotten to close the door. I've got no more ham left but I can make you a jam sandwich instead,' Jayne said, heading back towards the kitchen to get her phone. A plate whizzed past her, narrowly missing her head and smashing on the doorframe. A piece of the plate caught her cheek, drawing blood and she yelled in surprise and pain.

She turned and looked at Joel, who glared back at her. 'I don't want a jam sandwich, I wanted ham. I'm going to kill that fucking cat!'

Jayne picked up the broken pieces of crockery in silence and walked away, trying to ignore Joel's angry screams echoing along behind her.

39

'I've got good news and bad news,' Les told Alex. 'The good news is that Vicky Wilson's phone was switched back on. The bad news is that it's somewhere in Wombourne Woods.' Les indicated the area on his computer screen.

'That's a massive search area! Can't you narrow it down any more than that?'

'I can try, but it won't be by much.' Les looked as fed up as Alex felt.

'Print me off some copies of that map, I'm heading down to uniform for some spare bodies to assist in a search. We can divide the area up when we get there. Keep trying to narrow down the location and keep me informed. Gary, you're with me.' He headed to the door.

***

Wombourne Woods was a dense area with over fifty square miles of protected parkland, much-loved by dog-walkers, mountain-bikers and joggers alike. There were hiking trails clearly marked, and Alex wondered who was responsible for their upkeep. Usually peaceful and secluded, the woods were alive with the sound of volunteer police officers poking and prodding at the thick undergrowth, hampered by the deluge of rain that had begun shortly before they arrived.

So far, nothing that could be deemed of interest had been found, but Alex had to wonder why it was that there were always solo shoes in these places. No-one ever lost both shoes; it was always just the one. And why didn't people come back and look for them? Surely, you'd notice your shoe coming off if you were outside? It was one of those things that had always baffled him. He remembered when he'd been in uniform, he'd found one in the cells, but no-one had ever claimed it, not even the person who'd been held there. He found it very bizarre.

'Boss, over here!' Alex jumped as his name was called from somewhere over to his left. He trampled his way through the sodden leaves and twigs to where PC Penny Griffiths was standing. She held a large, muddy object in her gloved hand.

'I've found a handbag, sir,' she said. 'Not looked inside yet, I thought you might want to do that.'

Alex pulled on a pair of gloves and took it from her. 'Well done. Let's have a look, shall we?'

The bag was so badly caked in mud it was impossible to tell what colour it was. He tugged at the zip, but it was stuck fast. He looked at her in frustration and she smiled as she handed him a folding pocket-knife.

'Here you go, sir, this was still in my pocket from the last time I went hiking.'

Alex took it and cut a long slit in the handbag. He handed the knife back and peered inside. There was a jumble of items, but no mobile phone. He passed the bag back to Penny and told her to log it as evidence. He pulled his own phone out to call Les, but the signal was very weak, and he couldn't get a connection.

'Penny, walk back up to the clearing and see if you can get through to DC Morris. Ask him to start ringing Vicky

Wilson's phone at one-minute intervals. With any luck, the sound will be on and we'll be able to locate it.'

'Yes, guv.' She started up the incline towards the dirt path, slipping and sliding as she went. Alex scratched his head, adding more mud to what was already in his hair. Gary came and stood with him, equally as muddy and looking as fed up as Alex felt.

'How's it going, boss? We found a few bits and pieces that may or may not be relevant, a couple of items of clothing, a woman's shoe and a hairbrush. I've logged it all in case it belongs to Vicky Wilson. What about you?'

'PC Griffiths found a handbag, it's too dirty to be certain of the colour but we know that Vicky's handbag was missing, so it's hopeful. No phone inside though. This rain and mud aren't helping either.'

Gary jerked his head up, his hair flicking raindrops into Alex's face. He cocked his head to one side, listening intently.

'Can you hear that, boss?'

Alex concentrated hard. He could just make out a faint tinny noise. 'It's coming from down there,' he said, pointing down the bank towards a large clump of bushes.

'I'll go.' Gary was off before Alex could stop him, almost diving headfirst into the undergrowth. Within a few minutes he was back, covered in mud but grinning from ear to ear. He waved a small object in triumph.

'Good man,' Alex grinned, pulling a plastic evidence bag out of his pocket. 'Let's get back to the station.'

He glanced at his watch. 'On second thoughts, I'll take it, I'll drop you off at yours on the way back. No point in you coming back to HQ, it's almost 5 p.m. now and everyone else will either be heading home or thinking about it.'

'Cheers boss.' Gary found a crumpled tissue in his pocket and tried to wipe his face, but just made it even muddier. 'Jo will be pleased I'm home; we're having our presents tonight then going to her parents tomorrow. What are you doing?'

'We're at Dave and Carol's, so it will be a laid-back affair. Carol and Jayne won't let us men in the kitchen, so me, Dave and the boys will probably slob in front of the telly until after dinner, when we get the washing up. I'm not drinking just in case there are any incidents, but I'll be making up for it when Charlie Baldwin is back off sick leave.'

Alex threw his car keys to Gary. 'Go and start the car and sit in the warm. I'll just finish up with everyone here. There should be some carrier bags in the back, spread them on the seats first before you sit down.'

40

'We're finally getting somewhere,' Alex announced as he strode back into the office. 'We've got Vicky Wilson's phone and digital forensics are looking at it now. With any luck we should be able to pull some information off it. Well done Gary, you're relieved from tea-making duty today. Les, put the kettle on.'

'But I made the last one,' Les protested.

'Well, I wasn't here then, so you can make me one now,' Alex laughed, slapping him on the back as Les went off to boil the kettle.

'Two sugars in mine please mate,' Gary called after him. Les stuck his fingers up in reply.

'Laura Morrison said that the bracelet was Vicky's,' Dawn said. 'She recognised some of the charms on it.'

'Okay, thanks Dawn.'

'Wow, that's a lot of mud,' Mo remarked, glancing at Alex's trousers. Alex looked down. His trousers had clods of mud clinging to them, some of it still wet. His shoes were in a state too.

'Well, it was pretty bad out there, but it'll wash off. We got the phone, which is the main thing. What are you up to?'

Mo looked up from her computer. 'I'm going over the

case so far and something doesn't make sense.'

Alex perched on the edge of Mo's desk. 'I'm listening.'

Mo scrolled up to the top of the screen. 'Helen Whittaker positively identified Vicky in the morgue, but when we spoke to Ray Diamond, he swore blind that Vicky was at his house on the Monday. We've all assumed that Ray was lying, but what if he wasn't? The body was in a bad way, and her face was all but obliterated, yet Miss Whittaker said straightaway that it was her. What's bothering me is how could she know, when she hardly glanced at her?'

Mo clicked on the photo of Vicky from Laura Morrison's phone and put the post-mortem photo up next to it. She pointed at the screen. 'I'd be hard-pressed to say that was the same woman, even with both photos side by side like this.'

'You think she made a wrongful identification? Well, it does happen I suppose, but she seemed pretty certain at the time.'

Mo pushed her pen behind her ear, where it usually lived. 'Call it another one of my famous hunches, but something seems hinky to me.'

Alex mulled it over for a minute. 'Forensics are already running DNA, but whether they will ever get back to us is a mystery. Go over there Mo, tell them I'm on the warpath.'

Mo grabbed her jacket and left. Alex watched her go, hoping she was successful. He wanted to get the loose ends tied up before he went home, so he could concentrate on Christmas with his family. The way things were going he'd be hard-pressed to see them before New Year.

The phone on Mo's desk rang, and Alex picked it up.

'Finally!' Faz's cheery voice echoed in his ear. 'I thought you were coming to see me?'

'Sorry mate, we got a hit with Vicky's phone, so rushed

off to try and locate it – which we did,' Alex said.

'Did you? Well done. Now get yourself along to my office before I eat all the mince pies. I've got the full post-mortem and toxicology report for Miss Wilson, and I'm about to turn your world upside-down.'

'I'm not sure I like the sound of that. I'll be there in ten minutes.' He put the phone down.

'Tea up, boss,' Les called in a cheery voice, but Alex was already on his way out of the door.

'Sorry Les, I need to go. You can have mine,' and he was gone, leaving Les holding two mugs and cursing Alex under his breath.

41

Alex knocked loudly on the door before walking in. 'You'd better have saved me one,' he said, pointing to a tin on the desk.

Faz looked up, his phone pressed against one ear and his mouth full of food. He grinned and pointed to the far wall, covering the mouthpiece with his hand.

'No chance, but there are some chocolate Hob Nobs left. I'll be with you in a minute.' He pointed to the record player on the sideboard to his far left. 'Can you switch that off for me? Ta.'

The office was warm and inviting, the walls decorated with dark oak panelling on the lower sections, the upper sections painted sage green. Cream curtains hung at the window, and various certificates decorated the walls. A battered-looking brown leather sofa stood against the wall just inside the door, above which were Faz's collection of vintage movie posters.

Alex walked over to the expensive-looking turntable, currently playing Motorhead's Overkill album and carefully lifted the arm off the record. On the wall above the sideboard, Faz had hung a selection of family photographs. The photo in the centre showed Maisie with Luna, her Boxer dog. She had her arms wrapped tightly around Luna's huge neck and the dog's tongue lolled out of its mouth. Alex couldn't decide which one of them had the biggest grin.

He dropped into the chair in front of the large oak desk, helped himself to a biscuit and waited as Faz finished his phone call.

'Sorry about that,' he said. 'Just sorting out last-minute Christmas shopping. Bloody hell, you look like you've been mud wrestling. Please tell me it was with topless twins and you have photographs.' Faz's face took on a dreamy expression.

'You wish. What have you got for me?'

Faz handed Alex the file he'd been looking at. 'I've got a Christmas puzzle for you. Have a look at this and tell me what you see.'

'I don't need any more riddles, I've already got Mo questioning everything we've got so far,' Alex said as he took the file and opened it.

'Post-mortem results on Vicky Wilson – or are they?' Faz teased. 'You tell me,' he said and sat back with his hands laced across his stomach, waiting patiently as Alex read the file.

Alex scanned the pages, then re-read them before looking up again. 'Is this right? The skin under Vicky's fingernails was her own? Are you saying that she scratched herself?'

Faz shook his head. 'No, I'm not. My guest has no scratches at all.'

Alex looked at Faz, the penny finally dropping. 'It's not Vicky Wilson. Mo was right. She said something felt off and wondered if we'd got an incorrect ID. That means that Vicky Wilson must be alive.'

'It looks that way to me,' Faz said, taking a biscuit and eating it in one bite. 'So, that leaves one question. Who is the young lady currently occupying my fridge?'

Alex closed his eyes and rubbed his temples. He could

feel a headache coming on.

Faz walked over to the door. 'Go home Alex, spend some time with your family. The dead will wait for a day or so. You've got loads going on. If there's anything to report, I'll ring you at home. Merry Christmas, mate.'

'Yeah, you too.'

Alex looked at his watch. It was already 7 p.m. He pulled his phone out, mentally preparing himself for a bollocking when he told Jayne it was going to be a late night.

42

Christmas Day passed without incident in the Peachey household, apart from Dave almost burning the house down when he put extra brandy on the Christmas pudding without telling Carol.

Dawn had phoned to say there had been no new developments, and for Alex to stop worrying, as she had everything in hand. With detectives from Charlie Baldwin's team drafted in to cover those who were off, she seemed to be in her element running the show.

Much of Boxing Day had been taken up with Alex and Dave moving the last of the furniture into the new bungalow. They had taken Joel along on the first trip, so he could show them where he wanted his desk, bed and so on. He was delighted to have his own kitchen area. He didn't have a cooker in case he burned himself, but he had a fridge and toaster so he could make his own breakfast and lunch.

The following morning, Jayne, Carol and Joel had gone to the new house early in order to get as much done as possible before so that they could move in that day. They helped Joel unpack his many files and folders containing his family tree documents first, then left him to sort them alphabetically into his new filing cabinets while they concentrated on the rest of the house.

'You're finally in, chick.' Carol said a couple of hours later as they took a break for a coffee. 'I bet you can't wait to sleep in your own bed again.'

'I can't,' Jayne replied. 'Alex and Dave worked so hard yesterday getting everything in its rightful place, which made it so much easier. Thanks for helping me to put the curtains up and make the beds, it's a huge help.'

'It was my pleasure. I'm looking forward to having you all as neighbours.'

Jayne pulled a face. 'I'll remind you of that next time Joel kicks off.'

'Hopefully he'll stop doing that now and you can all just relax.' Carol drained her mug and put it in the sink. 'Come on, we may as well unpack the rest of these boxes while we wait for your shopping to be delivered.'

She started pulling things out of boxes and stacking them on the counter for Jayne to put away.

Joel appeared in the doorway, gliding almost silently in his electric wheelchair. Carol looked up from her task. 'Look at you! I bet it feels good to be able to use your chair indoors instead of being on your hands and knees.'

'Yes, and I can attach a tray to this one so I can carry things,' Joel said.

He looked at Jayne. 'Mum, I've invited Tom over for tea so he can see the new house. Can you order us a Chinese takeaway please? He likes sweet and sour chicken.'

He drove away again without waiting for a reply.

Carol looked at Jayne. 'He seems to have settled in already.'

'He does,' Jayne agreed. 'Let's just hope he stays that way.'

43

'You've all read Faz's report, so you know that the victim was wrongly identified,' Alex said to his team at the morning briefing. 'Vicky Wilson's skin was found under the victim's fingernails, so we need to find out not only who the victim is, but also the whereabouts of Vicky herself. She could be a missing person or the main suspect, we just don't know yet. Meanwhile, I need you lot to start at the beginning. Comb through everything we have so far, someone must be missing this woman, so find out. It's the 28th now, and I'd like to tie this one up before New Year's Day if possible. I want a fresh incident board set up next to the original one, so things can be cross-referenced.'

'Do you want us to re-interview everyone, boss?' Craig asked.

Alex shook his head. 'Not necessarily. Re-read all the interviews and if something doesn't sit right, then get that person in. If you're satisfied, move on. Cross-check each other's work in case something jumps out.'

'Mo, can you do a thorough background check on Ray Diamond? I know you've already done one but go back further and spread the net wider. I've crossed paths with him before, I know I have, but I'm damned if I can remember where it was.'

A voice from the doorway called to Alex. It was the same young officer as last time. Alex wondered whether they kept sending him because he was the only one fit enough to run up the two flights of stairs.

'Excuse me, sir, there's a Mr Sanderson in reception, asking for you. He's got Mr Diamond with him.'

'Thank you, Constable. Tell him I'm on my way down,'

Alex looked at his watch. 'He's right on time. Dawn, you're with me. The rest of you crack on.'

**

Geoffrey Sanderson sat patiently in reception, reading a copy of *The Metro* while Ray Diamond sat next to him, idly thumbing through what looked like a brand-new phone. Ray looked smart and sober, his hair was freshly washed and brushed back into a ponytail, he wore a brown suit, white shirt with the collar open, and black boots. Mr Sanderson wore a tired-looking grey suit with a faded yellow shirt and brown tie. His black brogues looked old and hadn't seen any polish for a while.

Alex soon had them settled in an interview room. He explained he would be taping the interview and both men nodded in acknowledgement. Dawn knocked on the door and entered. She sat next to Alex and opened her notebook expectantly.

'Thank you both for coming in. Mr Diamond, but it wasn't necessary for you to bring your solicitor with you, as this is an informal interview,' Alex said.

Ray shrugged. 'I wanted to make sure you lot don't try and stitch me up for something I didn't do.'

'I can assure you that wouldn't happen, but it's your prerogative. I believe you've met my colleague, Detective Sergeant Dawn Redwood. She came out to your house and took a statement, but you seemed a little off-colour that day, so we'd like to get a clearer picture if you don't mind.'

'Sorry, I don't remember you,' Ray said to Dawn.

He nodded to his solicitor, who produced a book out of his briefcase and placed it on the table. Ray pointed at it.

'That's my work diary. Shelley – Michelle – said I should bring it, in case I forgot anything.'

After they had gone through the events of the evening in question, Alex opened the folder he'd brought with him.

'These are DS Redwood's notes from your last interview,' he said. 'In it, you said that Vicky Wilson had been at your house on the Monday after the show. Is that correct?

'Yes, she turned up with breakfast for both of us, BLT's I think. I wasn't expecting her, I didn't even know she knew my address, but I wasn't going to turn away free food. We had sex a couple of times, then she left.'

Ray looked at his hands and picked at a loose cuticle.

'I see. Was anyone else in the house?' Alex asked.

'Shelley had gone to the supermarket; she goes every Monday. She went to the bank as well, to pay some bills I think, or to put some money in. Anyway, she didn't get home until just before 1 p.m. I was meeting someone, so I barely saw her for five minutes.'

'Does Vicky Wilson have any unusual markings, like tattoos or birthmarks, that you are aware of?' Alex asked.

'I'm not certain about birthmarks, but she has a tattoo of a black rose on her arse – I mean, bottom.' Ray corrected. 'She was laughing and saying her old man had gone mad when he found out, he said she may as well go on the game and be done with it.'

'Do you know when she got the tattoo? Was it recent?'

'No, she got it when she was on holiday a few years ago. She said she and her mates all had matching ones.'

230

'Do you know which friends?'

Ray shrugged. 'I don't know their names, but I think they were the same ones that were with Vicky that Friday night. I've seen the blonde before, she's friends with the drag queen, but not the brown-haired one. I don't think she'd been to a strip show before, she looked terrified when I jumped onto her lap.'

The grin slipped from his face when he realised that no-one else was smiling.

'What happened when Vicky went backstage with you?'

Ray appeared to think hard for a moment, but Alex was sure it was a delaying tactic. He was beginning to lose his patience already. He cleared his throat and looked hard at the solicitor, who nudged his client.

'Sorry, I was lost in thought there. Vicky was all over me like a rash, and I got very turned on. The drag queen was getting fed up with it and told her to pack it in. Vicky told her to go and fuck herself, if you'll pardon my French. In the end I took Vicky outside and we had a quickie. I told her I'd see her after the show, and I went back inside.'

'So, you left her outside in the dark on her own?'

'Yeah. She was fine, she said she couldn't wait to see me later, she promised me all kinds of kinky stuff and I nearly gave her another one because it made me horny again.'

'Did you see her again later?'

'No. To be honest, I don't remember leaving. I was very drunk by then.'

'Did you receive any phone calls or texts messages from Vicky Wilson after that?' Alex asked.

Ray shook his head. 'I didn't hear anything from her until she showed up at my house on the Monday, wearing nothing but a long coat and a smile.'

Dawn and Alex exchanged glances.

'Thank you, I think that's all for now, but we may need to come back to you at some point. Do you mind if we hang on to this for a while?' Alex asked as he picked up the diary. 'We'll get it back to you as soon as we can.'

'No problem. Shelley has another copy in case I lose it.' Ray said. 'I'm always losing things.' He stood up and started to walk towards the door.

'Oh, before you go, would you mind providing us with a sample of your DNA? Just for elimination purposes?' Alex asked.

Ray looked at his solicitor. 'Do I have to?' he asked him.

'Not at all, but...'

'In that case, no I won't.'

Ray turned on his heel and walked out of the room, with his solicitor following behind him.

Dawn let out a breath she'd been holding. 'Wow, talk about being sensitive! I think we need to talk to Vicky's friends again.'

Alex followed Dawn out of the interview room. 'I'm interested in why they said Vicky had no identifying marks. If they knew about the tattoo, why not mention it?'

Dawn shrugged. 'I guess we'll find out later. I'll ring them and get them to come in. I'll ask them to bring an outfit for Vicky to wear. That way their suspicions won't be aroused.'

'Good idea. I would say just bring Helen Whittaker in, she saw the body so would have known it wasn't her. The question is why would she falsely identify someone?'

'What are we missing here? And where do I know that squirrelly bastard from?'

Alex looked exasperated and Dawn shared his frustration. 'I don't know. If there was anything to find, Mo would have found it by now. Maybe you're confusing him with someone else.'

'No, I'm not, that's just it. His mannerisms are so familiar, but I know I've never come across the name Ray Diamond before.'

'Maybe that's his stage name.' Dawn suggested. 'His mates all have them, perhaps Ray Diamond is his.'

'It's a possibility,' Alex said. 'But his face isn't ringing any bells at all.'

'Maybe he dyed his hair or grew it long since you saw him last.'

A memory gnawed at the back of Alex's brain, urging him to recall it and it was driving him mad.

Dawn's phone beeped. She looked at Alex. 'That was Les. Forget about Ray for now, the security man has just walked in.'

44

Arjan Bakshi sat in reception staring straight ahead, hands in his jacket pockets, clenching his teeth. He was tall and muscly, with black crew-cut hair, a goatee beard and cold dark eyes.

'Mr Bakshi? Sorry to have kept you waiting,' Alex held his hand out in greeting and tried not to wince at the man's firm grip, made more painful by the gold rings he wore.

'Please come this way. My colleague is on his way down to join us, then we can get started.'

Alex sorted out the tapes while they waited for Craig, who arrived a couple of minutes later. 'Now, Mr Bakshi,' Alex began, 'We've had quite a job tracking you down. Can you tell us who hired you to work the door that night?'

'Sure, it was Ray Diamond.'

He spoke in a thick Black Country accent, which belied his Indian heritage. 'He said the usual crew had let him down and asked if I'd do it as a one-off. I'm wishing I hadn't though, the bastard hasn't paid me yet.'

Alex and Craig exchanged looks. 'I understand you had an altercation with Miss Vicky Wilson. What happened?'

'She was a nasty cow. She looked like butter won't

melt, but she was a bitch to everyone. Not just me either. The bar staff were less than impressed with her. She threatened that Ray would get them fired if they didn't serve her first, and when I wouldn't let her through to the changing room, she kicked off at me big-time.'

'That must have been humiliating.' Alex said.

'Nah, not really, I'm a bouncer at The Grey Goose, so I'm used to people calling me Paki and stuff like that, even though I'm not Pakistani, I'm Indian. That sort of racist crap is water off a duck's back to me. What pissed me off was that she made out she was so important. She wasn't, she was one of many scrubbers that Ray lets backstage. He's normally got a queue a mile long. Don't ask me how he does it, but he's never lonely, know what I mean?'

'Did you see her after she went through to him?' Craig asked.

'Nah, she never came out again, unless she came along the path and back in through the front. I stayed until Ray said I could go, that must have been around 11 p.m. The drag queen was still onstage when I left. I went to The Goose; I was on the door with Benny till 3 a.m. You can ask Cheryl, she's the manager. There was a fight and we had to call you lot in to break it up.'

'Thanks,' Craig said as he wrote down the information. 'When you left did you notice anything unusual, anyone hanging around or acting suspiciously?'

'No, I was concentrating on getting to work on time. Speaking of which,' Arjan said as he looked at his watch. 'I really need to get going. I'm on the early shift tonight, and I must pop to my Mum's to pick up a load of food. She still insists on cooking for me, even though I left home ages ago.'

'No problem, we've got your details now, so we'll be in touch if we need to speak to you again. Have a good night.'

Arjan sauntered out of the room without a backward glance.

'He's a big bloke,' Craig said. 'Did you see the size of his hands?'

'I bet he packs a hefty punch,' Alex replied. 'He's built like Jack Reacher.'

'I take it you mean the book version, because he looks nothing like Tom Cruise,' Craig laughed.

***

Alex's phone was ringing when he got back to his office. 'Hey honey. I'm just leaving now. Okay, order it now and I'll pick it up on the way. Love you too.'

Alex hung up the phone and grabbed his keys. He was about to leave when Craig called him over.

'Here you go boss, enjoy your first night in your new home.' Craig said, taking a bottle of champagne out from his desk drawer and passing it across to him. Gary handed Alex a card, signed from them all and Mo presented him with a bunch of flowers.

Alex felt himself getting emotional, they were a great bunch of people and he knew how lucky he was.

'Thanks guys, that means a lot. You've all had my back these past couple of years, and I want you to know that I appreciate each and every one of you.'

Alex sniffed back tears, and Dawn hugged him.

'Bugger off, before Jayne sends out a search party for you,' she said, pushing him towards the door.

45

Alex walked into the office the next morning feeling brighter than he had in a long time. Last night had been lovely, sitting in the new house with his wife, enjoying a takeaway and drinking the champagne together.

Joel had been thrilled to have all his things unpacked and was enjoying his new office. Jayne and Carol had worked hard, and all the essentials had been unpacked and put away, leaving the boxes containing books and ornaments for a later date. The shower in their bathroom was ten times more powerful than the old one, leaving Alex feeling like a new man, and he'd slept like a baby until Jayne had nudged him to tell him his alarm was going off.

'Good morning team, I hope you all slept as well as I did, and thank you all again for the champagne. Right, let's get cracking.'

Alex looked at the list he'd made while he was eating his breakfast. 'Les, ask uniform to send someone over to Vicky Wilson's flat and see if she's been home. She's devoted to her cat, so I can't see her just abandoning him. Mo, check her financials and see if she's used any of her cards recently. Unless someone's holding her against her will, she'll be needing money soon. Craig and Gary, can you check on the two friends that Vicky Wilson was out with that night? Excellent, thank you. Can anyone think of anything I've not covered? Good, then go and get on with it.'

***

Alex popped along to see his boss and bring him up to speed. DCI Andrew Oliver was a tall, slim man with dark brown eyes and a halo of grey hair. He was firm but fair, and knew Alex was more than capable of running his team without too much interference from him. Alex admired his faith; it made his life so much easier not having a condescending boss. They sat drinking coffee and eating homemade samosas that Andy's wife had sent in.

'So, we had a victim, then we didn't, and we had a suspect but then we didn't,' Andrew said over the rim of his mug. 'I hope you've got more to report than that.'

Alex swallowed a bite of samosa before he answered. 'Yes, we've got lots of small threads, we just need to pull them all together. I'm hoping that once Vicky's friends know of her resurrection, they will be able to shed some light on where she might go. Laura Morrison has been looking after Vicky's cat, so she might have noticed if someone's been in the flat.'

'I agree that Helen Whittaker definitely knows more than she's letting on,' Andrew said, 'But how sure are you that Laura Morrison is not involved as well?'

'I'm not 100% of anything at the moment but she did seem genuinely upset about Vicky's death.'

'As did Helen Whittaker,' Andrew pointed out. 'Yet she made a wrongful identification. If she'd had any doubts when she saw the victim's face, she would have mentioned the tattoo.'

'Good point. No-one that close a friend would make

that mistake. Something really doesn't sit right with any of this and it all comes back to Ray Diamond.'

'Perhaps you should focus on Ray Diamond. Perhaps someone is setting him up.'

Alex thought about it for a moment. 'Maybe you're right. Given his attitude, I assumed that Ray had killed Vicky, he's certainly arrogant enough to make you think he could commit murder and get away with it. He was sleeping with her, that much we know. Vicky's phone turned up in the woods behind his house and the bracelet that was found in his bag. Michelle Simmons said she had driven him home and he'd gone straight to bed. Do you think someone's trying to frame him?'

'It certainly looks that way,' Andrew agreed, 'You just need to find out who hates him enough to do it. From what you've told me it's quite a list.'

'It is. He steals work from fellow strippers on a regular basis, then brags about it when he's drunk. He viciously assaulted the drag artiste, he treats his assistant like dirt and he's a serial cheater. Add to that he's living in a house that will one day belong to his daughter. She may have told her godfather that Ray treats the place like crap.'

'He sounds delightful. Maybe you could use his oversized ego to your advantage. Get him to come in again and play the sympathy card,' Andrew suggested. 'Tell him you think someone's trying to frame him and that you want to help him find out who it is. He will probably tell you a lot more if he thinks you're on his side.'

'I like it,' Alex grinned. 'Make him feel like the good guy.'

'Exactly.'

46

Michelle folded Ray's freshly pressed costumes and towels and placed them carefully in his bag, along with a new bottle of baby oil, two boxes of tissues, a new pack of hair bobbles and hairbrush, and finally the old battered pornographic magazines. She'd flatly refused to buy him new ones so until he did, he would have to manage with what he already had.

As Michelle reached for a bottle of baby lotion, the doorbell rang, causing her to jump and knock the bottle off the counter. It hit the tiled kitchen floor and exploded with a loud pop, showering almost everything nearby, including her jeans and trainers. She swore loudly as she kicked her shoes off and hurried to the door to see who it was, wiping her hands on a tea towel as she went.

'Hi babe, I lost my key again. You took your time,' Ray breezed as he pushed past her and into the hall. He saw the state of her jeans and laughed. 'Were you wanking over my photos again? Really Shelley, I'll be happy to let you look at me naked, you'd probably come faster too.'

He bounded up the stairs two at a time, leaving the door wide open and Michelle seething in the doorway. Loud music began blaring out from behind his bedroom door almost immediately.

As Michelle turned to close the front door she shrieked. Si had approached while she wasn't looking. He stopped short and put his hands out as the door nearly hit him in the face.

'Whoa, easy tiger, you nearly squashed me then!' he exclaimed. He saw the expression on her face, grabbed her arms and pulled her towards him, covering her face in loud sloppy kisses. She laughed, hugged him fiercely then burst into tears.

'Hey, what's the matter? Has that twat upset you again? Do you want me to knock him on his arse?'

Michelle shook her head. 'He was being his usual charming self, nothing I can't handle. You know how he gets just before a big show.'

'That's no excuse. If he upsets my favourite girl, he upsets me. I don't suppose you'll let me go up there and batter him, will you?'

'You know I won't. If you do that he can't work, then I don't get paid.'

'Fair enough, but I can do this.' Si stuck his tongue out and waved two fingers at the stairs several times, making childish noises at the same time. He grinned at Michelle, then followed her back through to the kitchen.

'Bugger me, what happened?' Si looked at the mess.

'I dropped a bottle of baby lotion. It went on my jeans, so Ray assumed I'd been wanking over his photos and offered to get naked for me. I don't know why it upset me so much, he's said worse before.'

Michelle grabbed a roll of kitchen towel and started tearing sheets from it. Si took it from her and pushed her gently towards the kettle.

'I'll sort this out, you make us some coffee. I used to work in a butcher's shop, so I'm used to cleaning up all kinds of stuff. I'll have this done in no time, then I'll show you my new tattoo,' he said, dropping to his knees and mopping up the spilled lotion.

By the time the coffee was ready, Si had cleaned up all the mess. He tried to wipe Michelle's jeans, but she stopped him.

'Leave it, it's soaked in now. I'll stick them in the wash later. Thanks Si, you're a real darling to me.' Michelle looked on the brink of tears again and Si put his arms around her, lifted her up and spun her around, making her giggle again. He set her back down with a grin. 'That's more like it,' he said.

'Hey, check this out,' Si said, unbuttoning his shirt and slipping it off. He turned around to show her his back. 'Sweet or what?'

A new tattoo covered almost the whole of his back and depicted Botticelli's *Birth of Venus*. The attention to detail was stunning and Michelle whistled.

'Wow, that's incredible. Where did you get it done?' She touched the delicate lines, still raised from the tattoo artist's needle. 'Can I take a picture of it?'

Si grinned and posed for her. 'I had it done at Undertone in Codsall, by Lee. He specialises in works of art. You should see some of the other ones he's done. He's pretty awesome.'

'He certainly is. I've been wanting something done for my dad for ages but haven't decided what to have yet.'

'If you have a design in mind, give them a call. Tell Lee I said to give you one of my slots, I always book a few at a time because I know how busy he is.'

'I can see why; the quality is exceptional,' Michelle said. 'Is there something wrong with your tea? You've hardly touched it.'

'No, I'm fine, but can you just put some of this cream on my back for me? It's healing well but it's still a bit tender.'

Si handed her a tube of cream and Michelle applied it for him. He put his shirt back on and gave her a hug.

'My, don't you two look cosy?' Ray said as he bounced

into the kitchen, dressed in his favourite white designer jeans, tight-fitting black T-shirt and black biker jacket. His hair was freshly washed and blow-dried, and he carried his trademark biker boots under his arm. He stopped to take a mouthful of Michelle's coffee.

'Ugh, no sugar. I'm off to sort some stuff out, so I'll meet you at the venue. Make sure you've got everything, we don't want any fuck-ups like we had in Sheffield, do we?'

He pulled his boots on and walked towards the front door. Michelle nudged Si and pointed to the scattering of dark mud on the floor where Ray had stamped his feet to clean his boots. Si frowned at Ray's back and stuck his tongue out again. Michelle bit her lip to stop the laughter that was threatening to burst out. She made a funny noise and Ray turned around to look at her just as Si pulled her to him to hide the smirk on her face.

'Are you staying to play hide the sausage with Shelley? Be careful mate, she's a bit of an animal, if you get my drift.'

He winked broadly at Si and flounced out of the house, slamming the door behind him. A few seconds later they heard his car start up and, with a screech of tyres, he was gone.

'I wish I had someone like you to look after me,' Si said. 'I'll tell you something, he doesn't know how lucky he is. Why do you put up with it? We all think the world of you, and none of us can figure it out.'

Si started to smile. 'I know, you've got incriminating pictures of him wearing ladies' knickers, a woolly hat and a pair of wellies, haven't you?'

Michelle snorted into her coffee and Si roared with laughter, pleased that he'd made her smile again.

He spotted Ray's holdall on the floor and gestured towards it. 'Is that his gear for tonight?' he asked, standing up and walking over to peer in the bag.

Michelle nodded. 'Yes, all ship-shape and Bristol fashion. Not that he will appreciate it.'

Si gave her a wicked grin and pulled out Ray's new silver G-string. 'He's always saying how he's the best dancer, so let's make the fucker dance.'

47

Backstage at The Aurora Club, Kitty McLean was getting very stressed. How the management expected two drag queens and four strippers to get changed in such a small office was beyond her. She propped her mirror up against a computer on the larger desk and started to cleanse her face before applying her make-up. Ruby had hung up Kitty's costumes and had gone to get some bottled water from the shop across the road.

A bald, heavyset black man with no neck threw the door open and hit the back of Kitty's chair. Kitty tutted loudly and removed the line of eyeliner she'd smeared across her cheek. He threw her a look of contempt and glanced around the small room.

'Good evening Lavinia,' Kitty said, drawing a fresh line of pencil on her lower eyelid.

'It's a bit poky isn't it?' he said in a deep voice. He dropped his bag on the floor and pulled out a creased dress, throwing it casually across the back of a chair. He kicked his trainers off, revealing bare feet that were filthy. Kitty shuddered inwardly as he pulled his dirty green T-shirt over his head, revealing a very hairy chest and flabby stomach. He dropped his grey jogging bottoms, bending down just as Ruby came back in from the shops.

'Lord a mercy!' Ruby screeched in a fake Jamaican accent. 'Me nearly dropped me eyeballs down de drain!'

'Very funny,' the man said. He pulled a makeup bag out of his holdall and rummaged around inside.

'I did ask for a bigger room, but they said it was either this or the gents toilets. Trust me, you don't want to go in there.' Kitty sat back and looked in the mirror. Satisfied with the results, she started to undress, feeling Lavinia's eyes on her.

'What happened to your back? Bit of rough, was it?' Lavinia made a snorting sound.

'None of your business, Bob,' Kitty snapped, knowing full well that using her real name would wind her up.

'My name is Robert, and I was only asking,' Lavinia replied. He emptied his make-up bag out on the desk top, scattering tubes of lipstick and cotton balls everywhere. He looked around on the floor. 'Have you seen my tits?'

Kitty sighed. 'No, I have not seen your tits. Now go and get a drink from the bar and let me get ready in peace!'

'What's up with you? Lavinia sneered, scratching his armpit and releasing a cloud of B.O. Kitty picked up a bottle of perfume and sprayed it in the air.

'Fucking hell, when was the last time you had a bath? You stink like a docker! And do something about your toenails, will you? They're disgusting!'

'Fuck off, you vile bitch! You think you're something special, don't you?' Lavinia bellowed, storming up to Kitty and getting in her face.

Kitty glared back. 'You want to watch that someone doesn't shut your fat mouth for you!'

'Yeah? You and whose army?'

Kitty wafted a hand in front of her face. 'It would take a brave army to cope with your foul breath. It smells like you've licked a dog's back end.'

Lavinia stepped closer. 'One of these days someone

will put you on your arse, Lady. I hope I'm there to see it.'

'Hey, that's enough!' Ruby shouted as the two queens squared up to each other.

She got in between them and pushed them apart. 'Lavinia, put some clothes on, and Kitty, go outside and have a cigarette. Now!' she said, thrusting a packet of cigarettes into Kitty's hand. She pointed at the door and Kitty marched outside. Then she looked at Lavinia and sucked her teeth. 'I said, get dressed, then get out front and mingle with the punters.'

Lavinia said nothing, despite being big, she knew that Ruby would knock her out given half a chance. She silently put her make-up on then got dressed. By the time Kitty came back in she had gone into the function room.

'I'm sorry I threw you out, but trust me, she got both barrels as well.' Ruby handed Kitty a bottle of water and a straw. 'Now, sit down, have some water and tell me what's going on. It's not like you to lose it like that.'

Kitty sighed and rested her head in her hands. 'The nursing home rang me this morning. Mum's dementia is getting worse. Yesterday they found her crying in the bathroom. She was convinced she'd had a miscarriage.'

'Oh, bless her heart,' Ruby said, taking Kitty's hand and squeezing it. 'Are you going to see her?'

'I'm heading up there tonight, after the show. I spoke to John this morning and asked him to find cover for the New Year's Eve show. I'm not sure when I'll be back, it depends on how Mum is. I'll pay you for the missed show though.'

'Hey, don't worry about that, you stay as long as you need. It'll be a good excuse to catch up with my own stuff. Keep me in the loop though, yeah?'

'I will. Thank you honey.' Kitty exchange air kisses with Ruby. 'Now, I'd better finish getting ready, the boys will be here any minute.'

Ruby smiled. 'The show must go on.'

'Indeed, it must,' Kitty agreed.

48

The hen party had decided to meet up at Alex's place, so they could get the official tour before heading off on Jo's hen night. They had gone with French maids as a theme for their fancy dress, but Jo's mum had decided to dress as the Queen instead.

No-one minded at all, Martha was a tiny woman with a huge personality, with strawberry-coloured hair, blue eyes and some very raunchy stories up her sleeve. She looked very regal in her diamante tiara and long white dress with a blue sash that read: Mother of the Bride.

'Martha, you look stunning,' Alex said, kissing her on the cheek.

'Hello, bonny lad,' she said, her Geordie roots still showing loud and proud, despite having lived in Shropshire for years. 'The new house is amazing, when can I move in? I should warn you, if you wander about in your nuddy-pants I might have a stroke!' she cackled with laughter, cracking them all up.

'Here, is there any more of that Prosecco?' She held up her glass and Alex refilled it.

'Who are we waiting for? The minibus will be here in a minute.' Jo straightened her maid's cap and drained her glass.

'Just Deb I think.' Jayne did a quick head count. 'Yep, everyone else is here. Let's have another drink while we wait.' She opened another bottle and they all cheered.

'Wow, check out that foxy babe,' Mo said, looking out of the window. Deb strode up the path, looking a million dollars in her outfit. She looked just like Magenta from the Rocky Horror Show. Craig followed behind her, a huge grin on his face.

She threw the kitchen door open and struck a pose. 'What do you think?' she purred.

'I'm thinking of a threesome,' Isobel said, getting an elbow in the ribs from Mo.

'Behave yourself, or I'll have to spank you,' she scolded.

'Ooh, me first,' Deb said, bending over and showing off her frilly pants. Mo nearly choked on her drink and Isobel wolf-whistled.

'Come on you lot, get out so we can get on with our game,' Alex opened the front door and they filed out.

The minibus driver's face was a picture of delight as he helped them climb in.

'God help those strippers tonight,' Alex mused as they watched them drive away. 'I've a feeling it's going to get very messy.'

'That's why I wore old clothes,' Craig said. 'I don't want to ruin my good stuff.'

Alex looked him up and down. He wore grey designer jeans, a cream-coloured cashmere jumper and burgundy-coloured loafers. 'That's your old stuff?'

'Yeah. I do dress down sometimes, you know.'

Alex shook his head, laughing as they went through to the lounge.

'Did the women get off alright?' Gary asked. He had the table set up with roleplaying sheets, notebooks and pencils. A box containing various types of dice stood in the middle, next to a plate of home-made cake that

Martha had brought for them.

'Yes, I've said we'll pick them up at 11.30 p.m.' Alex said. 'Now, who's turn is it to go first?'

***

As the function room gradually filled up, the atmosphere backstage had become calmer with the arrival of some of the strippers. Lavinia was sitting on the floor on one side of the room, eating a Cornish pasty. She glared at Kitty as if daring her to comment as she tore another chunk off and pushed it into her half-full mouth. Kitty shuddered and turned away.

On the other side of the dressing room, Chad, Si and Des were leaning against the wall, talking quietly and sipping beer. Their costumes were neatly laid out ready for their acts, so they had plenty of time to relax. It was the first time they'd seen each other since being interviewed and were deep in conversation about the murder and speculating over who'd committed the crime.

Ray flung the back door open, startling everyone and causing one of Kitty's wig stands to go flying. Ruby grabbed it just before it hit the floor and set it back on the table, looking daggers at Ray as she did so. Ray seemed to find it hilarious; he was giggling like mad. Michelle staggered in with Ray's holdall and Si rushed to take it from her. Ray blew him a kiss and laughed manically.

'Ah Shelley, I think Si fancies you. Look at him carrying your bag for you like a little schoolboy. It's so sweet.' Ray taunted, but to the surprise of the other lads, Si just winked at Michelle and said nothing.

Ray was a bit taken aback by this; he was expecting Si to throw a couple of insults back at him. Si placed Ray's bag down in the centre of the room and walked back over to the other lads.

Des glanced at him. 'That's not like you, Si, having

nothing to say. Bit early for New Year's resolutions isn't it?'

Si gave him a beaming smile. 'Wait and see son, wait and see. Karma's a bitch.'

Ray loudly announced he was taking the last spot before the interval and the last spot in the second. He didn't expect anyone to argue with him and no-one did. That said, he walked through the curtain and headed for the bar, certain that his fans would be only too eager to buy him drinks if he turned on the charm. Ray never paid for anything; if his fans didn't keep him topped up, then he made sure Michelle did.

Michelle hung Ray's costumes up on a coat rack behind Kitty's area and carefully arranged his accessories on a stool below it. She kept glancing at Si, who kept winking back at her. Ruby noticed the exchange and went over to where Michelle was wrapping up a bottle of lotion in a flag for Ray's final spot, when he would do his full strip.

'What's going on with you and Si?' she asked with a grin. 'Are you two at it?'

Michelle giggled. 'No, nothing like that. Let's just say that Ray's routine will be extra hot tonight.'

'Sounds intriguing,' Ruby smirked, hoping for more, but Michelle said nothing and got on with her work.

'I reckon he did it, he thinks he's untouchable,' Si said, as the conversation returned to the murder and Ray's possible involvement.

Des shook his head. 'Nah, he may be many things, but I can't see him killing anyone. It's one less adoring fan if he did and he needs as many as he can get at his age.'

'True,' laughed Chad. 'But in the heat of the moment and all that. Crimes of passion aren't unheard of, and he gets his fair share of that. I heard that her face was battered in and she was strangled. Ray's a two-minute wonder from what I've heard, so he wouldn't have time to do all that before he shot his load. Unless he's into necrophilia.'

Si shuddered. 'He's a weird fucker; I wouldn't put anything past him. Let's face it; we've seen him do some strange shit in his time. Do you remember that time we went to Greece? It was a case of anytime, anyplace, anywhere with him. I'm surprised he didn't end up in prison after he hijacked that bus full of pensioners and waved his cock around. I'm sure he only got away with it because he was so pissed.'

'Ray would never go to prison for anything, he's too good at talking himself out of trouble,' Chad said. 'He only got off that rape charge back in the 80s because his mates gave him an alibi.'

'What? When was that?' Des looked stunned. 'I know he's a prick, but rape? That's bang out of order, man.'

'Yeah, it was when he first got started and was getting a lot of interest. This woman accused him of rape and assault, she said he jumped her after she left the train station in Wolves. I remember reading about it. Poor thing was beaten up pretty badly too. He swore he'd never even been in town that night, but she said he'd followed her back from Birmingham and grabbed her as she walked through the underpass from the station.'

Si scratched his head. 'I know I said I wouldn't put anything past him, but I'd never have thought that even he'd do something that bad.' He looked over as Michelle dropped the glass she'd been holding and rushed out of the back door.

'Will you lot never learn to keep your voices down?' Kitty barked as she followed Michelle outside. She was back a few minutes later. 'She's fine, she just needs a few minutes.'

'Oh shit, I thought she knew about it. I'm sorry, Kitty,' Chad said, looking ashamed.

'It's not me you need to apologise to!' Kitty looked at

her watch. 'Chad, you've got half an hour, so get ready. Des, go and get us a bottle of wine from the bar will you, we could all use a drink. Tell them to put it on my tab.' She smoothed her dress down and picked up her microphone. 'Lavinia, you're on in fifteen minutes, so stop stuffing your face and get your frock on.'

49

Deb nudged Jo and nodded towards Ray as he mingled with the crowd, looking confident and relaxed. He scanned the room and made a beeline for the bar where he was immediately surrounded by women pressing up against him, some openly groping him. He accepted all the attention with an Oscar-winning smile.

'Hey ladies, you all look gorgeous tonight. I hope you're all looking forward to seeing my new act. Now, who wants to buy me a drink? There's a kiss for the fastest to the bar.'

Deb pointed towards him. 'Look at him sucking up to everyone. That's Ray Diamond, Craig said he was a bit of a prick.'

Jo almost inhaled her glass of white wine, setting off a coughing fit. Jayne had to thump her on the back till she could breathe again.

'I'm hoping he's going to be more than a bit of a prick, he's supposed to be huge!' Jo giggled as she took another slurp of her drink.

The others roared with laughter, causing Ray to turn and look at them. He must have thought he was onto a good thing as he sauntered over to them, fake smile plastered in place.

'Are you having fun, ladies? If not, I guarantee you will be soon once you see my performance. I always make a special effort for my fans.'

Jayne rolled her eyes at Deb and they started laughing. He looked puzzled; he wasn't used to not being fawned over. Dawn saluted him with her glass and he suddenly realised who she was. He started to pull away, but Martha grabbed his wrist.

'Actually, we're on a hen night so we want to see loads of cocks, not just one,' she told him, giving him a broad wink. 'I hope you're all hung like donkeys.'

Ray beamed and assured her she was in for the night of her life, then he bowed and was gone, circling the room like a shark in search of new prey.

'He probably takes it up the arse,' Martha said, starting them giggling again. The bar manager came over with a tray laden with glasses and an ice bucket containing a bottle of champagne.

'Compliments of the local constabulary, I have five more bottles of champagne on ice for you, and I'm instructed to inform you that if it's not consumed by the end of the night, you'll all be in handcuffs.'

'Sounds like my kind of night,' Deb told him.

Loud whoops of delight caused Ray to look their way. He spotted Dawn and looked away again quickly, then made his way back to the stage and disappeared behind the curtain.

Dawn did a wanker sign behind his back, causing everyone to start roaring with laughter again. They got stuck into the bubbly with gusto and had downed two bottles before the lights dimmed and Kitty appeared on stage. She was dressed in a white sequinned gown which caught the light beautifully, long white satin gloves and a huge feather boa. Jo sighed and wondered out loud whether she could borrow it to get married in.

'No problem babe,' Jayne assured her, 'We'll get Dawn

to pop backstage afterwards and nick it for you. Or she can arrest Kitty and lock her up till after the wedding.'

Dawn did a mock salute. 'Your wish is my command,' she said, waving her feather duster at them, 'But not until after we've drunk this place dry. Hey, you boy, bring us more champagne or I'll beat your ass with my tickling stick!'

The barman grinned and did as she asked, even bending over and taking six slaps on his backside after he'd deposited another bottle in the ice bucket.

'Good evening ladies, I hope you're having a good time so far,' Kitty began, glancing around the packed room. She pointed at Jo's party. 'It looks like you lot are anyway. What's the occasion or are you just pissheads in general?'

Dawn waved Kitty over and the drag queen came over to their table. 'Well, I've never been summoned in such a manner before, this had better be good. You're not all lesbians, are you? Only if so I should confess that I'm a cock in a frock, I don't eat fish.'

Deb presented Kitty with a glass of champagne and kissed her on the cheek. 'My friend's hen party,' she mumbled, 'And she loves your dress. Can she borrow it for her wedding?'

Kitty laughed and drained the glass before handing it back to Deb.

'Well, if you want to get into my clothes it'll take more than a glass of bubbly!' she drawled, sashaying back towards the stage among gales of laughter.

'How about a kebab then?' Dawn yelled, and Kitty smiled at her.

'Now that's more like it, we're not all anorexic you know. Talking of which, it's time I introduced your first act of the evening. This poor woman is a trainee bulimic. She stuffs herself with food, but she keeps forgetting to throw up. Please put your hands together for the wonderful Lavinia Longtime!'

The audience clapped and cheered as Lavinia bounded onto the stage, dressed as one of the Spice Girls. It was hard to miss the sneer she gave Kitty as they passed on the stage. Despite her obvious miming, Lavinia soon had them all up and dancing to some of the band's most popular hits.

After half an hour of jumping around and singing, Lavinia took a bow and bounced off the stage again, sweating profusely but with a huge smile on her face.

Kitty walked past her and wrinkled her nose. 'Ooh love, I think you need to wash your fanny,' Kitty announced over the mike, 'You smell like a barrel of kippers!'

Everyone laughed as Lavinia stuck two fingers up at her. Kitty raised one eyebrow. 'Happy New Year to you too darling. They don't call me the KitKat Queen for nothing so if you can't give me four fingers, don't bother' she said.

The audience cheered, and Kitty took a bow.

'Now ladies, are you ready for your first stripper? Then let's have a big warm welcome for the wonderful Black Velvet!'

Chad swaggered on to the stage dressed as a pirate, waving to the screaming crowd. He wore a white silk shirt which billowed when he moved, black satin trousers that clung to his slim frame, leaving very little to the imagination, and a long black velvet coat. Under his tricorn hat, his dreadlocks came down to his shoulders and were festooned with beads and small bones, and an eyepatch finished the look.

He soon had the crowd clapping along to his soundtrack as he danced for them. He took his shirt off to reveal a stunning body and the women went wild. Martha was delighted when he came over and straddled her. She grabbed at his bum and licked his rippling six-pack, making everyone squeal.

He gave her a kiss and ran back onstage to take the rest of his clothes off. Martha started shouting 'Off, off, off' and the whole room joined in. Chad was only too happy to oblige and was soon down to his flag. He ran into the audience, grabbed Martha and took her up onstage. He made her kneel in front of him and wrapped the flag around her head.

Jo was horrified. 'Oh my God! I hope Mum's okay under there!'

When Martha emerged, she had baby lotion all over her face like a face pack. She was laughing her head off and waving Chad's thong in the air. As she returned to her seat amid whoops of admiration, Chad opened his flag and revealed himself. The women all screamed – he was huge.

'Blimey Mum, that must have been a surprise,' Jo shouted above the noise.

Martha shook her head as she downed her drink in one. 'No, I guessed he'd be in proportion.' She pointed at Chad, who was now gyrating on the lap of another bride-to-be in the audience. 'I had one as big as that once, it wasn't pleasant. I couldn't walk for a week and I swear that's why I needed a new hip.'

Jo fell off her chair and everyone laughed.

'Don't look so shocked, I was a bit of a wild one in my day you know,' she went on. 'I can still get my legs behind my head. I just choose not to for incontinence purposes.' They all roared with laughter when Dawn announced she didn't fancy her champagne any more.

Deb tipped the bottle up. 'Just as well, it's all gone. I'll go and get some more.'

Martha thrust a couple of twenty-pound note into her hand. 'Put this in the kitty pet, I'm off to get my photo taken with that gorgeous young man.' She took off across the floor towards Chad, waving her camera.

50

Backstage, things weren't quite so pleasant. Lavinia was furious at Kitty's jibes in front of the crowd and didn't waste any time tearing into her when Kitty came offstage.

'Who the fuck do you think you are, you vile cow? How dare you take the piss out of me like that in front of the fans? I'll be having serious words with John tomorrow, you can count on it!'

Lavinia stood almost nose to nose with Kitty and jabbed an accusing finger at her face. The whole room went quiet. Kitty, to her credit, didn't even raise her voice. She knew she didn't need to. She spoke quietly but her words dripped with venom.

'Listen sweetie; if you put in half the work I do you'd have an act worth watching. Maybe if you stopped stuffing your fat face for five minutes you'd realise that. No, don't even think about hitting me, bitch,' Kitty warned, stepping back and holding her hand out as Lavinia lunged at her.

'I may look like a pushover, but I will knock you the fuck out if you lay a finger on me. For your information, you're only on this show because I felt sorry for you. John didn't want you, but I insisted. Now, be a good girl, pack up and piss off unless you want me to put your wages in the charity tin on the bar out there.'

Lavinia went back to her corner of the room, grabbed her costumes and shoved them into a bin liner. She looked around the room with a scowl and stormed out, slamming the door behind her.

'Oh dear, that was unpleasant. I'm sorry everyone,' Kitty said, bending down to pick something up from the floor. 'That showdown has been a long time coming. I knew she'd be upset, but she needed telling. She lost it ages ago, and now she's lost one of her tits.'

Kitty held the offending item up, making them all smile and breaking the tension. 'Now, it sounds like Chad's almost done. Who's on next?'

'Is there room for a little one?' a deep voice asked. Des whooped with delight and hugged the young man who had walked in through the back door, which Lavinia had left open.

'Ricky, my man! What are you doing here?'

Des clapped him on the back. 'Let me introduce you to everyone. Guys, this is Ricky Palomino, he works for Vince Patterson in Brighton and is already proving to be a big star on the circuit.'

Ricky grinned as they all shook hands with him. Kitty flushed with delight as Ricky took her hand and kissed it.

'Oh my, I can see you're going to break some hearts. Your reputation precedes you, I've heard great things from my south coast sisters. What brings you to our neck of the woods?' she asked.

'John asked me to come and work for him,' Ricky explained. 'Apparently, one of his lads has had some trouble with people stealing his gigs.' His eyes flicked quickly towards Ray and back. 'So, I've agreed to switch places with him for a few months,' he said. 'John suggested I come along tonight and say hello. I was hoping you might be able to squeeze me in.'

He looked around for approval, getting smiles from

everyone except Ray, who stood quietly at the back of the room, watching him like a hawk. Ricky made a point of walking over to him and holding out his hand. Ray didn't shake it but looked him up and down with disdain. At six feet six, Ricky was at least four inches taller than Ray, so Ray had to look up to meet his eyes.

'So, you're what all the fuss is about,' he said in a flat voice. 'Well, just remember your place and you won't go far wrong. There's no room on this show, but feel free to stay and watch. Who knows, you may learn something.'

Ray turned his back and pretended to look for something in his bag. Ricky raised his eyebrows in amusement and sauntered back to the rest of the lads and told them about his act while Ray pretended not to listen.

Kitty was impressed, a lot of the newer lads would have been upset by Ray's attitude, but Ricky seemed to thrive on it. He certainly was gorgeous to look at. Apart from being tall, he had long dark hair and a broad, well-muscled body. His hair was smoothed back in a neat ponytail, and his designer suit, shoes, shirt and tie were all black, which made his olive skin glow.

Ricky saw Kitty checking him out and smiled, showing perfect white teeth. He went outside and returned with a promotional photo, which he handed to Kitty with a small bow.

'Vince said I should give you one of my new promo pictures, and get your opinion,' he said with a wink.

Kitty caught her breath as she looked at the picture. Ricky was draped on an antique four-poster bed, in a tangle of black silk sheets which barely covered him. His hair was spread out on the pillows behind him and his body glistened with oil.

'Wow,' was all she could manage to say. She showed the picture to Ruby who was equally impressed. Ricky laughed at their reaction and offered to buy a round of drinks.

Michelle had popped to the toilet, so had missed Ricky's arrival, but Ricky was quick to notice her as she slipped back into the crowded room. He walked up to her and bowed low.

'Ciao bella, you are quite a beauty. A real English rose,' he purred as he kissed her hand. She blushed to the roots of her hair, making Ray seethe. He walked over and snatched Michelle's hand away from Ricky.

'Michelle belongs to me, so keep your hands off her,' Ray ordered.

Ricky put his hands up in defence and took a step back, the mirth in his eyes clear as he apologised for overstepping the boundaries. He winked at Michelle again before turning to speak to Des.

Michelle tried to smooth things over. 'Ricky was just being friendly, Ray. There's no need to be rude.'

'Who do you think you are, my fucking mother?' he replied. 'You work for me, you'd do well to remember it. I don't pay you to be a slag.'

Michelle said nothing at all, but put down the flag she'd been folding, picked up her handbag and walked out of the back door. Ray realised everyone was watching him, so he tried to turn it into a joke. 'Must be that time of the month,' he joked.

Ricky clapped his hands together. 'Right, seeing as I'm the new boy, the drinks are on me. What's everyone having?

'Nothing for me thanks, I'm on last and I like to keep a clear head,' Ray announced.

Si snorted, and Ray threw him an angry look.

'No skin off my nose, it makes it a cheaper round,' Ricky said.

He and Des left the room, leaving an awkward silence hanging in the air. When they returned Chad followed them in, still wrapped in his flag and sweating profusely.

He shook hands with Ricky then pulled a towel out of his bag and rubbed himself dry.

'Christ almighty, you've got a huge dick,' Ricky said. He winked at Chad before adding 'It's almost as big as mine.'

Chad placed his hand on his own chest. 'Why, thank you Massa Rick,' he said, copying Ruby's fake accent and making everyone else laugh.

The lads fell into conversation with Ricky, who was very easy to get on with. He made them laugh at stories from the Brighton shows, including one about an old lady who took her teeth out and handed them to him just before she disappeared underneath his flag.

Ray said nothing, he was still sulking in the corner, pretending not to listen. Eventually, he took his phone out and made a point of announcing he had an important call to make, but no-one paid him any attention, so he went back through to the bar, suddenly feeling very alone.

51

The booze had certainly done its job; the hen party were all plastered. Dawn sat grinning inanely, Black Velvet's hat parked at a rakish angle on her head, while Martha was happily sporting his G-string around her neck. Deb was sitting on Isobel's knee serenading her, much to Mo's amusement, and Jayne had gone to the bar. Mo was taking photos ready to upload to her computer. Jayne returned with a grinning barman in tow, carrying a tray laden with shots. He set the tray down, accepted kisses on the cheek from everyone and took away some of the empty glasses. Jayne downed her drink in one go and offered a shot of something bright-pink to Mo, who frowned in horror then downed it, to the cheers of her friends. 'Jeez that's vile, but what the hell, it's a party!' she said.

They all followed suit and agreed that it was. Jayne signalled to the barman, who seemed to have become their own personal waiter. He was having a great time and had slipped Dawn his phone number when Martha had loudly announced that she was single.

'You need a big stiff one,' Martha shouted over the noise. 'Like that one there.' She pointed towards the stage, where Si was juggling with lit torches. 'He wants to be careful; he'll toast his rissoles in a minute.'

Dawn laughed but was watching Si at the same time. His routine was very impressive, and so was his body.

'Are you religious? I bet he'd give you a burning bush!' Martha flipped her hair back and sent her crown flying. Jo fell over as she leaned to retrieve it.

'You wear it, pet,' Martha said. 'Seeing as you're my princess.' She kissed Jo on the cheek and ruffled her hair.

Deb came over and sat on Mo's knee, stroking her hair with a silly grin on her face. 'I love you Mo, you're so beautiful. I wish I looked like you.'

Mo kissed her on the cheek. 'I love you too Deb, and you're gorgeous. Craig's a lucky bloke, I hope he knows that.'

Deb winked at her, 'Trust me he'll know it when I get home! I'm going to shag his brains out and he'll say thank you too!'

Mo let out a huge snort and made them all cry with laughter.

'Hey, what about me? You can't kiss my girlfriend and not me,' Isobel protested.

Deb smiled, walked over and kissed her full on the lips.

'That's better,' she grinned.

They all cheered when Kitty announced the next stripper was coming on. Dawn stood on her chair waving her hat then promptly fell off. She lay on the floor holding her stomach, tears of laughter running down her face. 'Fuck me, that was class,' she said. 'But I'll have some right bruises on my arse in the morning.'

Mo finally caught her breath. 'Nothing compared to the bruises Craig will have when Deb's finished with him!'

Deb nodded vigorously. 'You can count on it,' she said with a wink. She laughed at Dawn's face when Des came out onto the stage, dressed in bike leathers, complete with helmet. 'I think someone should pick Dawn's chin up off the floor,' she commented. 'Fuck me, if he'd looked like that at Ray's house, I'd have frisked him there and then!' She made grunting noises as she rubbed her thighs lewdly.

'That's enough to turn a good woman straight,' Mo said. 'But he's not Bodie, so I'll have to decline.'

'What about your pirate friend?' Deb asked. 'I thought you were rather taken with him. Are you now saying that you prefer the biker?'

'At the moment I'd take either. It's been so long since I got laid that I'm chewing the legs off the table in frustration,' Dawn replied.

Dave was working his way around the room, discarding his clothes as he went. By the time he got to the hen party, he was down to his G-string. He laughed when he saw Dawn's pirate hat. 'Damn, he got there before me. Well, it will have to be you then,' he said, pulling Jayne up and pressing himself against her. She screamed in delight when he picked her up and threw her over his shoulder and carried her onto the stage, where he lay her down and writhed all over her, before turning her over onto her hands and knees and simulated doggy-style sex with her.

'Lucky cow,' Dawn sighed.

Mo laughed as she took photos. 'I dread to think what Alex will make of these.' She grinned.

'Don't worry, he knows it's all good clean fun,' Jo said as Jayne was carried back to her seat. 'At least, I hope he does.' She punched Jayne playfully on the arm. 'Hey, save some for me, it's my hen night.'

Jayne fanned herself with a beer mat. 'Oh, don't worry, there's plenty more to come yet. I don't know about you lot, but I'm having a great time!'

***

The evening flowed smoothly after Lavinia's departure, much to Kitty's relief. She couldn't cope with any more drama. Ricky's presence seemed to have brightened the atmosphere up, and both Chad and Si had been well-received by the audience. Apparently, the show was trending on Twitter as well, which would hopefully bring in more work for them all after New Year when it tended to go quiet.

Si was packing his costume and equipment away when Ray burst into the room. 'Where's Michelle? She's disappeared, and I need her!'

He'd been incensed when Ricky had turned up and needed a scapegoat. Si sensed that was why he wanted Michelle, so he played dumb.

Si pulled on a pair of denim shorts. 'Don't look at me mate.'

Ray grabbed his arm and Si pulled away angrily. 'What is your problem dude?'

'I'm not the one with the problem!' Ray grabbed Si's arm again. Chad stood up, ready to step between them but Si stood his ground and glared at Ray.

'Touch me again and you will have! She left when you had a go at her, remember? She finally got sick of your crap and fucked off. I can't say I blame her either, you treat her like shit!'

He bent down and grabbed a bottle of baby oil out of his bag, which he started applying to his arms and chest, readying himself for the fan photos which usually followed each show. He kept his eyes locked on Ray's, silently daring him to say something.

Ray was incensed. No-one had ever stood up to him like that and he was damned if anyone would start now. He was aware of Si's strength though and knew it was stupid to try and take him on in a fight. 'You're just jealous because I've got a bigger cock than you!' he sneered. He marched out of the back door, throwing Si a look of contempt as he went.

'Tosser,' Si laughed, shaking his head. He noticed Chad looking at him and grinned. 'I'm fine mate. He doesn't scare me, he's all piss and wind. Did you hear him? Bragging that his cock's bigger than mine? At least I know where mine's been. Do you and Des fancy a curry later? We could try that new place on the Stafford Road if you like.'

'Sounds good to me, dude,' Chad said. 'I'm not sure about Des, but I don't think he's got anything planned, unless he pulls one of those French maids out there.'

Si gave Chad his trademark grin. 'Let's ask Ricky too. If he's going to be working up here, we should at least make him feel welcome.'

Chad returned the grin. 'Sounds like a plan. I bet he's a good laugh, and he seems like a genuine guy.'

'Who's a genuine guy?' Ricky asked as he strolled back in. 'If you mean Ray, the only genuine thing about him is how angry he looked just then. He was muttering about revenge, so I guess he's a bit upset.'

'Fuck him,' Si replied. 'He was after Michelle, he's probably feeling lonely because we don't love him anymore, so he needs someone to stroke his ego.'

'I need someone to stroke my cock, but I'm not moaning about it,' drawled Ricky, making them laugh. 'I don't know him like you lot, but his reputation is well-known everywhere. Maybe his menopause has kicked in.'

'You could be right, but when he's like this he takes it out on Michelle.' Kitty filled him in on a few things and Ricky sat on the edge of the desk, his face stony.

'She can always come and work for me,' he said. 'My old man left me with a fortune when he died a few years ago, so I can afford to match or even beat whatever he's paying her.'

'If you're so loaded, why are you stripping?' Si asked.

Ricky grinned at him. 'Because I've got a great body and I know how to dance. It seems a shame to keep it all to myself.' He laughed. 'The truth is I once did it as a bet, but it went down so well I decided to take it up permanently. Having my Dad's money to fall back on is great, but I'm sensible. I've bought my house outright, so I've got no mortgage to worry about, and I invested the rest. I'm not just a pretty face you know.'

'Good man,' Chad said. 'Very few strippers remember that this life is a temporary gig, and that the work could dry up at any time. Well done, mate, if Ray had been as clever as you he'd be rolling in it by now.'

'The difference between him and me is that I don't need to buy my friends,' Ricky said. 'I have a few very close friends and some great mates who like me for who I am. Michelle would be a lot happier working for me. I'm surprised you've not made a move on her by now Des, it's not like you to let a great girl slip through your fingers.'

'Fuck off, she's like a sister to me, in fact, she's like a sister to all of us,' Des answered.

'Not to me she's not,' Si chipped in. 'I'd shag her six ways till Sunday, but she's not interested.'

'Maybe she's waiting for a man who's bigger in more ways than one,' Ricky said, cupping his crotch. He ducked as a pair of balled-up socks flew past his head. 'Hey, watch it, don't mess my hair up,' he laughed.

'We're going for a curry after the show if you fancy coming along,' Chad said. 'You can tell us what it's like working for Vince.'

'Sounds great. Now, who wants another drink?'

52

Ray stood outside in the frosty air, panting hard after the exchange with Si. He stood for a while, trying to calm himself down and watched his breath make clouds as he exhaled. He was furious with Si for speaking to him like that. Who the hell did he think he was? 'Nobody disrespects me like that, especially not a nobody like him! He forgets who gave him his big break. Without me he'd still be hauling barrels at the brewery,' he muttered.

Ray pulled a small packet of white tablets out of his jeans pocket and pressed a couple out onto his hand, tossing them back and swallowing hard. They went down better with a drink but there was no way he was going back in there until he was due onstage. He heard laughter emanating from the dressing room and it riled him even more.

He spotted Si's jeep parked nearby and wandered over to it. Si took great pride in his car and the newly-polished dark purple paintwork gleamed in the moonlight.

'I'll teach you, you little twat,' he said, quickly glancing around before taking his keys out of the pocket of his jeans and scoring a deep line along the side, all the way from front to back. He put the keys away and walked back towards the building, whistling softly to himself, completely unaware that he was being watched.

Kitty stepped out of the shadows as Ray went back inside. She'd seen what he'd done to Si's car and was going to confront him but thought better of it. Ray would wriggle out of it somehow, snakes like him always did. She dropped her cigarette on the ground and stepped on it, crushing the life out of it.

If only someone would do that to Ray, life would be a whole lot more enjoyable for all of us.

Si leaned out of the door. 'Kitty, Des is almost done if you want to come and take him off. Are you coming for a curry after the show?'

'Sorry chick, I'm off to my Mum's tonight,' Kitty smiled. 'But thank you for the invitation.'

Si winked at her and disappeared back inside, leaving the door open for her. She thought about sticking around to see what happened when Si saw his car but dismissed the idea very quickly. Kitty knew from experience what would happen and was glad she'd be long gone by then.

She grabbed her mic and walked back out to the audience. 'Ladies, have you had a good time tonight? I know I have; you've been a wonderful audience and this old queen thanks you from the heart of my bottom – oops, I mean the bottom of my heart. I hope you've enjoyed my lovely boys tonight; I know they've loved performing for you all. Now we come to the final act of the first half. This man needs no introduction; his reputation speaks for itself – in more ways than one – so without further ado, please welcome onto the stage the one, the only, Mr Ray Diamond!'

Kitty stepped down from the stage and headed towards the bar to chat to the manager as Ray, dressed in Army fatigues, slowly walked out onstage. As the lights formed a spotlight on him, he stood there for a moment and basked in the glory. As the music changed pace he went into his routine, clapping to encourage the audience to join in. He didn't notice that Si, Chad, Des and Ricky stood watching the show from the side-lines. Si had a big smirk on his face and waited for the fun to begin.

Des looked sideways at him. 'Why did you want us to come and watch Ray do this number? We've all seen it loads of times before. What makes this time so special?'

Si giggled. 'Trust me bro, this is one performance you won't want to miss. Let's just say happiness is a warm pair of pants.'

Ray had shed his jacket and hat and had run into the crowd to gyrate on several women's laps, including Jo's, who got the giggles and tweaked his nipples. He kissed her on the cheek, ran back onstage and went into the next part of his routine. Something was clearly wrong though; he was suddenly looking very uncomfortable and started scratching his crotch furiously. The women assumed this was part of the act and were cheering along, but Ray appeared to be in a lot of distress. He ripped his remaining clothes off as fast as he could, snatched a pint of beer from the nearest woman and poured it all over his cock. The crowd erupted into cheers, but Ray ran off the stage, narrowly avoiding crashing into his fellow strippers on the way.

Kitty was shocked by his sudden departure; she'd been chatting up a cute barman but picked up her mic and quickly took charge of the situation.

'Ladies, we seem to be experiencing some technical difficulties. I'll go and find out what the problem is, so go and get yourselves a drink, have a smoke, visit the little girl's room and normal service will resume shortly.'

There was a ripple of confused applause then people started milling around and talking loudly. Kitty vanished behind the curtain and angry voices were heard.

Si was almost on the floor in the corner, tears of laughter streaming down his face. Des and Chad were both doubled up too, though neither knew what had just occurred. Ricky stood with his hands in his pockets, smiling broadly.

'Man, that was fucking brilliant, like a Benny Hill sketch!' Chad said, when he could finally speak again. 'What did you do? I don't think I've ever seen him perform so well!'

Si wiped his eyes, but the tears kept coming. 'Just a little something I thought up this afternoon. He was being really nasty to Michelle, so I sprayed muscle rub on his G-string. He won't forget that performance, believe me, his bollocks will burn for a month.'

Des was shaking his head in disbelief. 'He's always horrible to her; I don't know how she puts up with it. Six years now she's been working for him and not once have I ever known her stand up to him. Anyone else would have walked out long ago. I mean, they've never been a couple, so it can't be out of any love she has for him.'

'The guys were telling me about it,' Ricky said. 'Maybe she needs the money, no-one would take that amount of crap otherwise.'

Chad drained his pint of fizzy pop, stood his empty glass on the windowsill and headed backstage. 'Don't ask me man, I haven't got a clue. I'll go and see if everything's okay back there. I've got a feeling that it's about to get nasty.'

It was indeed getting nasty. Ray was storming around the room, stark naked apart from his biker boots, and roaring like a wounded bull. Ruby was hastily packing Kitty's gear into bags, fearful that something would get damaged. Deep down she hoped he would pick on her, she was waiting for a reason to deck him, but she knew who Ray had set his sights on.

'Michelle, I don't know what you did to my costume, but you'll fucking pay for it and that's a promise!' he roared. 'No-one fucks with Ray Diamond and gets away with it! You're finished, bitch, so you'd better go and pack your stuff because if you're still at the house when I get back I'll fucking kill you!'

'Michelle's not here, she left ages ago, so I fail to see how she could have tampered with your costume,' Ruby said, but Ray ignored her. She sucked her teeth at him and carried on with her task.

Chad put a hand on Ray's arm, but Ray shook him off. 'Did you see what she did to my routine?' he bellowed. 'That took me months to put together and that little cow ruined it all! Have you seen her? No, I thought you'd defend her, you probably all will!' he shouted as the other guys came closer. 'I know you're all fucking her behind my back and think I don't know about it! Well, you can all fuck off as well; none of you will ever work again when I've finished with you!'

Si had had enough of his ranting. 'Listen Ray, if you must know it was me. I sprayed muscle rub in your pants – you deserved to be taken down a peg or two over the way you treat Michelle. We all know that it didn't take you months to learn that routine either, it's the same one you always do, just with a different costume.'

Ray's eyes were bulging, and his nostrils flared. He took a step towards Si, fists raised and ready to strike but Des and Chad grabbed his arms and pinned them to his sides. He struggled but to no avail; the two men were very strong. He had no choice but to stand still until Si had finished speaking.

'It's about time someone put you straight about a few things mate,' Si continued in a calm voice. 'Michelle is a lovely girl who does everything you tell her without ever questioning you. She'd jump out of the fucking window if you said she should. I don't know what hold you have over her but not anymore. If you ever lay a finger on her we'll break your fucking neck, so don't even think about it. And for your information, none of us are sleeping with her, but it would be none of your business if we were.'

Si's eyes never left Ray's; he wanted to make sure Ray knew he was serious.

'As for us never getting work again; we haven't nicked jobs from other strippers behind the boss's back, so I think we're safe enough. It's time you realised that you're not as powerful as you used to be, in fact you're an old has-been who needs to be put out to pasture,' Si said. He nodded to Chad and Des to let Ray go.

Everyone stood still for a moment, then Ray snatched up his clothes in silence and stalked off outside, still naked and not caring.

A few minutes later they heard his Porsche zoom off with a squeal of tyres.

'Wow!' said Des, clapping Si on the back. 'That was a hell of a speech, dude. I thought he was gonna burst a blood vessel for a minute. Brave though, nobody's ever stood up to him before.'

Chad shook Si's hand and pulled him in for a hug. Kitty stood at the edge of the room. She'd heard the whole exchange and had tears of pride in her eyes, for Si finally having the guts to do what she should have done years ago, but also of fear for Michelle. She hoped the little love was safe, she knew herself what Ray was capable of, and voiced her concerns. Si came over and hugged her, his trademark smile plastered firmly back in place.

'Don't worry about Shelley,' Si said. 'I'll ring her and warn her. That is, if he doesn't crash his car on the way. We can pop in and check on her later as well.'

'Thanks love. Well then Ricky, it seems there is a vacancy after all. Why don't you go and grab your gear, and you can show us how it's done down south?' Kitty said with a smile. 'I'll go and warm them up for you.'

53

Alex, Gary and Craig sat on a bench outside the club, waiting patiently to take the revellers home. Alex had suggested they take the added precaution of covering their car seats with towels in case of accidents. They had been waiting for over an hour, but none were brave enough to risk going inside to see if the women were ready to leave. They'd seen Ray depart earlier and had wondered whether the fact that he'd stormed out stark naked and driven off was anything to do with the hen party.

A local fast-food van had parked up nearby and Alex had treated them all to a burger while they waited. The doors of the club opened, and people started to stream out in groups, some heading towards the burger van and some getting into the various taxis that had formed a queue at the side of the club.

'Oh heck,' Gary said in a worried voice, pointing towards the door as a group of rowdy women emerged, all singing loudly. 'Look at the state of them.'

Craig was glad he'd not had the car cleaned yet that week. Deb was hanging onto Mo and Jayne, all three of them swaying dangerously. Jo and Isobel stumbled out behind them, closely followed by Dawn, who appeared to be wearing a pirate's hat and dreadlocks. She was swigging from a wine bottle and doing her best impression of Jack Sparrow. They spotted the waiting men, cheered loudly and made a beeline for them. Martha came around the rear, draped in a feather boa and wearing a G-string on her head. She seemed to have lost her crown.

'Hooray, the calvary, no, the clevery, erm, what's the fucking word I need?' Jayne slurred.

'I think you mean cavalry dear,' Alex said, trying to hold his wife up but being pulled over by the other two. 'Craig, sort your wife out, will you?'

'Excuse me!' Deb shouted in a fake haughty voice, 'I'll have you know that I don't need sorting out – but he will when I get him home. Come here, lover boy,' she whooped, grabbing Craig around the neck and licking his face. Craig pretended to be horrified.

'Help, boss! Give me a cell to sleep in for my own safety!' He tried to pry Deb off, but she clung on tight, attempting to stick her tongue in his ear and half-strangling him in the process. He wiped slobber off his face with a grimace.

'In your dreams, mate, most men would kill to be jumped on by Deb,' Mo laughed, 'And a fair few women wouldn't kick her out of bed either.'

She winked at Deb, who blew her a kiss.

'Jeez, look at the state of you all,' Alex exclaimed, trying hard to keep a straight face, 'You're a disgrace to the Force! Come on, let's get you all home.'

All the women made whooping sounds. 'We're having a gang bang!' someone sang.

'I've been molested by an Indian chieftain,' Jo stuttered. 'And very nice it was, too.' She pulled her dress up. 'I think I've got feathers in my knickers.'

Martha laughed until she snorted. 'He certainly tickled her fancy, bonny lad. You should have seen the size of his tomahawk.'

Gary was mortified. 'Jo, stop it.' He tried in vain to pull Jo's dress down again, but Jo wrapped one leg around him and shoved his head in her cleavage. Alex nearly choked because he was laughing so much.

Gary went very red and eventually managed to get Martha and Jo into his car. Deb, Mo and Isobel climbed into Craig's, leaving Alex to take Jayne and Dawn. He bundled Jayne into the back seat and turned to Dawn, who was striding around the car park, brandishing her feather duster like a sword.

'Nice hat. Pulled yourself a pirate, have you?'

Dawn took her hat off with a flourish and bowed low, then fell forwards onto her face with a crunch. She made a snorting noise and stood up again slowly, refusing his offer of help. Her nose was bleeding and she had gravel stuck to her face. She jammed her hat back on and grinned at him. 'Aar Captain!' she beamed.

54

There was more than just sore heads to complain about the next morning. Mo couldn't explain the huge bruises on her knees and elbows, and Dawn sported two stunning black eyes and a very swollen nose, which she swore was broken. As a result, she talked as if she had cotton wool shoved up both nostrils, which amused Gary greatly.

'I don't know, I'd have thought you lot could handle your drink,' he chuckled. Dawn stuck two fingers up at him and he roared some more.

Craig hobbled in, looking grim. He lowered himself into his chair with relief. 'That's better,' he sighed. He pointed an accusing finger at Mo and Dawn. 'You two have a lot to answer for, getting Debs so drunk. I nearly crashed the car on the way home because she was trying to climb onto my lap. I can't remember the last time we had that much sex. It's alright for her, she booked the day off work, so she's still snoring her head off. I can hardly stand up straight.'

He looked genuinely aggrieved, but he got no sympathy at all from anyone.

'Lucky you! If I were single, I'd be more than happy to go all night with your missus,' Mo called, winking at him.

'I bet she's got hidden talents.'

Craig grinned back at her. 'I'm saying nothing. But I seriously think I need a chiropractor to sort my back out.'

All amusement ceased when Alex came in. The look on his face told them he was not in a joking mood.

'We've just had a shout from Traffic Division. A homeless man was killed and two of his friends have been injured in what looks like a hit and run late last night. Gary, you and Mo get down there and talk to the officers on the scene. Witnesses are saying the car involved was a red Porsche. Craig, you and Les go and pick up our friend Mr Diamond and bring him in for a little chat. I have a feeling he may be able to shed some light on the situation.'

The phone rang in Alex's office, making him swear. He strode across and snatched it up, making short work of the conversation, then came back out and called for everyone to wait.

'We have another misper report just come in,' he announced to the team. 'Elizabeth Callendar hasn't been seen since before Christmas. Her parents are downstairs.'

He looked around the room to find someone who didn't look like they'd been in a fight to go with him to interview the parents. 'Dawn, you go with Gary, Mo can come with me.'

The desk sergeant had put the parents in an interview room, and Alex quickly put them at ease.

'How long exactly has your daughter been missing?' Alex began.

Mr Callendar fidgeted in his seat. He was a small thin man, with close-cropped grey hair and blue eyes. His grey trousers and pullover looked too big for him, as if he'd shrivelled up inside them. His wife was of a similar build, her reddish-grey hair was pulled back in a loose bun and her brown eyes looked sad. She wore a blue skirt and blouse, with a jacket that was a slightly different shade, as if it was from another suit.

'We're not entirely sure,' Mr Callendar said. 'We thought she'd gone on holiday with her boyfriend, but he rang us yesterday looking for her. It seems they had a huge bust-up, so she told him she was going alone.'

'I see. Did he say what they argued about?'

'No, but they argue a lot. To be honest, I'm surprised they've stayed together this long.'

'I'll need to speak to her boyfriend to get more details about the timeline, but if you could provide us with a photograph of Elizabeth, we can get it circulated.'

'I thought you might want one, so I printed this off for you.' Mrs Callendar took a picture out of her handbag. 'Betty's a social media fanatic, so thought this one would be the most up-to date one. It must have been taken on a night out because she's had her hair done.'

'We always call her Betty because she loved Betty Boop when she was little,' Mr Callendar explained.

Alex took the photo and looked at it before passing it to Mo. The young woman in the selfie smiling back at him was the spitting image of Vicky Wilson.

'What's the name of Betty's boyfriend?' Alex asked.

Mr Callendar looked at him. 'Sorry, I thought I mentioned it. His name is Arjan Bakshi.'

55

Michelle looked at the devastation around her. After walking out of the show last night, she'd gone for a long drive and had got home very late and had overslept. She cursed herself as she rushed around the supermarket, wishing she'd remembered to pick up her shopping list. She parked near the kitchen door but noticed the front door was wide open as she passed it. There was no sign of Ray's car, so she assumed he must have got a lift back from the show the night before.

'Ray, you left the front door open again!' she called as she staggered in, weighed down with shopping bags. When Ray didn't answer, she left the bags on the kitchen floor and went into the lounge, but there was no sign of him. She headed upstairs, listening for any signs of life. Ray's bedroom door was open, so she held her breath and walked in, bracing herself for a torrent of abuse for daring to enter his domain.

There was no sign of Ray, but his room looked as if a hurricane had torn through it. The dark red drapes on his bed hung in tattered shreds and his wardrobe doors stood open, the contents destroyed and scattered everywhere. Instinct made Michelle pull her phone out of her bag and call the police, but halfway through the conversation she heard someone running down the stairs. She hung up and gave chase, knowing it was a stupid thing to do, but determined to see who it was.

As she got to the bottom of the stairs, she saw someone run out through the front door. Michelle gave chase, regretting her decision as a sharp pain in her side brought her up short. The figure disappeared around the side of the house, but Michelle was in no fit state to follow them. She was still bent over clutching her side when a car pulled up and PC Penny Griffiths and PC Phil Marshall got out.

'Are you okay?' she asked, but Michelle pointed in the direction that the assailant had gone. PC Marshall took off around the corner while PC Griffiths stayed with Michelle. He was back a few minutes later, talking on his radio.

'No sign of anyone there now,' he told Penny.

'I checked downstairs, but they must have been hiding in the downstairs toilet,' Michelle said. 'I looked in all of the other rooms.'

'You should have stayed outside and called us instead,' Penny scolded. 'They could have attacked you.'

'I'm sorry, I didn't think,' Michelle replied. 'I just thought that Ray hadn't closed the door properly.'

Michelle sat in her car while the two officers surveyed the damage, then went to the station with them to give a statement. By the time she was done it was getting late. There was still no sign of Ray when she went back to the house, so rather than spend the night there alone, she packed a bag and checked into a budget hotel near Wolverhampton train station.

***

The following morning, she went home and made a start on clearing up the mess. Ray still hadn't surfaced, she figured he must have gone on a bender somewhere. He was unravelling fast, and Michelle guessed that the new stripper showing up two nights ago had probably pushed him over the edge.

Armed with bin bags and rubber gloves, Michelle began by bagging up all of Ray's clothes and shoes and stood them outside the bedroom door. She took the bed drapes down and added them to the pile before turning her attention to the shoe boxes on the floor of the wardrobe. Most of them had spilled their contents on the floor of her wardrobe, but some remained intact. Most of them contained photographs of women, probably conquests, Michelle thought. She sat on the floor and carefully sorted through the various photographs and bits of paper, dividing them into separate stacks for Ray to check when he got back from wherever he'd gone.

One photograph caught her eye and she smoothed it out carefully to take a better look at it. It was quite old and faded and showed three young men posing in a crowded bar on New Years' Eve. Behind the men was a group of women, oblivious that they were in the shot. Someone had drawn a circle around one of the women, who seemed to be leaning in towards her friend as if to hear what she was saying. Michelle threw it back on the pile and picked up an envelope marked Forbidden Fantasy. Peering inside, she pulled out a bundle of photographs and flicked through them, her horror increasing with each picture. Her phone rang, making her jump. She listened for a moment, then hung up. She put the photographs back into the envelope, stuffed it into her pocket and left the house.

56

'I want Arjan Bakshi found – now. Ray Diamond too. He's mixed up in this mess somewhere, I just know he is.'

Alex pinched the bridge of his nose in frustration. He knew the team were working flat out but his patience was wearing thin. He and Jayne had argued last night when he'd got home to find her with more bruises. The situation with Joel was getting out of hand, but she refused to let him call in social services. They had ended up having a full-blown row and it had been nearly 1 a.m. by the time they went to bed.

'Boss, take a deep breath and calm down before you burst a blood vessel,' Craig said, handing Alex a mug of coffee. 'You'll give yourself a heart attack in a minute.'

Alex slumped into the chair next to Craig's desk. 'I'm just pissed off that we're no further forward than we were before Christmas.'

'Yes we are,' Craig argued. 'We've had a positive ID on the woman from the club and we know that Vicky Wilson is alive. I agree that Ray Diamond seems to be mixed up in all of it, but if he is we'll get him in the end.'

Alex drank half of his coffee in one go. 'You can bet your life we will. You and Mo go and speak to Vicky's friends and see what else you can find. Don't let on that she's alive though. Get Gary and Dawn to go and check out Arjan Bakshi's place of work, and then go and see his mother. Find out if he belongs to a gym or some other form of club. Forensics should have finished processing Elizabeth Callendar's house by now, so get Les to get onto them and see what they've come up with.'

'Righto,' Craig said. 'Oh, I meant to tell you, they caught the guy responsible for the hit and run incident. It was an accountant on his way home from a Christmas party.'

'Finally, something Ray Diamond didn't do,' Alex muttered.

57

Neil Stone finished outlining his lips in a rich magenta shade before patting his face with a fixing powder. He carefully put on his long black wig and became Kitty once more. The end of year lunch at the LGBT headquarters was a huge affair, with all ticket proceeds going to various local charities. As one of the founders it was important to Kitty that she looked her best. She had chosen a long, red, Chinese-style dress with a Mandarin collar, which buttoned up to the neck, and plain black satin pumps instead of high heels. Kitty looked out of the bedroom window, hoping that the rain had stopped, but it was still teeming down. She went downstairs, grabbed her coat and umbrella from the cupboard in the hall and opened the front door. Ray's daughter Hope was standing there, soaked to the skin and visibly shaken. Her fair hair was plastered to her pale face and her clothes clung to her slim frame.

'Good Lord, child, come in before you catch your death of cold!' Kitty hurried her through to the lounge and switched the gas fire on. 'Take those wet clothes off and sit down, I'll get you a hot drink.'

She threw her coat and umbrella back in the hall cupboard, removed her wig, then put a pan of milk on the stove to heat through before calling her friend Tony to explain that she wouldn't be able to make the lunch.

Hope moved over to the fire and crouched down in front of the artificial flames. She was still staring into them when Neil came back in with a mug of hot chocolate. He gently eased her to her feet, helped her undress and sat her down into an oversized armchair. He pressed the mug into her hands, pulled the throw on the back of the chair around her and sat opposite, watching her face carefully. The woman was in shock, that much was obvious, but Neil sat patiently, knowing she would speak when she was ready. As she sipped at her drink, Hope's colour started to come back but she was still miles away.

'I'll just go and take my slap off,' Neil said, indicating his face. 'But I'll only be a few minutes. There's more milk in the pan if you want a top-up, love.'

He sped upstairs, hastily removed his make-up and changed into a pair of black trousers and a white shirt. Hope had fallen asleep in the huge armchair, which made her look even smaller than she was. Neil carefully took the empty mug from her hand and crept out of the room. He sent a text to Michelle, sat at the kitchen table and waited.

'Sorry I'm late,' Michelle said when Neil opened the door an hour later. 'I had to run an errand first, and it took longer than I expected. What's wrong?'

Neil pressed his finger to his lips, gestured her through to the kitchen and made her a hot drink. He explained how Hope had shown up on his doorstep, and that she seemed to be in shock.

'I'm not surprised, to be honest. I don't know what Hope was looking for in her father's room, but I think she found these,' Michelle said. She took a packet of photographs out of her bag and slid them across the table towards Neil.

He picked them up, looking puzzled. Each one showed a series of women lying either across a bed or on the floor. They all appeared to be unconscious and their clothes were in disarray, leaving them sexually exposed. Some of the photos were very graphic, and as Neil flicked through them, the look of horror on his face grew and he put them down and fanned his face with his hand.

'I think I'm going to be sick,' he croaked. Michelle got him a glass of water and he sipped at it slowly.

'That's better, thank you,' he said weakly. 'I know that nowadays people take photos of pretty much everything on mobile phones, but why would you do that on a normal camera? I'm surprised that any company would process these though, you think they would have reported them to the police.'

'Maybe he was shagging the film developer,' Michelle said. 'The question is, what do I do about them? The logical thing to do is to go to the police, but I'm more inclined to confront him with them and see what he has to say about them.'

Neil looked scared and gripped Michelle's hand across the table. 'Promise me you won't do that,' he begged. 'You don't know how he will react, and I couldn't bear it if he were to hurt you.'

'Don't worry about me, I'm a big girl and can take care of myself,' Michelle said. She glanced at her watch and stood up, scooping up the photos and stuffing them back into her bag. 'Can I leave Hope here with you for now? I'm going to meet some friends for lunch, and I don't want her going back to the house by herself. I'll call you later and let you know what I decide to do.' She kissed Neil on both cheeks and hugged him tightly. 'Thank you for being so wonderful,' she said.

'My pleasure honey, my door is always open to you.' Neil watched her drive away and wondered whether he should call the police himself. In the end, he decided to give Michelle the benefit of the doubt and headed back to the kitchen to start preparing lunch.

58

Craig leaned against Laura Morrison's door frame and pressed the bell once more for good measure. He shrugged and wrote a message on the back of a card before dropping it through the letterbox. Jogging back to the car, he climbed in and settled himself against the soft leather.

'Let's try Helen Whittaker's next, then we may as well go to Vicky's flat,' he said.

Mo pulled away from the kerb with a roar. Craig grinned at her. 'Can I drive on the way back?'

Mo raised her eyebrow at him. 'What do you think?' she said as she drove smoothly through the city centre. It was busy at this time of day, but Mo's car was powerful enough to slip in and out of the tightest gaps with ease. Before too long they were in Bilston, Helen's address being easy to find due to it being around the corner from the famous Robin 2 Club.

'If you've never been there, you're missing out,' Craig said as they drove past. 'They have some cracking musicians, famous ones as well as tribute ones. Many bands got started there.'

'Sounds good, I'll check it out,' Mo said.

She pulled up outside Helen's house, which stood in

the middle of a row of terraced houses. 'No car in the driveway,' she commented.

'Maybe she doesn't have one,' Craig replied as he climbed out of the passenger seat and shut the door with a solid *thunk*. It would have been easy to miss the upstairs curtains moving very slightly, but Mo had spotted it. She shared the observation with Craig, and he responded with a slight nod.

After knocking a couple of times, the next-door neighbour came out. She was a short skinny woman, with very short grey hair, a leathery face, and blue veiny legs that looked like a road map. She wore a floral apron over her faded orange dress, blue slippers and had a dustpan and brush in her hand. 'Who am yow after then?' she said in a broad Black Country accent. Craig showed her his ID and explained they were looking for Helen.

'Her ay in, is her?' the woman said, looking at them both, her curranty eyes full of suspicion. When she pursed her lips, she looked like she was gurning.

'What did she say?' Mo whispered.

'She said that Helen's not in. It's the accent, you do learn to tune into it after a while,' Craig muttered back.

The woman was still standing on her doorstep, waiting for them to say something. Craig just smiled, wrote a note on the back of a card and went to put it through the letterbox.

'What yow doing that fer? Helen ay there, but her mate is. Noisy cow she is an' all. Playing bleeding Abba all night, drives me saft it does. I'll be glad when her buggers off home.'

Mo looked at Craig, who suddenly looked very interested in the old lady. 'Really? What does Helen's mate look like?'

The old woman pursed her lips again. 'Ginger hair, big tits and a fat arse. Pretty wench though, got a crackin' smile.'

Craig pulled his phone out and showed the woman a photo. 'Is this her?'

'Ar, that's her. What's her done? Has her bin on the rob, or is her a druggie? She looks like a druggie with all that bling.'

'No, she's not a druggie,' Mo said. 'Thank you for your help, Mrs . . .'

'Chanter. Ivy Chanter. So her's a prozzie then, is her? Is there a reward? For information, like?' The woman looked hopeful, but Craig shook his head.

'No, we're just making some enquiries, Mrs Chanter. You've been a big help though, thank you.' Craig walked towards the car, his phone pressed to his ear.

'Bleeding charmin', that's what yow get when yow 'elp the police – sod all!' Mrs Chanter went back inside and slammed the door.

Mo looked up at the windows again, but the curtains stayed still.

59

Gary and Dawn drove back to Wolverhampton in silence, both frustrated at the lack of progress they had made. Mrs Bakshi had been no help at all, first insisting that her son was a good boy and would never hurt anyone. Then she swore at them, calling them pigs and finally she pleaded with them not to take him away from her, and it had taken them a while to explain that they just wanted to talk to him. Eventually, she had suggested they go and see his boss; she sometimes gave him extra work if there was any available.

'God, my face hurts,' Dawn said.

'It's hurting you? It's killing me,' Gary laughed, earning him a thump in the ribs.

Gary drove through the city and parked at Piper's Row, near to the newly refurbished bus station. Once a hang-out for drunks and junkies, it was now very smart and modern. A couple of new restaurants had opened nearby, meaning that the area was almost always busy. The rain had stopped but the pot-holes were still full of water, as Gary found when he stepped in one and the water went over the top of his shoes. Dawn laughed and winced at the same time. 'Serves you right,' she grinned.

Dawn pointed across the street to Mac's Bar. The

basement doors were propped open and the dray lorry was being unloaded by a familiar figure.

'There he is, let's go and speak to him,' she said. 'Don't mention Elizabeth is dead, let's see what he has to say first.'

Arjan looked up as the two approached. For a split second, panic spilled across his face, quickly replaced with a look of resignation. He signed the dray man's paperwork and closed the basement doors with a loud clang.

'You're a hard man to track down,' Dawn said.

'I've been keeping my head down because Elizabeth's parents have been badgering me,' he replied. He pulled an old bar towel from his apron pocket and wiped the sweat off his face. 'I keep telling them I don't know where she is. She went on that holiday we were meant to share, so she should have been back a few days ago. They ring me every damned day – speak of the devil!' he said as his phone went off.

He pulled it out of his shirt pocket and turned it off. 'There, now maybe they will get the message.'

'We have a lot to discuss with you, like why you failed to mention that your girlfriend was Vicky Wilson's double,' Gary added.

'Was she? Yeah, I suppose they do look a bit alike. I never really thought about it.'

'You didn't really think at all, did you?' Dawn said, letting him know that she was not impressed. 'We've been running around like blue-arsed flies and all this time . . .'

'Let's just get back to the station so you can fill in the gaps for us,' Gary interrupted. He could see that Dawn was about to blow her top. 'Then you can tell us everything from the very beginning.'

***

310

Arjan Bakshi had gone to pieces when they broke the news to him about his girlfriend.

'Well, that didn't go as planned,' Gary said afterwards. 'He seemed genuinely heartbroken.'

'I agree, but I don't buy that he didn't know his girlfriend was at the club that night, unless she did a great job of avoiding him.'

'I suppose she would if they'd had a bust-up,' Gary added as they headed back to the office. 'Maybe an argument broke out and he killed her, but I don't think he did.'

'What makes you so sure?' Dawn asked.

'What makes who so sure?' Alex asked as he caught them up on the stairs.

'Gary thinks that Mr Bakshi is innocent, he was about to tell me why,' Dawn told him.

'Well, let's get everyone together and you can enlighten us all,' Alex said as he pushed the office door open.

'I reckon that Arjan Bakshi being at the club was either a coincidence or he was set up,' Gary began once the team were assembled. 'He said that he was called in at the last minute, so he wouldn't have known his girlfriend was there because he thought she was on holiday. The staff said he never left his post at the stage door at all, apart from a quick smoke break. He didn't have enough time to cause so many injuries, plus he would have been covered in blood.'

'Good point,' Alex said. 'What makes you think he was set up?'

'Maybe whoever killed her found out that Arjan was her boyfriend so decided to frame him.'

'Well, he's a hefty bloke, I bet he's handy with his fists. It would be easy for us to assume that he'd seen her, and they'd argued again,' Les admitted.

'Vicky's skin was found under Elizabeth's fingernails, so we know they came to blows at some point. Perhaps Vicky was jealous because Elizabeth had the same hairstyle, I've known women fall out over less,' Gary suggested.

'We know that Helen Whittaker's involved in this too, so maybe she broke up a fight between the two of them,' Dawn said. 'The fact that Vicky has let everyone, including her own parents, think that she's dead is beyond me. Once Helen gets home, both she and Vicky will be brought in for questioning, so hopefully we'll find out just what the hell is going on.'

'I do have one theory as to why the two women might have had a fight,' Gary said. 'Maybe they were both knocking off Ray Diamond.'

Alex nodded, deep in thought. 'Faz did find semen present, so let's get DNA samples from both Mr Bakshi and Mr Diamond so we can find out if it belongs to one of them.'

60

Alex ploughed his way through a bacon roll in his office while he prepared some notes. Laura Morrison had been puzzled as to why Alex had insisted that she accompany him to the station immediately, but after he'd assured her that all her loved ones were fine, she'd grabbed her things and gone with him. Alex had half-watched her as he drove back, not sure if her innocent expression was genuine, or she was just a great actress. He'd know soon enough, but first he was going to tackle Helen Whittaker.

'Mo,' he called as he went into the main office. 'You're with me. We'll be interviewing each woman in turn. The rest of you, sort out warrants and execute searches on Helen's house and Vicky's flat. Do Laura Morrison's house too, just in case. Uniform have said we can have six officers, so make good use of them. These women have messed us around long enough, let's take the gloves off now.'

He left the office and strode towards the interview rooms with Mo hurrying along behind him.

Helen Whittaker sat with one foot propped up on her knee, idly picking at one of the rips in her jeans. She wore an oversized blue shirt and white trainers, and her hair was brushed back off her face. She looked up but said nothing when Alex and Mo walked in.

This wasn't a cosy room like the last time, it was basic, with thinly cushioned metal chairs bolted to the floor and a scuffed table. The walls were painted in a shade that could only have come from mixing grey and beige together, and the only – reinforced – window was high up near the ceiling and didn't open. She remained silent but never took her eyes off Alex as he set up the recording equipment. She seemed surprised when Mo took the lead on the interview.

'Miss Whittaker, why didn't you inform us that Vicky Wilson was alive and well?'

Helen shrugged. 'I didn't see the point.'

'I see. Did you not think about what her parents were going through?'

'Not really. Her mum's got no backbone, she's never protected Vicky from that pig of a husband. He beats her up, you know. He used to hit Vicky too, till she hit him back. That's why he doesn't speak to her now, he's pretty much disowned her. Vicky's gran knew what it was like, she knew her daughter would never stand up to that bully, but she hoped that by leaving Vicky everything she owned, Vicky would walk away and maybe persuade her mum to go too. Mrs Wilson is nice but she's weak and wouldn't leave, choosing to stay and put up with his bullying. As far as I'm concerned, she's made her bed, so she can lie in it.'

'When did you know that Vicky was alive?' Mo asked.

'I've always known. I caught her scrapping with that other woman in the toilets, so I slapped them both, dragged Vicky outside and phoned for a taxi. When it arrived, I gave her my keys and told her to go to my place and stay put until I got home. I took her phone off her too, so she couldn't ring that dickhead. She left her handbag in the taxi, and they rang me about it because I'd booked it for her, so I collected it the next day, took it out to the woods near Ray's house and dumped it. I threw her phone as hard as I could into the undergrowth. I hoped that if you lot found it you'd think he was guilty.'

'So, when we called you both in and told you that she was dead, rather than come clean you kept up the pretence, even though you knew it was in your best interest to be honest with us? What kind of friend does that?'

Helen shot forward in her seat, her face red with anger. 'A fucking good one, that's who. I told her more than once that getting mixed up with that prick would end in tears, but would she listen? Would she fuck. When she overheard that other woman bragging that she was seeing Ray, she lost it and went for her. If I hadn't walked in when I did it would have got really bad.'

Alex finally lost his temper and slammed his fist on the table. 'It did get really bad, Elizabeth Callendar ended up dead. I don't care what your reasons were, you and Vicky are complicit in Miss Callendar's murder as far as I'm concerned.'

'If you lot had done your jobs properly and locked him up years ago, he wouldn't even be around. So, if you want to blame anyone, maybe you need to look in the mirror,' Helen spat back.

Alex looked stunned. 'What are you talking about?'

Helen's mouth dropped open. 'You don't know, do you?'

'Know what? Are you saying that Ray Diamond got away with a crime before?'

'That's exactly what I'm saying. Only he wasn't called Ray Diamond then, he was known as Keith Raymond.'

Alex closed his eyes in disbelief. He knew Ray had seemed familiar to him, and now he knew why.

Helen watched his reaction. 'Now you know what I'm on about, don't you?'

'Interview suspended at 11 a.m. Wait here, I'll be back

in ten minutes,' Alex told Mo as he left the room.

When he came back in, Alex was holding a thick folder. He placed it on the table, restarted the tape and turned to Mo.

'It was the first major case I worked on,' Alex began. 'Fifteen years ago, we picked up Keith Raymond on suspicion of a brutal rape in the ladies' toilets at Wolverhampton train station. He had short black hair back then, which is why I didn't recognise him. The victim was a young woman, who had been savagely beaten, raped and left for dead. The victim positively identified him, but he had a watertight alibi, so the case fell apart. The woman suffered severe facial injuries as you can see from the photos,' Alex said, opening the folder and showing Mo the photographs.

'What happened to her?' Mo asked as she flicked through the folder.

'She tried to commit suicide,' Helen said. 'I know this because she is my Mum. I was only four at the time, and I had to go and live with my nan for a few months while she recovered. Nan paid for her to have plastic surgery, but she still suffered from depression for a long time. It didn't help that I didn't recognise her after her surgery either.'

'How is your mum now?' Mo asked.

'She's fine now. I think that in the end, changing her face helped her to cope. She knew he would never recognise her if he saw her again, so in a way it was like wearing a mask.'

'How did you end up in a club with the man who ruined your mother's life? That can't have been a coincidence,' Alex said.

Helen gave a small laugh. 'Actually, it was,' she said. 'He had a different name for one thing, and he'd changed the way he looked. The only reason I knew it was him is because Vicky told me she had seen an old passport in his bedroom with the name Keith Raymond on it. He doesn't know she saw it because she was poking around while he was in the shower. I was nearly sick when she told me. I know she was upset when I went mad at her for seeing him, but she didn't know the reason why I hate him so much.'

'Did you kill Elizabeth Callendar in order to frame Ray Diamond, as revenge for what he did to your mother?' Alex asked her.

'No, I didn't. I wouldn't use anyone else to get to him, I'd just beat the shit out of him myself. The only reason I haven't is because it would hurt my Mum. She doesn't need all that crap dragging up again. I tried to keep Vicky away from him though. I did hear Elizabeth talking about him though, so I told Vicky he was two-timing her. She went to the toilets to confront Elizabeth and they started fighting, so I sent her to my place. I hoped that Vicky would see him for what he was after that, but she still went on about how much she loved him.'

'Why did you wrongly identify Elizabeth as Vicky?'

'I don't know, it just seemed like a good idea at the time. She looked so much like Mum after he beat her that I thought he had done it. I told Vicky that Ray had done it and she believed me.'

Alex blew out a long breath. 'I'm going to ask someone to come and take a formal statement from you, but for now this interview is suspended.'

61

Vicky Wilson was in a similar room to Helen, but her expression was more of fear than defiance. Her blue cut-off trousers and long-sleeved orange polo-neck jumper looked far too big for her, and her hair was dragged back off her face in a rough ponytail. She couldn't look either officer in the face as they set everything up, instead she concentrated on trying to read the faded graffiti scored into the table top.

'Miss Wilson,' Mo began, 'we've already spoken to Miss Whittaker, but we'd like to hear what you have to say.'

Alex watched the young woman's expression but said nothing.

'I didn't kill anyone, I swear!' Vicky began, as tears started to form in her eyes. 'I don't know who did, but it wasn't me.'

'Tell us about the fight with Elizabeth Callendar,' Alex said in a firm voice.

'Was that her name? It was her fault. I was in the cubicle when she came into the loos, she was on her phone, talking all lovey-dovey with someone. I came out and nearly walked into her. I mentioned that we had the same hair pins in, she said her bloke gave them to her. I said he had the same great taste as mine and we laughed. It was only when she said it was Ray that I flipped out. I told her that I was seeing him, but she laughed and said she doubted Ray had ever been exclusive with anyone. She said Ray had lusted after her for months, ever since she'd met him at the pub where her boyfriend was a bouncer. Ray had been with someone at the time, but it hadn't stopped him trying to get into her knickers.'

Mo wrote everything down. 'So, rather than get angry with Ray Diamond for cheating on you, you chose to take it out on Elizabeth Callendar instead.'

'Ray is a sweetie; he's easily led where women are concerned. I know him and he's not a cheater at all. She was just out to get laid, she admitted that her and her chap had broken up recently, so she thought it would be a good laugh. That's when I lost it with her, but I swear I didn't kill her.' Vicky chewed on her false fingernails, looking everywhere but at the two officers.

'Show me your arms.' Alex said. Vicky looked taken aback, so Alex repeated his request so she pulled her sleeves up. There were faded scratches on her forearms and bruising around her wrists. 'Explain those injuries to me please,' he said.

'The scratches are from the fight with that slag, I'm surprised I didn't catch something from her, the skanky cow.' She stopped speaking when she saw the expression on Alex's face. 'Well, she asked for everything she got, stealing someone else's man.'

'What about these marks?' Mo asked, leaning forward and taking Vicky's hand. She pointed to the bruise that circled Vicky's wrist. 'Were these from the fight too?'

Vicky blushed. 'No, they were from one of the times I was with Ray. He wanted to try a bit of bondage, and I like to make him happy, so I said yes. He had these handcuffs, which were fun. I wasn't too keen on the noose at first though, but he said it gives you the most

321

intense orgasms, so I was willing to give it a try.'

'He had a noose?' Mo asked.

Vicky nodded. 'Yeah, he keeps it in his car, it used to be part of his costume when he did his Highwayman routine. We went out into the woods behind his house where it's secluded. If you've never done it outdoors, I highly recommend it. He pulled the noose quite tight and I was a bit scared, but Ray was right when he said that having your breathing restricted intensifies the orgasm. It was pretty amazing.'

Mo looked as if she was going to be sick. Alex leaned forward and studied Vicky hard for a moment. 'So, you went into the woods with Ray and had sex with him while being partially strung up from the nearest tree. Have I got that right?'

'I was wearing the handcuffs too, and he insisted that I was naked,' Vicky added. 'To get the full experience, you know? Ray said it was the best sex he'd ever had too. He's so sweet, you have no idea how lovely he is. There's no way he killed that slag, it's not in his nature to hurt anyone.'

Mo wrote *WTF?* on her notepad and Alex had to agree with her. They both pitied Vicky, Ray had her eating out of the palm of his hand, and she wouldn't hear a word against him.

'We will need to verify all the things you've told us, so I'll be keeping you here for a while. If it all checks out, I'll let you go home. In the meantime, maybe you'd care to explain to your mother why we ruined her holiday by wrongly informing her of your death,' Alex said as he stood up.

There was an audible creak from his knees and Mo winced on his behalf. Alex opened the door to find Gary waiting with Vicky's mother. She pushed past, her arms around Vicky, crying and shaking as she hugged her daughter. Vicky broke down and hugged her back, repeating how sorry she was. Alex ushered Mo out, closed the door and left them to it, leaving Gary to supervise.

'How come you didn't tell her about the things Helen Whittaker told us?' Mo asked.

'I will, but let's give Vicky's mother some time first. That poor woman has been through enough. I'm too knackered to think straight at the moment, I need a caffeine hit.'

***

Alex sank back in his office chair, closed his eyes and sighed deeply. Dawn and Les were currently interviewing Laura Morrison, but Alex wasn't too concerned. If what the other two had said was to be believed, Laura was an innocent bystander. She had been horrified that her two best friends had deceived her. Alex rubbed the bridge of his nose in frustration. Ray Diamond – that man seemed to be the root of all the problems, and Alex was sick of hearing his name. He looked up when Gary knocked the door. Alex waved for him to come in and sit down.

'I've got the reports on what we found as a result of the search warrants,' Gary said. 'Nothing really of substance as expected. The Forensics report said that Vicky Wilson's place yielded nothing of significance. Several photos and a couple of videos of an . . .' Gary went red and cleared his throat '. . . explicit nature were recovered, which we'll have to ask her friends about. There are no faces shown on any of them, so we don't know who the people are. There were other indications that a man, or men, had been at the flat.'

'Such as?' Alex asked.

'Men's shower gel, razors, that kind of thing. Of course, they could be hers. Jo uses my razor all the time, she says they're a better shave.'

'Anything else?' Alex asked, impatiently.

'Helen Whittaker's place had nothing at all to offer. Craig is still at Laura Morrison's place, but he should be back very soon. What do you want me to do now?' Gary asked, trying to look at his watch without Alex noticing.

'Go home, get some sleep and we'll start fresh tomorrow. God knows I could do with getting my head down. See you tomorrow.'

'Cheers boss.' Gary was off like a shot.

Alex smiled and shook his head. Gary was a great team player, solid and dependable. He'd been very shy when he'd first joined the team but pairing him with Craig Muir on a regular basis had brought him out of his shell, and since meeting his fiancée Jo, Gary had grown in confidence and ability. He still had his faults, but Alex believed in playing to someone's strengths instead of their weaknesses.

On a whim, Alex rang Jayne from his personal mobile phone. It was a while before she answered, and she sounded breathless.

'Ooh, heavy breathing – I like it, Mrs Peachey. Very kinky,' he grinned. 'What colour knickers are you wearing?'

'Sorry, I couldn't find my phone,' Jayne panted. 'I can't talk now, my husband will be home soon, so I need to have his dinner ready for when he gets in. He can be a grumpy old bastard when he wants to be, especially where food is concerned. How about you ring back another time and we can indulge in some phone sex?'

Alex laughed. 'It's a date. Will wine be served or is he picking a bottle up on the way home?'

'I'm hoping he will pick a nice bottle of red up, unless he's happy with water tonight?'

'I'm sure he'll bring something back with him.'

'Can you also tell him that his son is away overnight, so all I'm wearing is a frilly apron, stockings and high heels? Thanks, bye.' The line went dead, leaving Alex to wonder how he was supposed to drive home with a raging hard-on.

62

Les arrived early the following day, having been up half the night with a vomiting dog. The sickness had eventually stopped, only to be replaced by diarrhoea, so after clearing up again at 5 a.m., Les had abandoned any hopes of sleep and headed into work, leaving Ruth in charge of the mop bucket.

He studied the board carefully, tilting his head this way and that, trying to see the bigger picture. He had rearranged the evidence several times and it still pointed to Ray Diamond.

'Hey, you're in early, did you shit the bed?' Craig called when he walked in. Today's attire was a midnight-blue suit, ivory-coloured shirt and grey tie. The trademark matching handkerchief peeked out of his breast pocket.

'No, but Millie did,' Les replied. 'I mean, she didn't do it in my bed, just her own – and in the hallway, the kitchen and probably the lounge by now. The dopey dog swallowed a peach stone and has been trying to shift it ever since. Ruth's taking her to the vets as soon as they open. It'll probably mean surgery and a large bill to go with it.'

Craig shuddered. 'That's why we don't have any pets, I couldn't be dealing with stuff like that. I'm sure she'll be okay, though.' He walked over and stood next to Les, eyes scanning the board. 'You see something?'

'Not sure,' Les admitted. 'I've shuffled things around to try and see things from a different perspective, but it all keeps coming back to Ray Diamond.'

Craig squinted at the board. 'You're not wrong mate. It looks that way to me too. The problem is he's a slippery customer, and we can't get anything to stick.'

'I think the key is the relationship between him and his assistant,' Les said. 'Everyone we've spoken to has mentioned it. Either he's holding something damning over her head, or she's a bloody masochist. Either way, I'd like to know what's going on.'

'You and me both, mate,' Craig agreed. 'Michelle Simmons seems like a sensible woman, I can't see her working for someone who treats her so badly unless she has a bloody good reason to. Maybe he's blackmailing her.'

'Craig, you are a bloody genius!' Les took the pictures off the board and rearranged them again, this time putting Michelle in the centre. He stood back with a grin. Craig looked puzzled, not knowing what Les was on about.

'Suppose for a second that Ray has a deep, dark secret and Michelle knows what it is. She forces him to give her a job and somewhere to live in exchange for keeping quiet. He resents her for having a hold over him, which is why he's so horrible towards her. She refuses to leave no matter how badly he treats her, because she knows that she's got him by the short and curlies.' Les looked very pleased with himself and Craig patted him on the shoulder.

'You're right, I am a genius. Let's do some digging and see what we find,' Craig said as he headed for his desk. 'I'll start with the electoral roll; you get cracking on phone records and financial stuff.'

After a few moments, Craig frowned and called Les over. 'Hey, look at this. It says that Michelle Simmons isn't on the electoral register.'

Les scanned the screen. 'Maybe she's opted out of the public one. Try the private one.'

'I have done, she's not on that one either. Has she been married? Maybe Simmons isn't her maiden name.'

'Maybe,' Les replied. 'See if she's got a social media account or anything like that.'

Craig hit a few more keys. 'Nada. Not even Myspace.'

Les laughed. 'Nobody has Myspace any more, but you could try another older site, like Friends Reunited. Do we know where she's from?'

Craig opened one of the folders on his desktop. 'I don't think we do.' He looked at Les. 'How long did she say she's worked for Ray Diamond?'

'Hold on a sec,' Les went to his own computer and looked for a copy of Michelle's statement. 'I don't think we asked her, and if we did, it's not recorded anywhere here. Mo and Dawn talked to her, perhaps they know.' He picked up his phone and rang Dawn, who walked through the door just as her phone started ringing.

'Where's the fire? I'm only ten minutes late,' she grumbled. 'Barney decided he needed an extra dump this morning.'

Les skipped the usual pleasantries. 'How long has Michelle Simmons worked for Ray Diamond?'

Dawn tilted her head to the side as she thought about it. 'Around five or six years I think, I can't remember off the top of my head, but it'll be in the paperwork somewhere. Why?'

Les filled her in on his conversation with Craig and explained that he couldn't find any trace of Michelle Simmons.

'What, no paper trail at all?' Dawn asked. 'What about the electoral roll?'

'First place we looked,' Craig said. 'Do you know where she's from originally?''

Dawn looked stumped. 'Now you've asked me. I have no idea. I just assumed that she was local. Hang on, I'll go through the interview logs. Scrap that,' she said as Mo walked in.

'Oi, Rainman, how long has Michelle Simmons worked for Ray Diamond?' Craig called.

Mo smiled at the use of her nickname. 'Six years and one month exactly, she started in late November.' She took off her jacket and hung it on the back of her chair then switched her computer on.'

'See, I told you she'd know,' Dawn said.

'Les thinks that maybe Michelle could be blackmailing Ray to make him keep her on, rather than Ray having something over her,' Craig said. 'I have to say, it's plausible. Plus, we can't find any trace of her on the electoral roll or social media.'

Mo mulled it over for a second. 'Try looking for her parents instead, chances are they still live in the same place.'

'We don't know where Michelle is from, we didn't ask her.' Dawn said.

'Well there must be someone who knows her better than we do, Neil Stone for instance, or maybe one of the strippers.'

Dawn picked up the phone to call Neil just as Alex arrived, and the team quickly bought him up to speed. He told Dawn to put the phone down.

'Don't ring any of Ray's colleagues, they may tip Michelle off and then we'll get nowhere.' Alex said.

'What do you suggest we do then?' Craig asked.

'I'll give John Jackson a call, he's pretty approachable and he's known Ray for nearly twenty years. Gary, stick the kettle on, will you?'

Alex went into his office and closed the door. Within a

few minutes he came back out.

'That was interesting. John says that Michelle turned up at his office around seven years ago, asking where she could find Ray Diamond. John said she told him she was a fan, so he told her where Ray was going to be appearing over the next few weeks, and she left. Next thing he knew, Michelle was working for Ray. He thought they were sleeping together but Michelle denied it. She said she wanted to find Ray because he'd promised her a job when she left University.'

'Did John know where she was from?' Craig asked.

'No, but he had a daughter in college at the time and had some university prospectuses on his desk. They got talking about them and Michelle told him that she'd studied Business Studies and Psychology at Birmingham City University.'

'I'll get on to the Uni,' Les said, 'They may still have a home address on their system.'

63

Ray strode into his house, threw his keys on the hall table and jogged upstairs. He was in a good mood, having earned nearly two hundred pounds from a couple of middle-aged housewives who had wanted a threesome, and another hundred from the hapless Liam, who still hung on his every word and believed all of Ray's bullshit.

Ray spotted the bin bags outside his bedroom and frowned. He opened his bedroom door and saw that all the clothes and shoes that had been on the floor were gone. The drapes had been removed as well. He noticed the boxes of photographs spewing their contents across the floor of the open wardrobe and scrabbled around among the contents in a panic, throwing clothes up in the air and scattering shoes and other belongings in his search but to no avail.

'Shelley you bitch. You've gone too fucking far this time,' he shouted at the top of his lungs, 'I'll fucking kill you!'

He took a small plastic bag containing a dozen pills out of his bedside drawer and removed two of them, swallowing them dry, then standing with his eyes closed, waiting for them to kick in.

His phone buzzed in his pocket and he sat on the edge

of the bed to answer it.

'Hey Liam, are you missing me already? Whoa, slow down. No, I don't know anything about any cheques. What do you mean you don't believe me? Why would I steal from you babe? Look, I'll come back round, and we can sort this out.'

Ray listened for a moment then laughed. 'Don't be a dick. You can't break up with me because we were never an item. Do you really think that I would voluntarily be with an ugly fat wanker like you? You're a means to an end, just like all the other clients that I provide a service to. Well, I don't need you, so stick your money up your fat arse, you little prick.'

Ray hung up and threw his phone across the room. It hit the wall and fell down behind the dressing table. He ran downstairs, went into the kitchen, retrieved a bag of cocaine from his kit bag and did two lines in quick succession, making his head spin. He found a bottle of vintage brandy at the back of the pantry, opened it and chugged down a third of the bottle.

He whistled. 'Fuck, that's good. Now, where was I before that little twat interrupted me?'

***

John Jackson was beginning to regret giving Shona two weeks off. January was a busy time as all the strippers' contracts were due for renewal. Between sorting those out and taking bookings for strippergrams and private parties, he was trying to set up dates for a UK-wide tour, something he'd never done before but was keen to try to get the exposure the firm badly needed. Sales had fallen last year so he wanted to recoup some of the losses. He also needed to do his tax returns before the end of the month deadline.

He held the phone in the crook of his bulky neck as he

scribbled on the notepad. 'Just to recap, you want a Fireman strippergram for the 17th of February for a 50th Birthday party, and you want a black guy? Yeah, you pay him when he arrives, he's not allowed to do the job until he's been paid. That's great, thank you very much.'

John put the phone down and wrote the job details in the big book in front of him. He scanned the list of available black strippers and settled on Calvin, one of the new lads. He added the job to Calvin's spreadsheet on the computer and put his initials next to the job to show that it had been allocated.

John picked up his mobile phone and scrolled down his contact list. The call from Alex had made him feel uneasy, and he was still in two minds whether to call Michelle and see if she was okay. It wasn't as if he knew her very well, but he liked her and felt sorry for the shit she put up with from Ray. He had no idea why the police would need information about her family unless something bad had happened to her. Would it do any harm to check?

'Ah, what the hell,' he said to himself, and clicked on her name.

64

Michelle surveyed the mess in the kitchen and figured that Ray was either drunk, stoned or both. She screwed the top back on the brandy bottle and put it back in the pantry. She used a wad of damp kitchen roll to remove the traces of white powder on the counter, filled the coffee machine with fresh water and set it to drip, then went upstairs.

Ray's bedroom door was open, so she peered in. He was lying on the bed on his back, eyes wide open. Michelle waited for him to shout at her to get out of his room, but he said nothing, just stared at the mirrored ceiling.

'Ray, can you come downstairs please? I need to talk to you about something.'

'Sounds ominous,' he drawled, sitting up and swinging his long legs over the edge of the bed. He stood up and wobbled, and Michelle went to steady him but he pulled away, clearly annoyed at her. 'Get your hands off me, I don't need your help.'

He went downstairs into the lounge and sat on the small sofa. Michelle went to the kitchen to get them both some coffee. She put his mug on the low table by the fireplace and curled up in the armchair nearby, pulled out her phone and started texting.

'Well?' Ray asked. 'Surely whatever you want to say is more important than texting your boyfriend, so spit it out.'

The drugs had long worn off, blackening his mood and his patience was thin.

Michelle put her phone down and pulled an envelope out of the pocket of her jeans. 'We need to talk about these.'

Ray gave her a blank look. 'What are they?'

'Photographs of women you've raped or assaulted. Would you care to explain?'

'I don't have to explain myself, least of all to you,' he sneered. 'I'd like to know why you thought it was okay to go poking around in my bedroom though. If you were looking for money, then you'll be disappointed because I'm broke.'

Michelle gave him a pitying stare. 'Oh Ray, you think you're so hard done by. It was your daughter that found your precious photos. I have no idea what she was looking for, but it clearly wasn't these. Neil rang me to say she turned up at his house, soaked to the skin and suffering from shock. I've asked him to keep her there for now, until I decide what to do next.'

Ray stood up suddenly and upended the table, sending everything on it flying across the room. 'Until *you* decide?' he roared. 'Who the hell do you think you are, Michelle? You think you can lord it over me? You've got a fucking nerve, telling me that you and that fucking poof will decide what happens next? How about I tell you to fuck off and not come back?

Michelle looked at him, her face filled with disgust. 'You're pathetic, Ray. I knew you were a maggot, but when I saw those photos, I realised just how much of one you really were. You deserve everything you get.'

Ray lunged at her, knocked the envelope out of her

hand and grabbed her by the neck, pinning her to her chair. 'You think you're so fucking clever! Do you think I don't know that you're trying to ruin my career?'

He squeezed hard, cutting off Michelle's air supply, and she kicked out furiously, catching him on the shins. He let her go and she shot out of the chair, gasping for air. Snatching up the envelope, she moved closer to the door.

'Fuck off Ray! You think you're a big man, loved by everyone don't you? Well, you're not. You're a sad, pathetic loser who doesn't know when to quit. Trust me, you'll get what's coming, and it won't be soon enough!'

'Bitch!' he shouted as he made another grab at her. She ran out of the room and slammed the door, hitting him full in the face. She rushed towards the front door and wrenched it open just as the doorbell rang. Si and Des stood there, both panting and looking anxious.

'I got your text and thought I'd better call for Des on the way. Are you okay?' Si pulled her into a hug as Michelle burst into tears. He stroked her hair gently and looked at Des.

'I thought he was going to kill me. He was so angry.' Michelle sobbed into his shoulder.

'Shh, it's okay now, we're here,' Si said. 'Tell us what happened.'

Michelle pulled away from him and wiped her eyes on her sleeve. She pulled an envelope out of the pocket of her jeans. 'Hope found these and was very upset. She ran off to Neil's house and he called me. I told him to keep her there and I came home to ask Ray about them. He just flipped and attacked me. You have to help me; I swear he's going to kill me.'

Si took the photos out of the envelope and looked through them. He rubbed his hand through his hair, trying to keep his temper. 'He's a sick bastard.' He handed the photos to Des, so he could look at them.

Des looked at the first few pictures, then shoved the

packet at Si. He stormed into the lounge and charged into Ray, the momentum carrying the two of them over the back of the sofa. Ray struggled to push him off but wasn't strong enough. Des dragged him to his feet and punched him hard enough to loosen Ray's teeth, causing him to stagger backwards and crash into the pool table. Des pinned Ray down and continued to rain blows down on him until Si dragged him off.

'Des, that's enough!' Si shouted. 'He's not worth it.'

'He's a cunt, that's what he is,' Des shouted back. 'Did you see their faces? Those women? What sort of sick fuck gets off on doing that?' He went back into the kitchen and stood at the sink, breathing hard.

Michelle got a bottle of vodka out of the fridge and poured him a large measure. He downed it in one go, then tried to push past Si to go back into the lounge. Si put a hand on his chest to stop him.

'He's not worth it, mate. He'll be finished once these get out. We'll make sure everyone knows about this and he'll never work again. Michelle, you're coming home with me, go and get your stuff.'

Michelle stroked Si's arm. 'Thanks babe. I'll take his car and meet you at yours.'

She kissed him on the cheek and went up to her room. Si left Des sitting on the countertop and went into the lounge. Ray stood by the pool table, the blood from his nose beginning to dry on his face. His eye was closed and starting to swell, and his hair was dishevelled. He looked up when Si entered the room.

'Don't say a word, Si, you don't know the full story,' Ray said quietly.

'I know enough to know that no-one will give you a job now, we'll see to that,' Si replied. 'I always knew you were rotten, but now I know just how much. You raped those women, or should I say girls, because half of them don't look old enough to even be at a show. Then you

339

humiliated them by taking photos as souvenirs! I bet the mighty Ray Diamond made sure that none of them went to the police either!'

Si looked Ray up and down as if he were vermin. 'You make my flesh crawl.'

Ray shook his head. 'Si, you don't understand, you've got it all wrong!'

'No, don't try and talk your way out of this,' Si said, holding up his hand. 'You're done.'

Ray tried to speak again but Si turned away and walked towards the door.

'Yeah, that's it, you run to Michelle like the good little boy you are,' Ray called after him. 'She snaps her fingers and you're there like a pig at a trough.'

Instead of leaving the room, Si closed the door and walked over to the side table where Michelle had laid a paper pattern out over some dress material. He picked up a large pair of scissors and approached Ray, who suddenly looked nervous.

'Are you finished? Because I'm only just getting started.'

65

'Right, let's assess where we are and what we've got since this morning,' Alex said to his team as they stood around the board. 'By the way Les, how's the dog?'

'She's fine now,' Les said. 'The vet removed the stone and she should be home later today.'

'Excellent news. After your epiphany this morning, we've turned everything on its head, and it does explain a few things,' Alex said. 'For a start, we know that Michelle Simmons isn't who she says she is. Craig, would you care to enlighten us?'

Craig took over. 'I spoke to Professor Wright at Birmingham City University, who positively identified Michelle from the photo I sent her, but says she was enrolled under the name Julie Kershaw. Julie got a degree in Psychology and Business Studies, and Professor Wright remembered Miss Kershaw emailing her to ask about getting her name changed on her certificates around seven years ago. She was told she would have to bring in official documentation, but Professor Wright never heard from her again.'

'I got an old address using the name Kershaw from the electoral roll,' Mo said. 'There were a few, but it didn't take as long as I'd thought to find the right one. They used to live in Bilston but moved to Wellington near Telford after Julie graduated. Her dad died a few months later, but her mum's still there. Julie changed her name to Michelle Simmons when she left home.'

'Dawn, you and Gary get over to Mrs Kershaw's and have a chat with her.' Alex said. 'Mo, you and Les dig deeper into Ray Diamond's background and see if he's ever crossed paths with anyone called Kershaw. Maybe Michelle has a grudge against him. Craig, you're coming with me to talk to Ray Diamond.'

'What if Michelle's there?'

'Then we'll ask him to come with us. I don't like the man, but we need to get him alone.'

As they walked through reception on the way to the car park, one of the desk Sergeants called out to Alex and he stopped. 'What's up?'

'Thought you'd like to know that we had a call to go to Wombourne Gardens just now. The call came from a Miss Simmons.'

'Thanks, we're on our way over there now. Are your lads on the way?' Alex asked.

'They left about five minutes ago.'

66

Dawn and Gary parked outside a neat row of terraced houses on a modern estate near the Princess Royal hospital in Wellington. It was one of those estates where the houses were of a decent size, not the usual rabbit hutches that one had come to expect with mass-produced housing. The Kershaw family home looked well-kept, the front garden was a little overgrown, but given the time of year, that was to be expected. A medium-sized grey saloon was parked on the square of tarmac in front of the garage.

'Looks like there's someone in,' Gary remarked.

Dawn punched him on the arm and rolled her eyes. She led the way up the path and rang the doorbell.

The door was opened by a tall slim man in black trousers and a short black tunic. His sandy-brown hair was clipped short at the sides and brushed back on the top and he had a friendly face.

'Can I help you?' he said in a soft, almost effeminate voice.

Dawn introduced herself and Gary to him. 'We'd like to speak to Mrs Kershaw please. Is she available?'

The man held the door wide and stepped back. 'Please come in.' He showed them into a bright, airy sitting room and offered them refreshments.

'Sheila is having a nap, but I'll go and get her.' He went to go upstairs but Gary stopped him.

'Before you do, would you mind telling us who you are please?'

'I'm so sorry, where are my manners? I'm Kevin Huntley, Sheila's carer. She's got early-onset dementia, you know.'

'I'm sorry to hear that,' Dawn said. 'Maybe you could help us then, rather than bother Mrs Kershaw.'

Kevin smiled and sat down. 'I'll certainly try,' he said. 'What would you like to know?'

'We're here about Mrs Kershaw's daughter, Julie,' Dawn said, remembering to use Michelle's birth name. 'Do you know her?'

Kevin nodded. 'Yes, of course I do. Is she in trouble?'

'We hope not, but we're just gathering information at the minute,' Dawn explained. 'When did you last see her?'

'She was here yesterday, she brought the shopping over,' Kevin said. He cocked his head and went to the foot of the stairs. 'Sorry about that, I thought I heard Sheila waking up. She can get a bit confused, so I like to be ready if she needs me.'

He perched on the edge of the armchair nearest the stairs.

'That's okay, we'll be quick.' Dawn continued. 'Julie changed her name by deed poll some years ago, from Julie Kershaw to Michelle Simmons. Do you know why she did that?'

'Did she?' Kevin looked as if he'd been slapped in the face. 'Now, why would she do something like that? You can't tell Sheila, she'd be devastated.'

He looked as though he might burst into tears and Dawn felt quite sorry for him.

'Did she have a falling-out with her dad, which may have prompted her to do that?' Gary asked.

Kevin shook his head. 'No, definitely not. Julie adored her step-father, she was heartbroken when he passed away.' He jumped up and snatched a photo frame from the mantelpiece. He thrust it towards Dawn. 'That's her with Bill, it was taken a few weeks before he died from liver cancer.'

Dawn and Gary exchanged glances. 'So, Mr Kershaw wasn't Julie's father then?'

'No, Sheila and Bill got married when Julie was around eleven years old. They had not long celebrated their wedding anniversary when he was diagnosed. He managed to hang on for five months, long enough to see her graduate.' Kevin realised he was still holding the picture frame. He placed it back on the mantelpiece and returned to his seat.

'What happened to Julie's father?' Gary asked him.

'He died when she was a little girl. Well, I say little, she was around seven or eight years old. I didn't meet the family until much later, when I became Bill's carer, but Sheila told me all about it.'

'Was it an accident?' Dawn asked.

Kevin looked around him then sat forward, as if about to impart a trusted secret. 'The official version says it was, but I don't really believe that. He was on his way home from work when he was hit by a car. The car didn't stop, and the police never managed to trace it. It happened right outside their house, Sheila told me that Julie was looking out of her bedroom window, watching for her Dad and saw the whole thing. She was so traumatised that didn't speak for ages afterwards, poor little thing.'

'What makes you think it wasn't an accident?' Gary asked.

'The road outside the house where they used to live is perfectly straight. The tyre tracks showed that the car mounted the pavement and sideswiped Steve, who was

346

walking directly towards the house before swerving back onto the road and driving away. I suppose back then the forensics or whatever weren't as good as they are today.'

Dawn felt something scratching at the back of her memory, something familiar about what Kevin was telling them. 'What was Julie's father's name?' she asked.

'You might have heard of him actually, he's something of a local legend,' Kevin said. 'His name was Steve Gifford.'

67

Alex and Craig got to Ray Diamond's house in less than fifteen minutes, Alex channelling Mo's boy-racer skills but with a much less capable car. Alex hope his trusty Astra would be okay, it hadn't sounded very healthy as he raced along the dogleg. A police car was parked near the front door and the two officers got out when they saw Alex coming up the driveway.

'We were told that you were on your way, sir, so thought it best to wait,' PC Griffiths said. 'We've checked around the outside, no signs of disturbance, but PC Marshall said he could see someone inside through a gap in the curtains.'

'I saw someone sitting on the floor in the lounge, sir.' PC Marshall confirmed. 'I couldn't tell if it was a man or a woman though.'

Craig leaned on the doorbell but got no response. Alex tried the handle and the door swung open.

'Hello, Mr Diamond? Is anyone home?'

Alex nodded to Craig and the two of them led the way, followed by the two uniformed officers. Craig and PC Griffiths went towards the kitchen and Alex and PC Marshall headed to the lounge, where they found Ray sitting on the floor, leaning against the back of the upturned sofa. He had a nasty bruise on his cheek and his nose looked as if it was broken. His long blond hair had been hacked off and lay scattered on the floor all around him. He was making feeble stab marks at the parquet floor with a pair of scissors.

Alex knelt in front of Ray, both knees cracking loudly and making him wince. 'Ray, how about I take those?' he said gently.

Ray didn't look up as he placed the scissors in Alex's outstretched hand. Alex passed them to PC Marshall and gestured for her to leave the room. Craig poked his head around the doorframe and waved an empty brandy bottle at Alex. Alex nodded, and Craig disappeared again.

'Why don't you tell me what happened, Ray? Who did this to you?' Alex asked. He sat down on the floor next to Ray to take the pressure off his knees.

Ray shook his head. 'They wouldn't listen,' he mumbled. He wiped his eyes on the back of his hand and winced when he caught the bruised part.

'Who did you fight with?' Alex asked.

Ray gave a snort of derision. 'Those fuckers jumped me. If it had been one-on-one, I would have wiped the floor with them. Trust me, there will be hell to pay. No-one does that to Ray Diamond and gets away with it. I'll make sure they never work again.'

'Which one of your friends did this to you?' Alex tried again.

Ray tried to stand up but stumbled and sat down again. 'Friends? Fucking leeches you mean. Always round here, being nice to my face then stabbing me in the back. I gave them their break and they repay me like this. Just because Michelle batted her fucking eyelashes at them. Well, she needn't come crawling back here because I'll fucking kill her, just like I killed her old man!'

He waved a fist in Alex's face and Alex jerked his head back but said nothing. Ray scratched his head and looked

350

surprised at finding bare scalp. He picked up a handful of hair from the floor and looked at it, then put it down again.

'What do you mean, you killed her old man? What was his name?' Alex shook Ray's shoulder.

'He approached me in a pub one night, after I'd got drunk and started taking my kit off. He gave me his card and said to call him as he had a job I might be interested in. I just laughed at him, I figured he was an old pervert who fancied his chances. I soon found out that he was a promoter, and he was looking to do something new. He gave me my big break. You are looking at the original male stripper, all others are cheap copies.' Ray laughed at the memory.

Alex said nothing and waited for Ray to continue.

'Steve Gifford thought he was something special, but he was just a user. He would have been nothing without me!' Ray seemed to realise he was shouting and stopped abruptly. 'He was at my place one night, we'd both had a bit to drink, and we were chatting about shit, as you do. I told him I wanted to be a photographer when I was at college. He seemed interested, so I showed him the photos I'd taken for my A-levels. He threw them at me and said I was a sick bastard. He tried to fire me, but I'd signed a five-year contract and it still had two years to run. Steve tried to get out of it, but it was watertight.'

Ray drifted off in a daydream and Alex shook him by the shoulder. 'What was so bad about the photographs that would cause Steve to try and fire you?' he asked.

Ray didn't answer but stared at a point on the far wall. Alex touched his elbow and startled him.

'You said that Steve tried to fire you,' Alex prompted.

'Steve knew he couldn't cancel my contract, so he started bringing newer guys in and cutting me out that way. He teamed up with that knobhead John, and between them they squeezed me out.'

'Do you mean John Jackson? I've met him, he seems very fair,' Alex said.

Ray shrugged. 'He might be now, but he was quite young back then and Steve had a lot of pull. If he said jump, John would ask how high. One night I'd turned up at a gig to watch my mate, but Steve wouldn't let me in the room. He got his goons to throw me out. The worst part was that he stood and laughed at me while they escorted me off the premises. I'll tell you now, no-one laughs at me. I went to another pub and had a few beers because I was so pissed off. I was heading home when I saw him walking along the road, like he didn't have a care in the world.'

'So you ran him over,' Alex said.

'I didn't mean to, I was just trying to scare him,' Ray insisted. 'The stupid fucker saw me driving towards him and he didn't get out of the way. What a twat.' Ray blinked heavily a few times then closed his eyes. 'God, I'm tired,' he said.

'What about the woman from The Leamore Club, did you kill her too?' Alex asked, watching Ray closely. He couldn't seem to focus properly.

'Vicky? No of course I didn't. I had sex with her, and she struggled a lot, but she was trying to make it feel real for me, she knows it turns me on.'

'Do you know a woman called Elizabeth Callendar?'

'Arjan's bird? Sure, I've seen her a few times. She had the hots for me, but you don't shit on your mates. He would have killed me if I'd touched her.'

'She was the woman who was murdered. Could you have mistaken her for Vicky? They looked very similar that night.'

'No, I'd recognise Vicky anywhere. I took a photo on my phone, it's here somewhere,' Ray looked around him but couldn't see his phone. He wiped his nose on the back of his hand, making it bleed again.

Alex winced when it made a crackly sound. 'That looks painful. We should get you to hospital.'

'No, I'm fine.' Ray said. He looked at Alex as if seeing him for the first time. 'The lads came around. They called me names and beat me up.' Ray looked angry. 'Don't they know who I am? I'm Ray Diamond, the best in the business, the number one. I just have to click my fingers and they'll be out of a job like that.' He let out a long, shuddering breath. 'Leave me alone, I need to sleep.' His eyes started to close so Alex shook him awake.

'Ray? Talk to me Ray, I can't help you if you don't,' Alex pleaded.

Ray looked up at Alex as if seeing him for the first time. 'I'm Ray Diamond, the one and only.' His face went slack, and he slid to one side.

Alex shook him again but got no response. 'Craig!' he shouted, 'Get an ambulance, now!'

68

Dawn drove across the city in her usual style, and Gary had to hang on to the door handle with one hand while holding his mobile phone to his ear in the other. After several attempts he gave up and tucked the phone back in his pocket. Dawn shot across the roundabout, narrowly avoiding an oncoming van. The driver blared his horn and made rude gestures at her. She ignored him and braked sharply before turning left at the next junction. Gary closed his eyes and prayed he wouldn't die before his wedding.

'Still no answer?' she asked as she slowed a fraction before driving into the station car park. She pulled up next to Craig's car. 'Well, he's not here,' she said, nodding towards Alex's empty space.

Gary climbed out of Dawn's car and straightened his tie. 'Maybe he's still in Wombourne,' he said. He opened the station door for her, and she gave him a mock curtsey.

They headed to the office but there was no-one there. Gary looked at his watch. 'It's only half past three. Don't say they've all gone home early.'

'Nah, they'll be around somewhere. Try the canteen,' Dawn suggested, sitting down at her desk. She tried ringing Alex but got voicemail. 'Bugger,' she said. She tried Craig and had no luck there either. She was about to try Alex again when her phone rang, so she snatched it up.

'Hello? Hi Jayne. No, Alex isn't here at the moment. Is there anything I can do? Okay, I'll be sure to tell him as soon as I get a hold of him. Thanks, 'bye.'

'No-one in the canteen,' Gary said as he came back in. 'Who was that?'

'That was Jayne. She's been trying to reach Alex, she says it's urgent. I told her I'd get him to ring her as soon as we track him down. She didn't sound very happy.'

'I hope everything is alright,' Gary said. He made them both a drink and had just sat down when Mo came in, a folder in her hand.

'What's that you've got?' Dawn asked.

'Alex wanted some background done on Ray Diamond, so I traced him back to his college days,' Mo said. She stuck her thumb up at Gary when he pointed to his mug. She opened the folder and took out the papers from within. 'He was a naughty boy, as you can imagine, with a few black marks against his name.'

'What sort of things did he get into trouble for?' Gary asked, handing Mo her tea.

'Cheers. There were some incidents of fighting, just minor scuffles, two reports for bringing alcohol in, and one for lewd behaviour. Apparently, he flashed his tackle at one of the female lecturers.'

'I'm not surprised he became a stripper. I'm amazed he wasn't expelled though,' Dawn remarked.

'Oh, he was very clever, and passed all of his exams with flying colours. He got a commendation for art, the only one in his class to do so,' Mo said.

'I was rubbish at art,' Gary admitted. 'What use is being able to draw bowls of fruit?'

'There are lots of different types of art besides

drawing, Gary,' Mo said. 'It seems that young Raymond chose photography as his medium.'

'I could have done that, I'm quite handy with a camera,' Gary admitted.

'Ray was pretty good at it too, he produced a series of photographs titled: Forbidden Fantasies. It was deemed very controversial at the time, but his tutor said he was a genius.'

The phone rang, and Dawn picked it up. After a brief conversation, she hung up and looked at her colleagues. 'That was Craig. Ray Diamond is in hospital, it looks like he's taken an overdose.'

'Blimey,' Gary said. 'Is he okay?'

'Not sure, the ambulance has only just left. Craig said Alex is trying to get a search warrant sorted out, and we're to head out there once it's been executed. Mo, you've to go to the hospital and stay with Ray. Oh shit, I forgot to tell him that Jayne called.'

She tried to call Craig back, but it went straight to voicemail.

69

Alex called his boss. 'That's right sir, he's on his way to hospital now. I've asked DC Ross to go to the hospital and stay with him.' He listened to the voice on the other end for a moment. 'I think a search warrant is a good idea. Something really fishy is going on.'

He hung up the phone and turned to Craig. 'DCI Oliver has authorised a warrant, it's on its way now. He says to wait here in case Michelle Simmons turns up.'

'No problem, boss,' Craig said. He handed an envelope to Alex. 'I found these photos in the kitchen bin. I think you need to look at them.'

'You should have left them there and waited for the warrant, you know that,' Alex said sternly. He fished a pair of gloves out of his pocket and put them on before taking the envelope from Craig. He opened it wide enough to see what it contained before pulling the first photo out.

'Jesus Christ!' he said when he saw the picture. 'How many are there?' he asked as he flipped his thumb along the stack.

'Around thirty I think,' Craig answered. 'There are numbers on the back of each one, but I don't know what they mean. Serial numbers perhaps?'

Alex turned the photo over and had a look. There was a six-digit number written in pencil, so it was very faded. He put the photo back in the envelope and handed it to Craig. 'Bag it and get it to the lab. Ask them to send us a list of the numbers so we can try and figure out what they mean. Ray mentioned some photos from his college days, I think these may be them.' Alex wrinkled his nose in disgust. 'It's a pretty sick topic though.'

PC Marshall came in. 'Excuse me, sir, DS Redwood and DC Temple are here with the warrant. There are also some more uniformed officers.'

'Great, let's make a start.'

***

Mason Manor was a hive of activity, with police swarming all over the house and gardens. Alex had been astonished to find out that Michelle was Steve Gifford's daughter, but it made a lot of sense. The search team had been instructed to seize anything drug-related as well as anything that could link either Ray Diamond or Michelle Simmons to the death of Elizabeth Callendar or Steve Gifford.

Alex sorted through the chest of drawers in Ray's bedroom. It was an unpleasant experience. Alex had queried out loud why a man of Ray's reputation would need so many vibrators until PC Marshall had explained that they were butt plugs. Alex had dropped them like they were on fire, thankful he was wearing two pairs of gloves. He found Ray's phone under the bed and checked the photo files.

Among the many unsavoury pictures was the one of Vicky Wilson at the Leamore Club. She was posed in a similar way to the women in the photos that Craig had found. Her clothes were pulled up, and her naked lower half was on show. Alex noted the rose tattoo that Ray had

360

mentioned, confirming that it was Vicky. The likeness between her and Elizabeth Callendar was striking.

A search of the wardrobes turned up half a dozen small bags, each containing a selection of multi-coloured pills, some tubs of white powder and several bags of weed. Everything was logged and taken away. Alex collected up a pile of photographs and looked through them. He found the one that Michelle had seen, the woman in the bar with her face circled. She looked very familiar, but Alex couldn't place her. He logged the photograph along with all the others in the wardrobe.

'Where next, sir?' Penny asked once they had finished. They walked out onto the landing. All the other doors were open and appeared occupied, apart from the one facing them at the end of the corridor.

'I guess we take that one,' Alex said.

70

Michelle started the car and held her breath, hoping that the noise of the engine turning over wouldn't wake Si. He'd fallen asleep on the sofa after dinner, partly due to the sleeping tablets that Michelle had slipped into his energy drink. She put the Porsche into gear and crawled slowly out of the quiet road, waiting until she was out of sight of Si's house before switching the headlights on.

Instead of taking the A460 from Cannock to Wolverhampton, Michelle drove along the smaller B-roads, taking extra care to avoid any traffic cameras. She circled New Cross Hospital, with its complicated parking system until she found a space in the East Car Park. Michelle followed the maze of corridors until she found the short stay ward that she'd been directed to by a harassed-looking porter.

She scanned the information board by the nurses' station to see whereabouts Ray Diamond's bed was, then walked down the hallway behind a small group of people, trying to look as if she belonged there, just another visitor on a drab January evening.

Ray was lying in bed on his back with a drip in his arm. His nose had been taped and his face was a palette of bruises. As Michelle approached the bed, he groped for the buzzer, but she grabbed it and moved it out of reach.

'Not so high and mighty now, are you?' she said in a low voice.

'Get lost Michelle, you're fired. I want you out of my house now.'

'Not gonna happen, big boy. I'm not done with you yet, I just wanted to tell you a few things so you might understand why I set you up.'

Ray closed his eyes again. 'Fine, tell me. Then fuck off.'

Michelle smiled at him in pity. 'That's what Vicky said when I tried to tell her the truth about you. Shame she didn't listen.'

Ray's eyes flew open. 'Are you telling me you killed her? Because if so, you got it wrong. Vicky's still alive, you murdered the wrong woman.' He settled himself back against the pillows with a smirk. 'You always were stupid, Shelley.'

Michelle leaned in close to his ear and lowered her voice. 'No Ray, I'm not. When I came back to the club to pick you and your car up, you were with a woman in the back alley. I knew Vicky had left because I'd seen her go. Don't worry, I gave your lady friend a good battering first before I strangled her. I wasn't even worried when you shouted at me to ask what I was doing, because I'd seen how much you'd had to drink and knew you wouldn't remember a thing. The only DNA they've got is yours.'

Ray shook his head. 'The police have no evidence that I did anything other than get her to suck me off. I'll tell them it was you who killed her.'

Michelle smiled. 'Do you really think they will believe you? It's possible, but they now know that you killed my dad, so at least you'll go down for that.' She patted him on the head and started to walk away before turning back to him. 'Oh, and I'm sure that a certain security man will want a word about you shagging his girlfriend.'

As she approached Bay Five, Mo Ross came from the opposite direction, her phone in her hand. For a split second their eyes met, then Mo started walking quickly towards her. Michelle turned and fled, almost knocking over a young couple coming the other way. She picked up her pace and ducked into the next ward.

A few seconds later, she saw Mo go past, so she doubled back, intending to go back into Ray's ward, but a shout from behind her made her run for the nearest exit. She flew out of the hospital, trying not to slip on the patches of ice that had formed, and ran towards the car park.

Mo cursed her and raced off in the other direction to where she had left her own car, shouting into her phone as she ran.

71

Alex and Penny searched Michelle's bedroom carefully, leaving no stone unturned. Penny found a journal under the bedside cabinet and Alex had discovered various objects of interest. Penny pulled the wardrobe doors open and whistled. 'Sir, look at this,' she said.

'What is it?' Alex asked, not looking up from the drawer of clothes he was currently sifting through. When Penny didn't answer him, he went to see what Penny had found.

The inside of the wardrobe looked like a shrine, with pictures of Steve Gifford plastered everywhere. On a lot of the photos he was with a small child, their sunny smiles lighting up the room. There was a framed obituary and a framed newspaper report with the heading: Local Legend Dies in Tragic Accident. There was an old T-shirt which had probably belonged to Steve and a small collection of stuffed toys. There was also a large scrapbook, full of pictures and press cuttings of Ray Diamond, along with flyers of where he was appearing. There were some photographs too, of him leaving various venues, shops and a couple of private homes. Michelle had clearly stalked her prey very thoroughly.

'It's so sad,' Penny muttered, indicating the largest

photo of Michelle and Steve, taken at a funfair. She was sitting on her dad's shoulders and he was looking up at her with a huge grin on his face. 'I lost my dad to a heart attack when I was young. The hurt never goes away.'

'It is sad, but it's no excuse for breaking the law,' Alex said. 'Michelle went after Ray with the sole intent of avenging her father's death. What she should have done is come to us.'

'Easier said than done,' Penny said. 'My dad was my world, and I simply can't imagine how she must have felt, watching him get mown down like that.'

'Mine left when I was young, not long after Dave was born,' Alex said. 'From what Mum says, we were better off without him.'

Penny flipped through the pages of Michelle's journal. 'Sir, I think I know how Michelle was planning to get her own back. Look at this,' she said, handing the book to Alex.

Alex read the entry out loud. 'I found Ray on the bathroom floor again this morning. He was high as a kite and I struggled to get him back to his room. On the upside, he had a load of cash in his jacket pocket, which is now safely tucked away in my bank account. I also found some blank cheques which I helpfully filled in and banked for him.'

A later entry read:

With any luck, Hope will never speak to him again after she saw those photos. I wonder how she found out about them — probably that anonymous email she got. Little by little, I'll make him pay for killing my dad.

'Wow,' Penny said. 'She really hates him, doesn't she?' She took the book from Alex and dropped it into an evidence bag.

'That kind of grief can eat a hole into you,' Alex replied.

Craig burst into the room. 'Boss, Mo just called. It seems that Michelle Simmons showed up at New Cross Hospital but took off when she saw Mo. Michelle is driving Ray's car, she smashed through the parking barrier at the hospital and is heading along the A460 towards the A449. Mo is in pursuit.'

'Jesus Christ, Mo will get herself killed! Get onto traffic, tell them what's going on. I'll see if I can get a helicopter on them.' His phone rang as he pulled it out of his pocket. 'Sorry darling, I've got an emergency, I'll call you back in a bit.' He hung up, rang DCI Oliver and filled him in.

'Alex, tell your DC to stand down, the traffic police will take it from here.' Andy Oliver said. 'We don't want the public put at risk. The helicopter will soon find Miss Simmons and track her wherever she goes. No need for heroics.'

'Understood, sir,' Alex said. He tried Mo's phone but there was no answer. 'Bollocks,' he said. He rushed down the stairs to his team. 'Have any of you heard from Mo in the last few minutes?' he asked.

'Not since just now,' Craig said. 'Why?'

'DCI Oliver has ordered her to cease her pursuit, he's sending the helicopter up and has asked Uniforms to intercept. Do we know where Michelle Simmons could be heading?'

Gary spoke up. 'Her mum lives in Wellington. My guess is that's where she'll go.'

'Your guess will have to do Gary, I'll let traffic know. If any of you hear from Mo, tell her she's to stop channelling her inner Bodie and get her arse back to the station.'

72

Mo drove as fast as she could along the A449, one eye on the Porsche in front and the other on the rest of the traffic on the dual carriageway. She blasted her horn at a driver who refused to move over, content to stay in the right-hand lane, so Mo dropped down a gear and flew past him on his left, leaving his rude gestures behind. Stamping on the pedal, she made her engine growl and punch the car forward hard enough to cause whiplash as she took the second exit at the Three Tuns roundabout, narrowly missing a lorry which was turning right.

***

The Porsche had gained some ground by the time they got to the industrial estate, and Mo had to put her foot down to close the gap. The traffic lights at the junction for the M54 turned red as Mo approached and she had no choice but to wait. She revved her engine in frustration and hoped the white van in front of her wouldn't give her any problems. She sped off as the lights changed and zipped around the van, taking the mini roundabout at the top of the slip road onto the motorway at 60 mph. Mo accelerated until the needle on her speedometer tapped

120 mph, causing the car to vibrate. She gritted her teeth and hung onto the steering wheel, anxiously searching for any sign of the Porsche up ahead. The heavens chose that moment to open, making visibility more difficult.

Mo floored the pedal, urging her car forward. The Porsche appeared to have slowed down and she managed to close the gap to three cars.

As they approached junction 3, Michelle's car exited left onto the slip road towards Albrighton and Shifnal. An old couple in a Mercedes changed lanes abruptly in front of Michelle's car, forcing it off the road and over the edge of the steep embankment. The car rolled over a couple of times and landed back onto the motorway on its roof, right in Mo's path. Mo stood upright on her brakes and swung the steering wheel hard, trying desperately to avoid it, but the gap was too small.

Everything seemed to happen in slow motion as the two cars collided. Mo felt the shockwaves travel up her spine as her car spun around, throwing her from side-to-side before coming to a stop. She tried to turn her head but the shooting pain in her neck persuaded her to stay still. She could see Michelle slumped awkwardly against the door pillar of the upside-down Porsche, her eyes closed and blood on her face. A pool of liquid caught the moonlight as it trickled out from underneath the wreckage.

Mo fumbled to release her seat belt, desperate to get to Michelle in case the spilled fuel ignited. Other cars had pulled over nearby and drivers had exited their vehicles, phones pressed to their ears. A few seemed to be filming, more intent on their fifteen minutes of fame on the internet than helping to get either of them to safety.

There was a scraping noise as someone slowly wrenched Mo's door open. She shuddered at the sound, thinking how all her brother's restoration work had been for nothing. Gentle hands helped pull her from her seat and she leaned heavily on her rescuers as she limped towards the embankment.

73

Alex clung on for dear life as PC Marshall drove as fast as possible, the blues and twos on her squad car warning other drivers to move out of the way. The helicopter had reported the accident and Alex prayed under his breath that no-one was badly injured, or worse.

'Nearly there, sir,' Penny said as she sped up the M54. 'Highway Patrol have closed the motorway and have set up a diversion at junction two to stop anything else joining the queues.'

Within minutes they could see stationary traffic up ahead, and Penny drove along the hard shoulder to get closer to the scene. A fire engine was parked next to the central reservation and the crew were spraying foam everywhere. Alex was out of the car before it had stopped properly, anxious about his officer. He ran over to a nearby ambulance, his face white as a sheet.

Mo lay on a stretcher in the back, a stiff collar fastened around her neck. A paramedic had her hooked up to a portable ECG machine. She opened her eyes slowly when she heard Alex's voice.

'Mo, what the hell were you thinking? You could have been killed!' The fury in Alex's voice was mixed with relief.

The paramedic gave him a sharp look. 'She needs pain relief, but she refused any until you got here,' she told him.

Mo whispered something and Alex leaned in close to catch what she was saying. 'Michelle,' she croaked. Alex glanced at the paramedic and she shook her head.

'Don't worry about Michelle for now, just be thankful you're lying down so I can't kick your arse. Thank God your brother fitted that roll cage when he rebuilt your car, otherwise it might have been a different story.'

Mo winced at the thought of her precious car, then mouthed something else.

'What was that?' Alex asked her.

'Visor,' she repeated.

'Visor? In your car? What about it?'

Mo nodded. 'Picture.'

'Okay, I'll find it. Now you take your meds and get going.' Alex squeezed her hand and went to look at Mo's car. It was a sorry sight, with nearly all the glass shattered and big holes in the bodywork. The driver's door had come clean off and lay on the road in a twisted heap. He reached inside the car and pulled the visor down. He smiled as he retrieved Mo's precious photo of Lewis Collins that was taped to the flap and tucked it safely in his jacket pocket.

He jogged over to Faz, who was waving at him. Michelle's body lay nearby, covered by a blanket.

'Poor DC Ross, she loved that car,' Faz lamented. 'I don't think she will be able to rebuild it this time.'

'Never mind that, what did you want?' Alex snapped. He apologised almost immediately but Faz waved it away.

'No need, I know you're frustrated. This bloody rain isn't helping either.' He pointed to the remains of the Porsche. 'That, my friend, is a death-trap. I have no idea how it got through its last MOT, but you should trace the garage and close them down.'

'What are you on about?'

'Look at this,' Faz said, indicating a portion of the crumpled door pillar where the paint had scraped off, revealing fine lines of welding. 'This looks like a cut and shut – two cars welded together.'

'Fucking hell, no wonder she didn't survive,' Alex said.

'Exactly. The car rolled over onto its roof and the pillars gave way under the weight, likely breaking her neck. I'll know more after the PM, but I think it's safe to say that your officer is not to blame, this young lady was dead before the collision.'

'That will be some small comfort I suppose,' Alex replied, 'But Mo will still be getting a bollocking for driving like a lunatic.' He looked at Mo's car again. 'Then again, maybe she's been punished enough.'

74

The team had gathered back at the station, and Craig was on tea duty. 'It's a shame we haven't got anything stronger,' he said as he handed the mugs out.

Les came off the phone. 'That was Isobel. Mo is okay, she's got whiplash, a couple of cracked ribs and a sprained ankle. It's a miracle, given the state of her car.'

'Thank God for that,' Alex said. 'We're going to have a serious word about her obsession with *The Professionals* when I see her next. She could have been killed.'

'Isobel told her the same. Mo said that Lewis Collins saved her life,' Les said.

'That'll be the drugs in her system,' Gary added. 'How's Ray Diamond?'

'He's recovering,' Dawn said. 'He's had his stomach pumped and his injuries have been treated. He decided not to make an official report concerning what his friends did to him. He's now claiming that he cut his own hair off. He said he was done with stripping so was going to reinvent himself.'

'I wonder what he will do now?' Les said.

'The first thing he will do is stand trial for killing Steve Gifford,' Alex said, sipping his tea. 'Although he's slippery enough to try and worm his way out of it. He's out of the frame for Elizabeth Callendar though. It looks like Michelle Simmons had it all planned out for years before. We'll never know if murder was on her mind from the start, but she was determined to make him pay for killing her dad. She doesn't appear to have been that sorry for killing Elizabeth by mistake.'

'What about Vicky and Helen? I hope they're not getting off scot-free,' Gary said.

'Oh, don't worry, they'll each be charged with obstruction and wasting police time,' Alex said.

'It was a pure fluke that Ray Diamond started dating Helen Whittaker's friend,' Les added. 'But I doubt Vicky Wilson will want to see him again once she finds out about him killing Steve Gifford.'

'Probably not, but that's their business. I for one will be glad to see the back of that man.' Alex rubbed his face. 'Now, I have to go and see Mr and Mrs Callendar. It's time they got their daughter back.'

'Leave it until the morning, boss,' Craig said. 'It's gone midnight now and they're probably asleep. One more night won't hurt, will it?'

'No, it has to be tonight,' Alex insisted. 'It won't take long and it will give them closure. Now bugger off home all of you.'

75

Ray Diamond sighed inwardly as he felt someone sit down on the edge of his hospital bed. 'For fuck's sake, will you lot leave me alone and let me sleep,' he snapped.

'That's no way to treat an old friend,' a gravelly voice replied, making Ray's stomach clench in panic. 'Especially not when you've been dossing in their house.'

Ray slowly opened one eye and Glyn Mason's face swam into focus. He had filled out while living abroad, and his hair was now the colour of steel wool. His tanned face creased into a smile, but his blue eyes remained as cold as ice.

'Looks like you've been in the wars, old son,' he said as he patted Ray's cheek. 'Now, before we discuss what you've done to upset my goddaughter, let's talk about the cheques that you stole from my nephew.'

76

It was after 1 a.m. before Alex managed to get home, and the house was in darkness. There was a faint glow coming from his son's office window, which afforded him enough light to see where he was going in the otherwise pitch black. Making a mental note to sort out some outside lighting, Alex slipped quietly inside and kicked off his shoes. He stood for a few seconds, enjoying the silence.

He padded to the kitchen and opened the fridge. Jayne had left a plate of food, covered with cling film for him, but he was far too tired to eat. He grabbed a bottle of beer instead, twisted off the cap and drank almost half of it in one go. Taking his beer with him, he headed straight towards the bedroom. He opened the door quietly but was surprised to see the bed empty.

Alex went back along the corridor towards Joel's room, figuring Jayne must be helping him with one of his many projects. He opened his son's office door and stopped dead.

The room looked like a bomb had hit it. Torn up posters lay scattered on the floor, CDs and pens were spilled over the desk and the curtains had been torn down.

Jayne lay still and quiet on the floor by Joel's bookcase, her eyes closed, her hair matted with blood. Alex felt a whooshing sound in his ears as he dropped his beer bottle, rushed over to her and anxiously checked for a pulse. He detected a faint fluttering under his fingers. Pulling his phone out of his jeans pocket, he dialled 999 with one hand while keeping the other hand on Jayne's neck. He looked around for his son, his face distraught.

Joel sat on the floor in the doorway of the adjoining room, staring at his bloodied fists. He looked up at Alex, his face streaked with tears, his eyes puffy from crying. He opened his mouth to speak and his words came out in a whisper.

'I'm sorry, Dad.'

77

After Alex dialled 999, he rang his brother, then sat on the floor next to Jayne and stroked her face, ignoring his son's constant screams of apology.

Dave and Carol had rushed in a few minutes later and quickly took charge. Dave checked Joel for injuries before scooping him up and carrying him out of the room, ignoring Joel's protests and flailing arms.

Carol stayed with Alex, crouching by his side and speaking in a low, calm voice, all the while keeping an eye out for the ambulance. As soon as it had arrived, she pulled Alex away from Jayne so the paramedics could do their job.

Carol sat Alex on Joel's bed and held his trembling hands.

Dave came back into the room just as the paramedics lifted Jayne onto a stretcher and started to wheel her out of the door. 'I've put Joel in Jayne's car, take him to our house and try to calm him down. I phoned the boys while I was outside, so they'll be there to help you with him. I'll take Alex to the hospital.'

Alex stood up and tried to push past him, but Dave held him firmly by the shoulders. 'Stay put, mate. Let me take a look at you first.' He peered into Alex's eyes. 'Nah, you still look as daft as usual.'

Dave caught Alex just as his legs gave way and he collapsed, sobbing, into his brother's arms.

78

There was a harsh bite of frost in the air as the funeral procession drove towards the churchyard. Ancient cedar trees lined the avenue beyond the gates, all the way to the car park at the bottom. The small party got out and started their procession between the rows of headstones to where a sympathetic priest with sad eyes and a delicate smile stood, waiting for them by a large mound of earth and an open grave.

Michelle's mum sat in her wheelchair and cried silently, flanked by her carer Kevin Huntley, and John Jackson and his wife. Chad, Si, Des and Hope stood on the other side of the grave, with Neil and Ruby at the foot. The priest said a few quiet words before the coffin was slowly lowered into the ground. After a few minutes everyone headed back towards the cars, looking forward to getting out of the cold.

'Well, that was awkward,' Des said as he slid into the passenger seat of Chad's car. 'I didn't know what to say to her poor mum. She looked so broken up. I'm almost relieved we can't go to the wake.'

'Well, she's lost her husband and her daughter because of Ray Diamond,' Si said, climbing into the back seat. 'How do you come back from something like that?'

'I have to be honest,' Chad added, putting his seat belt on and starting the engine, 'I don't think it will be long until she joins them. She looked very frail.'

Chad joined the M54, heading east. The traffic was light at that time of day, and they drove in silence for a while.

'Does anyone know what's happening with Ray?' Si asked. 'I've heard nothing.'

Des gazed out of the window. 'I heard the police were charging him for Steve Gifford's murder. I don't know if he's in custody or not, I couldn't care less to be honest.'

'You and me both, brother,' Chad said. 'I'm staying away from that mess. If he hadn't killed Steve, none of this crap would ever have happened. The only upside is that we got to know Michelle.'

'True, she was pretty great. Always had time for a chat and always happy to help us whenever we needed her,' Si said. 'She was like a little sister to me. I'll really miss her.'

They drove past the exit for junction 3 of the motorway. There were still faded flowers tied to the railings close to where Michelle had died.

Des saluted them as they drove under the bridge. 'Sleep well, sweetheart,' he said.

ACKNOWLEDGEMENTS

Firstly, let me thank you, the reader, for buying this book, it means so very much to me that you did. It was a long, hard process, but so worth it to see it out there in the big wide world. I hope you enjoy the next one too. I have a lot of people to thank, but if I've missed you off the list, please know this was not intentional.

Firstly, I want to say a massive thanks to my publishers, Dark Edge Press, for putting their faith in me, and for the incredible amount of hard work they have put in to make this happen. They may be a small company, but they have as much drive and dedication as bigger ones.

I also need to thank Susi Holliday, author and co-founder of Crime Fiction Coach, for putting me in touch with fellow author Louise Voss, who did such a wonderful job with the line editing and proofreading – you really did make it a much better book.

Every character in *What Goes Around* is fictitious, and any similarities to persons living or dead are coincidental. Ray Diamond was created from all the things that irritate me about people – heaven forbid such a man should ever exist! On the contrary, Kitty McLane was made up of some of the finest drag queens I know, these ladies work incredibly hard, and will always have my utmost respect and love. There are two exceptions – Chad is based on my good friend, Conrad Brissett. He is indeed a male stripper, but also a double black belt and teacher of Karate, a dance teacher, a mentor, motivational speaker, and teacher of Ryoko Mindset. We had great fun creating his alter ego, and my heartfelt thanks go out to him. Peace and love, my brother.

The second character, Joel, is based on my own son.

He has cerebral palsy and Asperger's syndrome, caused by birth injury, and I wanted to show some of the things that the parents and carers of these children live with on a daily basis. Most of the time my son is happy, funny and very loving but, like Joel, he is prone to violent outbursts and destructive phases. Almost every situation between Jayne and her son are ones I have personally experienced. It was difficult writing about them, but I wanted to show the full reality of living with a disabled child.

An extra special group of friends allowed me to use their names for my characters, and I asked them to read the book in its infancy, to make sure they were completely happy with the storyline. They are Craig and Deb Muir, Gary and Jo Temple, Les and Ruth Morris, Maureen Ross, David and Carol Peachey, Glyn Mason, Lee Masters from Undertone Tattoo in Codsall, Dean Smith and his excellent band Nowhere Fast, John Woodward, owner of Adrenalin Promotions and Pleasure Boys UK, and last but by no means least, Matthew 'Faz' Farrow, who is not a coroner, but actually a top sports physiotherapist and owner of Physio Wolverhampton. Many a plot was discussed as he pummelled my muscles and cracked my neck!

Special thanks to Rob Parker, Howard Linskey, Dan Stubbings, Louise Fairbairn, Sharon Birch, and Gail Williams for the help, advice and support you have given me along the way. Massive hugs to Dr Noir, AKA Jacky Collins, who showcased my book on air last year, giving me a chance to tell people about it. You really are a wonderful lady, and you work so incredibly hard to help everyone. Also thank you to Hannah Stevenson, aka The Book Detective, for interviewing me on her blog last year, when the book had a different title.

I owe a huge debt of gratitude to author Graham Smith for creating the hugely successful Crime & Publishment, crime writing workshop, where so many of us have since cut our teeth. The course has been running for eight years, and to date there are fourteen attendees who are now successfully published, with hopefully many more to come. I arrived for that first weekend alone, terrified and full of self-doubt, and left feeling confident and worthy, having made some amazing friends who offered me so much support with my writing that I uprooted my family and moved to Scotland, so I could continue to work with them. Of those people, I particularly want to thank my Twisted Sisters, Irene Paterson, Linda Wright, Fiona Quinn, Jackie Baldwin, Hayley Kershaw, Christine Huntley, Sonia Sandbach, Beth Corcoran, Kriss Nichol, Jo Abbott and Tess Makovesky. Of equal importance were Mike Craven, Les Morris, Douglas Skelton, Michael J. Malone, John Langley, Lucy Cameron and Janet Williamson, who all read the book in its infancy and steered me in the right direction. Special thanks to Les for formatting the manuscript – I had no clue what I was doing with that. He became DC Les Morris in the book (and the incident with the dog is a true story!).

To my friend Sharon Withers, thank you for taking me to my first ever ladies' night, and to many more afterwards. We really do have some fabulous memories, don't we? To Donna Jones, thank you for reading some of the very earliest chapters, I hope you're pleased with the final result. To Bev and Gail, I wish you were both here to read this book, I'm sure you would have loved it.

To Anthony (Mother), I love and miss you so much, my darling.

The biggest thank you goes to my wonderful family. Paul, you put up with my erratic moods, my crippling self-doubt, my shoddy housekeeping and my tears of frustration. You also agreed to move hundreds of miles away and start over again so I could fulfil my dream. You are an incredible man, and I love you from the ground up.

To my amazing children, you have been my guiding lights, my inspiration and you never stopped believing in me. You are my happy thoughts; I would not exist without you.

Lastly, to Jack. You will always be my favourite son. Not a day goes by when I don't miss you.

Ann is a married mother of four grown-up children. Her passions include books, cats and rock music.

She started writing around ten years ago, but struggled until she discovered a crime writing workshop, called Crime and Publishment, established by author Graham Smith, in Gretna Green. The support and encouragement she received from her peers on the course was fantastic and it prompted her to move with her family from the West Midlands to Scotland, so she could concentrate on her writing.

She has had short stories published in two anthologies, titled *Happily Never After* and *Wish You Weren't Here*, with all profits going to local charities.

Love crime fiction as much as we do?

Sign up to our associates program to be first in line to receive Advance Review Copies of our books, and to win stationary and signed, dedicated editions of our titles during our monthly competitions. Further details on our website: www.darkedgepress.co.uk

Follow @darkedgepress on Facebook, Twitter, and Instagram to stay updated on our latest releases.

Printed in Great Britain
by Amazon

86592115R00236